STO

Christine

# Good Housekeeping's Best Book of Bedtime Stories

# Good Housekeeping's

# Best Book of Bedtime Stories

Edited by
PAULINE RUSH EVANS

Illustrated by
DON SIBLEY

GOOD HOUSEKEEPING MAGAZINE

BOOK DIVISION
250 West 55th Street, New York 19, N. Y.

Library of Congress Catalogue Number 57-12953

Designed by Diana Klemin
First Edition

*Printed in the United States of America*
36029

# Acknowledgements

Thanks are due to the following authors, publishers, publications and agents for permission to use the material indicated.

American Book Company for "The King's Rabbit Keeper" from MERRY TALES by Eleanor and Ada Skinner, copyright 1915 by American Book Company. Dodd, Mead & Company, Inc. for The Lost Merbaby by Margaret and Mary Baker. Copyright © 1927 by Dodd, Mead & Company, Inc. Reprinted by permission of the publishers. J. M. Dent & Sons, Ltd. for "The Princess and the Pea" and "Thumbelisa" by Hans Christian Andersen, translated by Mrs. Alice Lucas. Doubleday & Company, Inc. for "Mr. Murdle's Large Heart" from A STREET OF LITTLE SHOPS by Margery Bianco. Copyright 1932 by Margery Williams Bianco; "The Picnic Basket" from THE POPPY SEED CAKES by Margery Clark. Copyright 1924 by Doubleday & Company, Inc. Reprinted by permission of the publishers. E. P. Dutton & Co., Inc. for "In Which Eeyore Has A Birthday and Gets Two Presents" from the book WINNIE-THE-POOH by A. A. Milne. Copyright, 1926, by E. P. Dutton & Co., Inc. Renewal, 1954, by A. A. Milne; "The Hare That Ran Away" from the book EASTERN STORIES AND LEGENDS by Marie Shedlock. Copyright, 1920, by E. P. Dutton & Co., Inc. Renewal, 1948, by Arthur C. Jennings. Reprinted by permission of the publishers. Harcourt, Brace and Company, Inc. for "A Fourth of July Picnic" and "What Happened to the Only Pear" from TWO AND TWO ARE FOUR by Carolyn Haywood. Copyright, 1940, by Harcourt, Brace and Company, Inc.; "Guineapigmalion" from THE TERRIBLE NUISSANCE by Peggy Bacon, copyright, 1931, by Harcourt, Brace and Company, Inc. and reprinted with their permission. Alfred A. Knopf, Inc. for "Sudden Mary" from TILL POTATOES GROW ON TREES by Emma L. Brock. Copyright 1938 by Alfred A. Knopf, Inc. Reprinted by permission of the publishers. J. B. Lippincott Company for "The Brownie of Blednock" from SCOTTISH FAIRY TALES by Elizabeth Grierson; "The Old Woman and the Tramp" (Nail Broth) from FAIRY TALES FROM THE SWEDISH by Nils G. Djurklov; "Mrs. Peck-Pigeon" from OVER THE GARDEN WALL by Eleanor Farjeon. Copyright, 1933, 1951 by Eleanor Farjeon; "The Green Kitten" from THE OLD SAILOR'S YARN BOX by Eleanor Farjeon. Copyright, 1934 by Eleanor Farjeon; "Mrs. Goose's Rubbers" from MRS. GOOSE AND THE THREE DUCKS by Miriam Clark Potter. Copyright, 1936 by Miriam Clark Potter. Reprinted by permission of the publishers. The Macmillan Company for "The Mischievous Monkey" from THE LION-HEARTED KITTEN AND OTHER STORIES by Peggy Bacon. Reprinted by permission of the publishers. Harold Matson Company for selections from POO-POO AND THE DRAGONS. Copyright 1942 by C. S. Forester. Reprinted by permission of Harold Matson Company. Frederick Muller, Ltd. for "Tattercoats" and "Jack and the Beanstalk" by Joseph Jacobs. Reprinted by permission of the publishers. Thomas Nelson and Sons for "How She Kept Her Geese Warm" from THE LITTLE OLD WOMAN WHO USED HER HEAD by Hope Newell; "How She Made the Baby Elephant Happy" from MORE ABOUT THE LITTLE OLD WOMAN WHO USED HER HEAD by Hope Newell. Reprinted by permission of the publishers. Story Parade, Inc. for MISS CRUMPET'S GREAT DAY by Frank Rosengren. Copyright, 1938, by Story Parade, Inc. Reprinted by permission. Frederick Warne & Co., Ltd. for THE TALE OF PETER RABBIT by Beatrix Potter. Reprinted by permission of the publishers. Ann Watkins, Inc. for "The Wishing-Shell" from DON'T BLAME ME, by Richard Hughes, copyright 1940, by Harper & Brothers; "Living in W'ales" from THE SPIDER'S PALACE by Richard Hughes, copyright 1932 by Richard Hughes. By permission of Ann Watkins, Inc.

The editor and publisher have made diligent efforts to trace the ownership of all copyrighted material in this volume, and believe that all necessary permissions have been secured. If any errors have inadvertently been made, proper corrections will gladly be made in future editions.

# To Those Who Read Aloud

Anytime is story time to a child.

There comes a period in most mothers' lives when they seem to go through the day with a plaintive little voice behind them saying, "Mommy, read me a story," and "Please read me another story." And after a while, I'm afraid, many mothers begin to yearn for the well-regulated old days when Longfellow could call "the children's hour" a "pause in the day's occupation."

The whole day is story time to a small child, but there is still something special about bedtime. That is the hour for the last story, the best of all, the favorite that is read over and over again. It can be long or short, funny or sad, new or old, but a bedtime story should be a "best story."

Reading bedtime favorites to a child is one of the great privileges of parenthood. There's a unique sense of participation in the child's world, a chance to share the wonderful experience of make-believe while it is still bright and new. And perhaps—if the truth is to be told—perhaps the deepest pleasure of all is the opportunity to return again to the magical storyland of your own childhood.

Here is a collection of nearly half a hundred bedtime favorites—enough, I hope, for a thousand and one nights' entertainment. You'll find most of the stories that you have tucked away in your childhood memories—*The Gingerbread Boy* and *Little Red Riding Hood, The Ugly Duckling* and *Puss in Boots, Tom Thumb, Rumpelstiltskin,* and a dozen others. And you will find as many modern stories—*Winnie-the-Pooh, The Green Kitten, How the Old Woman Made the Baby Elephant Happy, Poo-Poo and the Dragons*—stories that are on their way to becoming tomorrow's classics.

There's no reason, of course, for all of these stories to be reserved for bedtime. They weren't written for that special purpose, and certainly they are as good in the morning as they are after the sun goes down. But still, I hope that in your home at least some of them will receive the highest of all childhood compliments—that they are asked for again and again at bedtime.

P. R. E.

Danbury, Conn.

# Contents

*The stories in this volume are arranged alphabetically.*

# Contents 11

# Contents

from DINAH MARIA MULOCK'S

# The Adventures of
# a Brownie

*This brownie is a playful little elf, about a foot high, who lives in the coal cellar. The children in the household are the only ones who ever see him, for to grown-ups he is invisible. Brownie is mischievous and likes to play tricks. But he always helps the children—as he does in this story about the new pony.*

## BROWNIE'S RIDE

For the little Brownie, though not given to horsemanship, did once take a ride, and a very remarkable one it was. Shall I tell you all about it?

The six little children got a present of something they had longed for all their lives—a pony. Not a rocking-horse, but a real live pony—a Shetland pony, too, which had travelled all the way from the Shetland Isles to Devonshire—where everybody wondered at it, for such a creature had not been seen in the neighborhood for years and years. She was no bigger than a donkey, and her coat, instead of being smooth like a horse's, was shaggy, like a young bear's. She had a long tail, which had never been cut, and such a deal of hair in her mane and over her eyes that it gave her quite a fierce countenance. In fact, among the mild and tame Devonshire beasts, the little Shetland pony looked almost like a wild animal.

But in reality she was the gentlest creature in the world. Before she had been many days with them, she began to know the children quite well: followed them about, ate corn out of the bowl they held out to her; nay, one day when the eldest little girl offered her bread-and-butter, she stooped her head and took it from the child's hand, just like a young lady. Indeed, Jess—that was her name—was altogether so lady-like in her behavior, that more than once Cook allowed her to walk in at the back door, when she stood politely warming her nose at the kitchen fire for a minute or two, then turned round and as politely walked out again. But she never did any mischief; and was so quiet and gentle a creature that she bade fair soon to become as great a pet in the household as the dog, the cat, the kittens, the puppies, the fowls, the ducks, the cow, the pig, and all the other members of the family.

The only one who disliked her, and grumbled at her, was the Gardener. This was odd; because, though cross to children, the old man was kind to dumb beasts. Even his pig knew his voice and grunted, and held out his nose to be scratched, and he always gave each successive pig a name, Jack or Dick, and called them by it, and was quite affectionate to them, one after the other, until the very day that they were killed. But they were English pigs— and the pony was Scotch, and the Devonshire Gardener hated everything Scotch, he said. Besides, he was not used to groom's work, and the pony required such a deal of grooming on account of her long hair. More than once Gardener threatened to clip it short, and turn her into a regular English pony; but the children were in such distress at this, that the mistress and mother forbade any such spoiling of Jess's personal appearance.

At length, to keep things smooth, and to avoid the rough words and even blows which poor Jess sometimes got, they sought in the village for a boy to look after her, and found a great rough shock-headed lad named Bill, who for a few shillings a week consented to come up every morning and learn the beginning of a groom's business; hoping to end, as his mother said he should, in sitting, like the squire's fat coachman, as broad as he was long, on the top of the hammercloth of a grand carriage, and do nothing all day but drive a pair of horses as stout as himself a few miles along the road and back again.

Bill would have liked this very much, he thought, if he could have been a coachman all at once, for if there was one thing he disliked, it was work. He much preferred to be in the sun all day and do nothing; and he only agreed to come and take care of Jess because she was such a very little pony that looking after her seemed next door to doing nothing. But when he tried it he found his mistake. True, Jess was a very gentle beast; so quiet that the old mother-hen with fourteen chicks used, instead of roosting with the rest of the fowls, to come regularly into the portion of the cowshed which was partitioned off for a stable, and settle under a corner of Jess's manger for the night; and in the morning the chicks would be seen running about fearlessly among her feet and under her very nose.

But for all that she required a little management, for she did not like her long hair to be roughly handled; it took a long time to clean her, and though she did not scream out like some silly little children when her hair was combed, I am afraid she sometimes kicked and bounced about, giving Bill a deal of trouble—all the more trouble, the more impatient Bill was.

And then he had to keep within call, for the children wanted their pony at all hours. She was their own especial property, and they insisted upon learning to ride—even before they got a saddle. Hard work it was to stick on Jess's bare back, but by degrees the boys did it, turn and turn about, and even gave their sisters a turn too—a very little one—just once around the field and back again, which was quite enough, they considered, for girls. But they were very kind to their little sisters, held them on so that they could not fall, and led Jess carefully and quietly: and altogether behaved as elder brothers should.

Nor did they squabble very much among themselves, though sometimes it was rather difficult to keep their turns all fair, and remember accurately which was which. But they did their best, being on the whole extremely good children. And they were so happy to have their pony that they would have been ashamed to quarrel over her.

Also, one very curious thing kept them on their good behavior. Whenever they did begin to misconduct themselves, to want to ride out of their turns, or to domineer over one another, or the boys, joining together, tried to domineer over the girls, as I grieve to say boys not seldom do, they used to hear in the air, right over their heads, the crack of an unseen whip. It was not theirs, for none of them had got a whip; that was a felicity which their father had promised when they could all ride like young gentlemen and ladies; but there was no mistaking the sound—indeed, it always startled Jess so much that she set off galloping, and could not be caught again for many minutes.

This happened several times, until one of them said, "Perhaps it's the Brownie." Whether it was or not, it made them behave better for a good while: till one unfortunate day the two eldest began contending which should ride foremost and which hindmost on Jess's back, when "Crack—crack!" went the whip in the air, frightening the pony so much that she kicked up her heels, tossed both the boys over her head, and scampered off, followed by a loud "Ha, ha, ha!"

Which certainly did not come from the two boys. They had fallen—quite safely, but rather unpleasantly—into a large nettle-bed; whence they crawled out, rubbing their arms and legs, and looking too much ashamed to complain. But they were rather frightened and a little cross, for Jess took a skittish fit, and refused to be caught or mounted again, till the bell rang for school—when she grew as meek as possible. Too late—for the children were obliged to run indoors, and got no more rides for the whole day.

Jess was from this incident supposed to be on the same friendly terms with Brownie as were the rest of the household. Indeed, when she came, the children had taken care to lead her up to his coal-cellar door and introduce her to him properly—for Brownie was very jealous of strangers and often played them tricks. But after that piece of civility he would be sure, they thought, to take her under his protection. And sometimes, when the little Shetlander was restless and pricked up her ears, looking preternaturally wise under those shaggy brows of hers, the children used to say to one another, "Perhaps she sees the Brownie."

Whether she did or not, Jess sometimes seemed to see a good deal that others did not see, and was apparently a favorite with the Brownie, for she grew and thrived so much that she soon became the pride and delight of the children and of the whole family. You would hardly have known her for the rough, shaggy, half-starved little beast that had arrived a few weeks before. Her coat was so silky, her limbs so graceful, and her head so full of intelligence, that everybody admired her. Then, even Gardener began to admire her too.

"I think I'll get upon her back; it will save me walking down to the village," said he one day. And she actually carried him—though, as his feet nearly touched the ground, it looked as if the man were carrying the pony and not the pony the man. And the children laughed so immoderately that he never tried it afterwards.

Nor Bill either, though he had once thought he should like a ride, and got astride on Jess—but she quickly ducked her head down, and he tumbled over it. Evidently she had her own tastes as to her riders, and much preferred little people to big ones.

Pretty Jess! when cantering round the paddock with the young folk, she really was quite a picture. And when at last she got a saddle—a new, beautiful saddle, with a pommel to take off and on, so as to suit both boys and girls—how proud they all were, Jess included! That day they were allowed to take her into the market-town— Gardener leading her, as Bill could not be trusted—and everybody, even the blacksmith, who hoped by-and-by to have the pleasure of shoeing her, said what a beautiful pony she was!

After this, Gardener treated Jess a great deal better, and showed Bill how to groom her, and kept him close at it too, which Bill did not like at all. He was a very lazy lad, and whenever he could shirk work he did it; and many a time when the children wanted Jess, either there was nobody to saddle her, or she had not been properly groomed, or Bill was away at his dinner, and they had to wait till he came back and could put her in order to be taken out for a ride like a genteel animal—which I am afraid neither pony nor children enjoyed half so much as the old ways before Bill came.

Still they were gradually becoming excellent little horse-men and horsewomen, even the youngest, only four years old, whom all the rest were very tender over, and who was often held on Jess's back and given a ride out of her turn because she was a good little girl and never cried for it. And seldomer and seldomer was heard the mysterious sound of the whip in the air, which warned them against quarrelling—Brownie hated quarrelling.

In fact, their only trouble was Bill, who never came to his work in time, and never did things when wanted, and was ill-natured, lazy, and cross to the children, so that they disliked him very much.

"I wish the Brownie would punish you," said one of the boys; "you'd behave better then."

"The Brownie!" cried Bill contemptuously, "if I caught him I'd kick him up in the air, like this!"

And he kicked up his cap—his only cap, it was—which, strange to relate, flew right up, ever so high, and lodged at the very top of a tree which overhung the stable, where it dangled for weeks and weeks, during which time poor Bill had to go bareheaded.

He was very much vexed, and revenged himself by vex-ing the children in all sorts of ways. They would have told their mother, and asked her to send Bill away, only she had a great many anxieties just then, for their dear old grandmother was very ill, and they did not like to make a fuss about anything that would trouble her.

So Bill stayed on, and nobody found out what a bad,

ill-tempered, lazy boy he was.

But one day the mother was sent for suddenly to her mother, not knowing when she should be able to come home again. She was very sad, and so were the children, for they loved their grandmother—and as the carriage drove off they all stood crying round the front door for ever so long.

The servants even cried too—all but Bill.

"It's an ill wind that blows nobody good," said he. "What a jolly time I shall have! I'll do nothing all day long. Those troublesome children shan't have Jess to ride; I'll keep her in the stable and then she won't get dirty, and I shall have no trouble in cleaning her. Hurrah! what fun!"

He put his hands in his pockets, and sat whistling the best part of the afternoon.

The children had been so unhappy, that for that day they quite forgot Jess; but next morning after lessons were over, they came, begging for a ride.

"You can't get one. The stable-door's locked, and I've lost the key." (He had it in his pocket all the time.)

"How is poor Jess to get her dinner?" cried a thoughtful little girl. "Oh, how hungry she will be!"

And the child was quite in distress, as were the two other girls. But the boys were more angry than sorry.

"It was very stupid of you, Bill, to lose the key. Look about and find it, or else break open the door."

"I won't," said Bill. "I daresay the key will turn up before night, and if it doesn't—who cares? You get riding enough and too much. I'll not bother myself about it, or Jess either."

And Bill sauntered away. He was a big fellow, and the little lads were rather afraid of him. But as he walked, he could not keep his hand out of his trousers' pocket, where the key felt growing heavier and heavier, till he expected it every minute to tumble through, and come out at his boots—convicting him before all the children of having told a lie.

Nobody was in the habit of telling lies to them, so they never suspected him, but went innocently searching about for the key—Bill all the while clutching it fast. But every time he touched it, he felt his fingers pinched, as if there was a cockroach in his pocket—or a little lobster—or something, anyhow, that had claws. At last, fairly frightened, he made an excuse to go into the cowshed, took the key out of his pocket and looked at it, and finally hid it in a corner of the manger, among the hay.

As he did so, he heard a most extraordinary laugh, which was certainly not from Dolly the cow, and, as he went out of the shed, he felt the same sort of pinch at his ankles, which made him so angry that he kept striking with his whip in all directions, but hit nobody, for nobody was there.

But Jess—who, as soon as she heard the children's voices, had set up a most melancholy whinnying behind the locked stable door—began to neigh energetically. And Boxer barked, and the hens cackled, and the guinea-fowls cried, "Come back, come back!" in their usual insane fashion—indeed the whole farmyard seemed in such an excited state that the children got frightened lest Gardener should scold them, and ran away, leaving Bill master of the field.

What an idle day he had! How he sat on the wall with his hands in his pockets, and lounged upon the fence, and sauntered round the garden! At length, absolutely tired of doing nothing, he went and talked with the Gardener's wife while she was hanging out her clothes. Gardener had gone down to the lower field, with all the little folks after him, so that he knew nothing of Bill's idling, or it might have come to an end.

By-and-by Bill thought it was time to go home to his supper. "But first I'll give Jess her corn," said he, "double quantity, and then I need not come back to give her her breakfast so early in the morning. Soh! you greedy beast. I'll be at you presently if you don't stop that noise."

For Jess, at sound of his footsteps, was heard to whinny in the most imploring manner, enough to have melted a heart of stone.

"The key—where on earth did I put the key?" cried Bill, whose constant habit it was to lay things out of his hand, and then forget where he had put them, causing himself endless loss of time in searching for them—as now. At last he suddenly remembered the corner of the cow's manger, where he felt sure he had left it. But the key was not there.

"You can't have eaten it, you silly old cow," said he, striking Dolly on the nose as she rubbed herself against him—she was an affectionate beast. "Nor you, you stupid old hen!" kicking the mother of the brood, who with her fourteen chicks, being shut out of their usual roosting-place, Jess's stable—kept pecking about under Dolly's legs. "It can't have gone without hands—of course it can't." But most certainly the key was gone.

What in the world should Bill do? Jess kept on making a pitiful complaining. No wonder, as she had not tasted food since morning. It would have made any kind-hearted person quite sad to hear her, thinking how exceedingly hungry the poor pony must be.

Little did Bill care for that, or for anything, except that he should be sure to get into trouble as soon as he was found out. When he heard Gardener coming into the farmyard, with the children after him, Bill bolted over the wall like a flash of lightning, and ran away home, leaving poor Jess to her fate.

All the way he seemed to hear at his heels a little dog yelping, and then a swarm of gnats buzzing round his head, and altogether was so perplexed and bewildered that when he got into his mother's cottage he escaped into bed, and pulled the blanket over his ears to shut out the noise of the dog and the gnats, which at last turned into a sound like somebody laughing. It was not his mother, she didn't often laugh, poor soul!—Bill bothered her quite too much for that, and he knew it. Dreadfully frightened, he hid his head under the bed-clothes, determined to go to sleep and think about nothing till next day.

Meantime, Gardener returned with all the little people trooping after him. He had been rather kinder to them than usual this day, because he knew their mother had gone away in trouble, and now he let them help him to roll the gravel, and fetch up Dolly to be milked, and watch him milk her in the cowshed—where, it being nearly winter, she always spent the night now. They were so well amused that they forgot all about their disappointment as to the ride, and Jess did not remind them of it by her whinnying. For as soon as Bill was gone, she grew quite silent.

At last one little girl, the one who had cried over Jess's being left hungry, remembered the poor pony, and peeping through a crevice in the cowshed saw her stand contentedly munching at a large bowl full of corn.

"So Bill did find the key. I'm very glad," thought the kind little maiden, and to make sure looked again, when —what do you think she beheld squatting on the manger? Something brown, either a large brown rat, or a small brown man. But she held her tongue, since being a very little girl, people sometimes laughed at her for the strange things she saw. She was quite certain she did see them for all that.

So she and the rest of the children went indoors and to bed. When they were fast asleep, something happened. Something so curious, that the youngest boy, who, thinking he heard Jess neighing, got up to look out, was afraid to tell, lest he too should be laughed at, and went back to bed immediately.

In the middle of the night, a little old brown man, carrying a lantern, or at least having a light in his hand that looked like a lantern—went and unlocked Jess's stable, and patted her pretty head. At first she started, but soon she grew quiet and pleased, and let him do what he chose with her. He began rubbing her down, making the same funny hissing with his mouth that Bill did, and all grooms

do—I never could find out why. But Jess evidently liked it, and stood as good as possible.

"Isn't it nice to be clean?" said the wee man, talking to her as if she were a human being, or a Brownie. "And I daresay your poor little legs ache with standing still so long. Shall we have a run together? The moon shines bright in the clear, cold night. Dear me! I'm talking poetry."

But Brownies are not poetical fairies, quite common-place, and up to all sorts of work. So, while he talked, he was saddling and bridling Jess, she not objecting in the least. Finally he jumped on her back.

" 'Off,' said the stranger; 'off, off, and away!' " sang Brownie, mimicking a song of the Cook's. People in that house often heard their songs repeated in the oddest way, from room to room, everybody fancying it was somebody else that did it. But it was only the Brownie. "Now, 'A southerly wind and a cloudy sky proclaim it a hunting morning!' "

Or night—for it was the middle of the night, though bright as day—and Jess galloped and the Brownie sat on her back as merrily as if they had gone hunting together all their days.

Such a steeple-chase it was! They cleared the farmyard at a single bound, and went flying down the road, and across the ploughed field, and into the wood. Then out into the open country, and by-and-by into a dark, muddy lane—and oh! how muddy Devonshire lanes can be some-times.

"Let's go into the water to wash ourselves," said Brownie, and coaxed Jess into a deep stream, which she swam as bravely as possible—she had not had such a frolic since she left her native Shetland Isles. Up the bank she scrambled, her long hair dripping as if she had been a water-dog instead of a pony. Brownie too shook himself like a rat or a beaver, throwing a shower round him in all directions.

"Never mind, at it again, my lass!" and he urged Jess into the water once more. Out she came, wetter and brisker than ever, and went back home through the lane, and the wood, and the ploughed field, galloping like the wind, and tossing back her ears and mane and tail, perfectly frantic with enjoyment.

But when she reached her stable, the plight she was in would have driven any respectable groom frantic too. Her sides were white with foam, and the mud was sticking all over her like a plaster. As for her beautiful long hair, it was all caked together in a tangle, as if all the combs in the world would never make it smooth again. Her mane especially was plaited into knots, which people in Devonshire call elf-locks, and say, when they find them on their horses, that it is because the fairies have been riding them.

Certainly, poor Jess had been pretty well ridden that night! When, just as the dawn began to break, Gardener got up and looked into the farmyard, his sharp eye caught sight of the stable-door, wide open.

"Well done, Bill," shouted he, "up early at last. One hour before breakfast is worth three after."

But no Bill was there; only Jess, trembling and shaking, all in a foam, and muddy from head to foot, but looking perfectly cheerful in her mind. And out from under her forelegs ran a small creature, which Gardener mistook for Tiny, only Tiny was gray, and this dog was brown, of course!

I should not like to tell you all that was said to Bill, when, an hour after breakfast-time, he came skulking up to the farm. In fact, words failing, Gardener took a good stick and laid it about Bill's shoulders, saying he would either do this, or tell the mistress of him, and how he had left the stable-door open all night, and some bad fellow had stolen Jess, and galloped her all across the country, till, if she hadn't been the cleverest pony in the world, she never could have got back again.

Bill durst not contradict this explanation of the story. Especially as the key was found hanging up in its proper place by the kitchen door. And when he went to fetch it, he heard the most extraordinary sound in the coal-cellar close by—like somebody snoring or laughing. Bill took to his heels, and did not come back for a whole hour.

But when he did come back, he made himself as busy as possible. He cleaned Jess, which was half-a-day's work at least. Then he took the little people for a ride, and afterwards put his stable in the most beautiful order, and altogether was such a changed Bill, that Gardener told him he must have left himself at home and brought back somebody else. Whether or not, the boy certainly improved, so that there was less occasion to find fault with him afterwards.

Jess lived to be quite an old pony, and carried a great many people—little people always, for she herself never grew any bigger. But I don't think she ever carried a Brownie again.

# Androcles and the Lion

In Rome there once lived a poor slave whose name was Androcles. His master was a cruel man who treated him so unkindly that at last Androcles ran away.

He hid himself in a thick forest for many days. But there was no food to be found there, and wandering around in the trackless woods, he grew weak from hunger and was ready to die with fatigue. So one day he crept into a cave and lay down in despair. Soon he was fast asleep.

After a while a great noise woke him up. He saw a huge lion coming into the cave, roaring loudly. Androcles was terrified; there was no way to escape, and he felt sure that the beast would kill him. Soon, however, he saw that the lion was not angry, but was advancing toward him gently, and uttering a mournful wail, as if he wanted help. Androcles noticed that he limped as though his foot hurt him.

Then Androcles grew bold enough to examine his strange guest, and took hold of the lion's lame paw to see what was the matter. The lion stood quite still, and rubbed his head against the man's shoulder. He seemed to say,—

"I know that you will help me."

Androcles lifted the paw from the ground, and saw that a long, sharp thorn had worked itself into the ball of the foot. He took the end of the thorn in his finger; then he gave a strong, quick pull, and out it came. As soon as the lion felt the relief, he began to show his joy. He jumped about like a dog, and licked the hands and feet of his new friend.

Androcles was not at all afraid after this; and when night came, he and the lion lay down and slept side by side.

From that day on, the lion brought food to Androcles every day. The two became such good friends that Androcles found his new life a very happy one.

But one day while wandering through the woods Androcles met a company of soldiers who recognized him as an escaped slave. They took him prisoner and brought him back to Rome and his old master.

At that time, the laws of the country were very severe against slaves. Every slave who was found guilty of having run away from his master was sentenced to fight a hungry lion. So a fierce lion was shut up for a while without food, and the time set when he would be loosed upon poor Androcles.

When the day came, thousands of people crowded into the arena to see the sport. At that time they went to see slaves thrown to lions very much as people nowadays go to see a circus show or a game of baseball.

The door opened, and Androcles was brought in. He

was almost dead with fear, for the roars of the lion could already be heard. He looked up, and saw that there was no pity in the thousands of faces around him.

There was a dreadful yell and a huge hungry lion rushed in. With a single bound he reached the poor slave. Androcles gave a great cry, not of fear, but of gladness. It was his old friend, the lion of the cave.

The people, who had expected to see the man torn to pieces by the lion, were filled with wonder. They watched Androcles put his arms around the lion's neck; they saw the lion lie down at his feet, and lick them lovingly. They saw the great beast rub his head against the slave's face as though he wanted to be petted. They could not understand what it all meant and shouted to him to give an explanation.

So Androcles stood up before the spectators and, with his arm around the lion's neck, told how this same lion which stood before them had been his friend and supplied him with food after the incident of the thorn, and how he and the beast had lived together in the cave.

"I am a man," he said, "but no man has ever befriended me. This lion alone has been kind to me; and we love each other as brothers."

The people present were astonished and delighted with the story. They felt that they could not be cruel to the poor slave now when even this fiercest of beasts had been softened by gratitude to him. "Let Androcles live and be free!" they cried. "Let him live and be free!"

Others cried, "Let the lion go free too! Give both of them their liberty."

And so Androcles was set free, and the lion was given to him for his own. And they lived together just outside of Rome for many years.

ROBERT LOUIS STEVENSON

# Bed in Summer

In winter I get up at night
And dress by yellow candle-light.
In summer, quite the other way,
I have to go to bed by day.

I have to go to bed and see
The birds still hopping on the tree,
Or hear the grown-up people's feet
Still going past me in the street.

And does it not seem hard to you,
When all the sky is clear and blue,
And I should like so much to play,
To have to go to bed by day?

ELIZABETH GRIERSON

# The Brownie of Blednock

Did you ever hear how a Brownie came to the village of Blednock and was frightened away again?

It was one November evening, just when the milking was done and before the children were put to bed. The people of the village were standing by their doorsteps talking about their bad harvest and the turnips, and what chances there were of a good price for their cattle at the coming fair.

All at once the queerest humming noise seemed to come up from the riverside. It came nearer and nearer, and all the good people stopped talking and began to look down the road. And, indeed, it was no wonder that they stared, for there, coming up the middle of the highway, was the strangest little creature that human eyes had ever seen.

He looked like a wee, wee man. He had a long blue beard which almost touched the ground. His legs were twisted, his knees knocked together as he walked, and his arms were so long that his hands trailed in the mud as he came along. He seemed to be humming something over and over. As he came nearer, the good people of the village could make out the words:

> *"Have ye work for Aiken-Drum?*
> *Any work for Aiken-Drum?"*

Oh, how frightened the people were! The children screamed and hid their faces in their mothers' gowns and the milkmaids threw down the pails of milk they were carrying. Even the dogs crept in behind the doors, whining and hiding their tails between their legs. Some of the men who were not too frightened to look the wee man in the face laughed and hooted at him.

"Did you ever see such eyes?" cried one.

"His mouth is so big he could swallow the moon and never even notice it," said the other.

"Look at his long blue beard!" said a third.

And still the poor little man came slowly up the road, crying:

> *"Have ye work for Aiken-Drum?*
> *Any work for Aiken-Drum?"*

Good Grannie Duncan, the kindest old woman in the village, called out at last: "He's just a Brownie, a simple, kindly Brownie. I've heard tell of Brownies before. Many a long day's work will they do for the people who treat them well."

Gathering courage from her words, all the village folk

crowded around the little man. When they were close to him, they saw that his face was kind and gentle and that his tiny eyes had a merry twinkle in them.

"Strange little creature," said an old man, "tell us what you want and where you came from?"

"I cannot well tell thee whence I came," said the wee man. "My country is a nameless land and is very different from this land of yours. For there we all learn to serve, while here everyone wishes to be served. When there is no work for us to do at home, we sometimes set out to visit thy land to see if there is any work we can do there. If thou wilt, I will stay here awhile. I do not wish anyone to wait on me, and I want no wages, nor clothes, nor bedding. All I ask for is a corner of the barn to sleep in, and a bowl of broth set down on the floor at bedtime. If no one meddles with me, I shall be ready to help anyone who needs me. I'll gather your sheep on the hill. I'll take in the harvest by moonlight. I'll sing your bairns to sleep in their cradles. You'll find that the bairns all love Aiken-Drum. And, good housewives, I'll churn for you and bake your bread on a busy day. The men folk, too, may find me useful when there is corn to thrash, or untamed colts in the stables, or when the waters are out in flood."

No one knew quite what to say in answer to the little creature's strange request. It was an unheard-of thing for anyone to come and offer his services for nothing. Some thought it could not be true; others said it were better to have nothing to do with the little creature.

Then up spoke good Grannie Duncan again:

"He's but a Brownie, I tell you, a harmless Brownie. Many a story I've heard in my young days about the work that a Brownie can do, if he be treated well and let alone. Have we not all been complaining about bad times, small wages, and the hard work we all have to do? And now, when a workman comes ready to your hand, you will have nothing to do with him just because he is strange looking. And I've heard that a Brownie can stalk a whole ten-acre field in a single night! Shame on you, say I!"

"A ten-acre field in a single night!" cried out all the men of the village at once. "A ten-acre field!" repeated one. "And in a single night!" added another. That settled the matter. The miller at once offered the Brownie a corner of his barn to sleep in, and good Grannie Duncan promised to make him some broth at bedtime and to send her grandchild, wee Janie, down to the barn with it every evening. Then all the people of the village said, "Good-night," and went to their homes. But they were careful to look over their shoulder once in a while, for fear that the strange little man was following them.

But if they were afraid of him that night, they had a very different story to tell about him before a week had passed. Whatever he was or wherever he came from, he was the most wonderful little worker that these people had ever known. And the strange thing was that he did most of the work at night. Village folk came from all parts of the countryside to catch a glimpse of this queer little worker, but they were never successful, for he was never to be seen when one looked for him. They might have gone to the miller's barn twenty times a day, and twenty times a day they would have found nothing but a heap of straw and an empty broth bowl.

But whenever there was work to be done, whether it was a tired child to be sung to, or a house to be made tidy,

or a batch of bread to be worked up, or a flock of sheep to be gathered together on a stormy night, Aiken-Drum always knew of it and appeared ready to help just at the right time.

Many a time some poor mother who had been up all night with a crying child would sit down with it on her lap in front of the fire in the morning and fall asleep. When she awoke she would find that Aiken-Drum had made a visit to her house; for the floor would be scrubbed and the dishes washed, the fire made up and the kettle put on to boil. But the little Brownie would have slipped away as if he were afraid of being thanked.

The little children were the only ones who ever saw him when he was not working, and, oh, how they loved him! When school was out you could see them away down by the stream crowding around the little dark brown figure, and you could hear the sound of low, sweet singing; for Aiken-Drum knew all the songs that children love well.

By and by the name of Aiken-Drum came to be a household word among the good people of the village, for, although they seldom saw him near at hand, they loved him like one of their own people.

And he would never have gone away if everyone in the village had remembered what good Grannie Duncan told them about Brownies. "A Brownie works for love," she had said to them over and over again. "He will not work for pay. If anyone tries to pay him, the wee creature's feelings will be hurt, and he will vanish in the night."

But a good man of the village and his wife forgot all that had been said, and one day they planned to make something for Aiken-Drum.

"He should not work for nothing," said the good man.

"He has already worn out his coat and trousers slaving for us," said his wife.

So one day they made him a little pair of green trousers and a little brown coat. That night the two good people laid a parcel by the side of the bowl of broth in the miller's barn.

In the middle of the night someone heard the Brownie saying to himself, "A nice pair of green trousers and a little brown coat for me. I can come here no more till one of the children of this village travels the world over and finds me first."

So this strange little creature had to go away. He vanished in the night as any Brownie is sure to do if someone tries to pay him.

And all the good people of Blednock talked of the kind deeds of the little strange man who came one evening into their midst, and they wondered and wondered if he would ever come back to them again.

# The Cock, the Mouse, and the Little Red Hen

Once upon a time there was a hill, and on the hill there was a pretty little house.

It had one little green door, and four little windows with green shutters, and in it there lived A COCK, and A MOUSE, and A LITTLE RED HEN. On another hill close by, there was another little house. It was very ugly. It had a door that wouldn't shut, and two broken windows, and all the paint was off the shutters. And in this house there lived A BOLD BAD FOX and FOUR BAD LITTLE FOXES.

One morning these four bad little foxes came to the big bad Fox and said:

"Oh, Father, we're so hungry!"

"We had nothing to eat yesterday," said one.

"And scarcely anything the day before," said another.

The big bad Fox shook his head, for he was thinking. At last he said in a big gruff voice:

"On the hill over there I see a house. And in that house there lives a Cock."

"And a Mouse!" screamed two of the little foxes.

"And a little Red Hen," screamed the other two.

"And they are nice and fat," went on the big bad Fox. "This very day I'll take my sack and I will go up that hill and in at that door, and into my sack I will put the Cock, and the Mouse, and the little Red Hen."

So the four little foxes jumped for joy, and the big bad Fox went to get his sack ready to start upon his journey.

But what was happening to the Cock, and the Mouse, and the little Red Hen, all this time?

Well, sad to say, the Cock and the Mouse had both got out of bed on the wrong side that morning. The Cock said the day was too hot, and the Mouse grumbled because it was too cold.

They came grumbling down to the kitchen, where the good little Red Hen, looking as bright as a sunbeam, was bustling about.

"Who'll get some sticks to light the fire with?" she asked.

"I shan't," said the Cock.

"I shan't," said the Mouse.

"Then I'll do it myself," said the little Red Hen.

So off she ran to get the sticks. "And now, who'll fill the kettle from the spring?" she asked.

"I shan't," said the Cock.

"I shan't," said the Mouse.

"Then I'll do it myself," said the little Red Hen.

And off she ran to fill the kettle.

"And who'll get the breakfast ready?" she asked, as she

put the kettle on to boil.

"I shan't," said the Cock.

"I shan't," said the Mouse.

"I'll do it myself," said the little Red Hen.

All breakfast time the Cock and the Mouse quarrelled and grumbled. The Cock upset the milk jug, and the Mouse scattered crumbs upon the floor.

"Who'll clear away the breakfast?" asked the poor little Red Hen, hoping they would soon leave off being cross.

"I shan't," said the Cock.

"I shan't," said the Mouse.

"Then I'll do it myself," said the little Red Hen.

So she cleared everything away, swept up the crumbs and brushed up the fireplace.

"And now, who'll help me to make the beds?"

"I shan't," said the Cock.

"I shan't," said the Mouse.

"Then I'll do it myself," said the little Red Hen.

And she tripped away upstairs.

But the lazy Cock and Mouse each sat down in a comfortable arm-chair by the fire, and soon fell fast asleep.

Now the bad Fox had crept up the hill and into the garden, and if the Cock and Mouse hadn't been asleep, they would have seen his sharp eyes peeping in at the window.

"Rat tat tat! Rat tat tat!" the Fox knocked at the door.

"Who can that be?" said the Mouse, half opening his eyes.

"Go and look for yourself, if you want to know," said the rude Cock.

"It's the postman perhaps," thought the Mouse to himself, "and he may have a letter for me." So without waiting to see who it was, he lifted the latch and opened the door.

As soon as he opened it, in jumped the big Fox.

"Oh! oh! oh!" squeaked the Mouse, as he tried to run up the chimney.

"Doodle doodle do!" screamed the Cock, as he jumped on the back of the biggest arm-chair.

But the Fox only laughed, and without more ado he took the little Mouse by the tail, and popped him into the sack, and seized the Cock by the neck and popped him in too.

Then the poor little Red Hen came running downstairs to see what all the noise was about, and the Fox caught her and put her into the sack with the others.

Then he took a long piece of string out of his pocket, wound it round, and round, and round the mouth of the sack, and tied it very tight indeed. After that he threw the sack over his back, and off he set down the hill, chuckling to himself.

"Oh, I wish I hadn't been so cross," said the Cock, as they went bumping about.

"Oh! I wish I hadn't been so lazy," said the Mouse, wiping his eyes with the tip of his tail.

"It's never too late to mend," said the little Red Hen. "And don't be too sad. See, here I have my little work-bag, and in it there is a pair of scissors, and a little thimble, and a needle and thread. Very soon you will see what I am going to do."

Now the sun was very hot, and soon Mr. Fox began to feel his sack was heavy, and at last he thought he would lie down under a tree and go to sleep for a little while. So he threw the sack down with a big bump, and very soon fell fast asleep.

Snore, snore, snore, went the Fox.

As soon as the little Red Hen heard this, she took out her scissors, and began to snip a hole in the sack just large enough for the Mouse to creep through.

"Quick," she whispered to the Mouse, "run as fast as you can and bring back a stone just as large as yourself."

Out scampered the Mouse, and soon came back, dragging the stone after him.

"Push it in here," said the little Red Hen, and he pushed it in, in a twinkling.

Then the little Red Hen snipped away at the hole, till it was large enough for the Cock to get through.

"Quick," she said, "run and get a stone as big as yourself."

Out flew the Cock, and soon came back quite out of breath, with a big stone, which he pushed into the sack too.

Then the little Red Hen popped out, got a stone as big as herself, and pushed it in. Next she put on her thimble, took out her needle and thread, and sewed up the hole as quickly as ever she could.

When it was done, the Cock, and the Mouse and the little Red Hen ran home very fast, shut the door after

them, drew the bolts, shut the shutters, and drew down the blinds and felt quite safe.

The bad Fox lay fast asleep under the tree for some time, but at last he awoke.

"Dear, dear," he said, rubbing his eyes and then looking at the long shadows on the grass, "how late it is getting. I must hurry home."

So the bad Fox went grumbling and groaning down the hill, till he came to the stream. Splash! In went one foot. Splash! In went the other, but the stones in the sack were so heavy that at the very next step, down tumbled Mr. Fox into a deep pool. And then the fishes carried him off to their fairy caves and kept him a prisoner there, so he was never seen again. And the four greedy little foxes had to go to bed without any supper.

But the Cock and the Mouse never grumbled again. They lit the fire, filled the kettle, laid the breakfast, and did all the work, while the good little Red Hen had a holiday, and sat resting in the big arm-chair.

No foxes ever troubled them again, and for all I know they are still living happily in the little house with the green door and green shutters, which stands on the hill.

# The Doll in the Grass

Once upon a time there was a King who had twelve sons. When they were grown up he told them they must now go out into the world and find themselves wives, who must all be able to spin and weave and make a shirt in one day, else he would not have them for daughters-in-law. He gave each of his sons a horse and a new suit of armor, and so they set out in the world to look for wives.

When they had traveled a bit on the way they said they would not take the youngest son Ashiepattle with them, for he was good for nothing. Ashiepattle must stop behind; there was no help for it. The poor boy did not know what he should do or which way he should turn. He became so sad that he got off the horse and sat down on the grass and began to cry.

When he had sat awhile, he suddenly saw one of the tussocks among the grass beginning to move, and out of it came a small white figure. As it came nearer, Ashiepattle saw that it was a beautiful little girl, but she was so tiny, so very, very tiny.

She went up to him and asked him if he would like to come below and pay a visit to her in the grass.

Yes, that he would; and so he did. When he came

down below, the doll in the grass was sitting in a chair, dressed very finely and looking still more beautiful. She asked Ashiepattle where he was going and what was his errand.

He told her they were twelve brothers, and that the King had given them each a horse and a suit of armor, and told them to go out in the world and find themselves wives, but they must all be able to spin and weave and make a shirt in a day.

"If you can do that and will become my wife, I will not travel any farther," said Ashiepattle to the doll in the grass.

Yes, that she would, and she set to work at once to get the shirt spun, woven, and made; but it was so tiny, so very, very tiny, no bigger than——so!

Ashiepattle then returned home, taking the shirt with him. But when he brought it out he felt very shy because it was so small. However, the King said he could have her for all that, and you can imagine how happy and joyful Ashiepattle became.

The road did not seem long to him as he set out to fetch his little sweetheart. When he came to the doll in the grass, he wanted her to sit with him on his horse; but no, that she wouldn't. She said she would sit and drive in a silver spoon, and she had two small white horses which would draw her.

So they set out, he on his horse and she in the silver spoon; and the horses which drew her were two small white mice.

Ashiepattle always kept to one side of the road, for he was so afraid he should ride over her; she was so very, very tiny.

When they had traveled a bit on the way they came to a large lake; there Ashiepattle's horse took fright and shied over to the other side of the road, and upset the spoon, so that the doll in the grass fell into the water. Ashiepattle became very sad, for he did not know how he should get her out again; but after a while a merman brought her up. But now she had become just as big as any other grown-up being and was much more beautiful than she was before. So he placed her in front of him on the horse and rode home.

When Ashiepattle got there all his brothers had also returned, each with a sweetheart; but they were so ugly and ill-favored and bad-tempered that they had come to blows with their sweethearts on their way home. On their heads they had hats which were painted with black, and this had run from their hats down their faces, so that they were still uglier and more ill-favored to behold.

When the brothers saw Ashiepattle's sweetheart, they all became envious of him, but the King was so pleased with Ashiepattle and his sweetheart that he drove all the others away. And so Ashiepattle was married to the doll in the grass; and afterwards they lived happily and comfortably for a long, long while; and if they are not dead, they must be still alive.

From *Fairy Tales From the Far North*, edited by P. C. Asbjörnsen and Jörgen Moe.

# Drakestail

Drakestail was very little, that is why he was called Drakestail. But tiny as he was he had brains, and he knew what he was about, for having begun with nothing he ended by amassing a hundred crowns. Now the king of the country, who was very extravagant and never kept any money, having heard that Drakestail had some, went one day in his own person to borrow his hoard, and Drakestail was not a little proud of having lent money to the king.

But after the first and second year, seeing that he never even dreamed of paying the interest, Drakestail became uneasy, and, at last, he resolved to go and see his majesty himself, and get repaid. So one fine morning Drakestail, very spruce and fresh, took to the road, singing:

'Quack, quack, quack, when shall I get my money back?'

He had not gone far when he met friend fox, on his rounds that way.

'Good morning, neighbor,' said the friend. 'Where are you off to so early?'

I am going to the king for what he owes me.'

'Oh, take me with you!'

Drakestail said to himself, 'One can't have too many friends' . . . 'I will,' said he, 'but going on all fours you will soon be tired. Make yourself quite small, get into my throat—go into my gizzard and I will carry you.'

'Happy thought!' said friend fox.

He took bag and baggage and, presto! He was gone like a letter into the post. And Drakestail was off again, all spruce and fresh, still singing:

'Quack, quack, quack, when shall I have my money back?'

He had not gone far when he met his friend, ladder, leaning on her wall. 'Good morning, my duckling,' said the ladder. 'Whither away so bold?'

'I am going to the king for what he owes me.'

'Oh, take me with you!'

Drakestail said to himself, 'One can't have too many friends' . . . 'I will,' said he, 'but with your wooden legs you will soon be tired. Make yourself quite small, get into my throat—go into my gizzard and I will carry you.'

'Happy thought!' said my friend ladder, and nimbly, bag and baggage, went to keep company with friend fox.

'Quack, quack, quack.' And Drakestail was off again, singing, and spruce as before. A little farther he met his friend river, wandering quietly in the sunshine.

'My cherub,' said she, 'whither so lonesome, with arching tail, on this muddy road?'

'I am going to the king you know, for what he owes me.'

'Oh, take me with you!'

Drakestail said to himself, 'I can't have too many friends' . . . 'I will,' said he, 'but you who sleep while you walk will soon be tired. Make yourself quite small, get into my throat—go into my gizzard and I will carry you.'

'Ah, happy thought!' said my friend river.

She took bag and baggage, and glou, glou, glou took her place between friend fox and my friend ladder.

'Quack, quack, quack.' And Drakestail was off again, singing.

A little farther on he met comrade wasp's nest, maneuvering his wasps. 'Well, good morning, friend Drakestail,' said comrade wasp's nest. 'Where are we bound for so spruce and fresh?'

'I am going to the king for what he owes me.'

'Oh, take me with you!'

Drakestail said to himself, 'One can't have too many friends' . . . 'I will,' said he, 'but with your battalion to drag along, you will soon be tired. Make yourself quite small, go down my throat—get into my gizzard and I will carry you.'

'By Jove! That's a good idea!' said comrade wasp's nest.

And left file! He took the same road to join the others with all his party. There was not much more room, but by closing up a bit they managed. And Drakestail was off again, singing.

He arrived thus at the capital and threaded his way straight up the High Street still running, and singing, 'Quack, quack, quack, when shall I get my money back?'

to the great astonishment of the good folks, till he came
to the king's palace.

He struck with the knocker, *Toc! Toc!*

'Who is there?' asked the porter, putting his head out
of the wicket.

' 'Tis I, Drakestail. I wish to speak to the king.'

'Speak to the king! That's easily said. The king is din-
ing and will not be disturbed.'

'Tell him that it is I, and I have come he well knows
why.'

The porter shut his wicket and went up to say it to the
king, who was just sitting down to dinner with all his
ministers.

'Good, good!' said the king laughing. 'I know what it
is! Make him come in, and put him with the turkeys and
chickens.'

The porter descended.

'Have the goodness to enter.'

'Good!' said Drakestail to himself. 'I shall now see how
they eat at court.'

'This way, this way,' said the porter. 'One step farther.
There, there you are!'

'How? What? In the poultry yard?'

How vexed Drakestail was!

'Ah, so that's it,' said he. 'Wait! I will compel you to
receive me. Quack, quack, quack, when shall I get my
money back?' But turkeys and chickens are creatures who
don't like people who are not as themselves. When they
saw the newcomer and how he was made, and when they

heard him crying too, they began to give him black looks.

'What is it? What does he want?'

Finally they rushed at him all together, to overwhelm him with pecks.

'I am lost!' said Drakestail to himself, when by good luck he remembered his comrade, friend fox, and he cried:

> 'Reynard, Reynard, come out of your earth,
> Or Drakestail's life is of little worth.'

Then friend fox, who was only waiting for these words, hastened out, threw himself on the wicked fowls, and quick! Quack! he tore them to pieces; at the end of five minutes there was not one left alive. And Drakestail, quite content, began to sing again:

'Quack, quack, quack, when shall I get my money back?'

When the king who was still at table heard this refrain, and the poultry woman came to tell him what had been going on in the yard, he was terribly annoyed. He ordered them to throw this tail of a drake into the well, to make an end of him.

And it was done as he commanded. Drakestail was in despair of getting himself out of such a deep hole, when he remembered his friend the ladder.

> 'Ladder, Ladder, come out of your hold,
> Or Drakestail's days will soon be told.'

My friend ladder, who was only waiting for these words,

hastened out, leaned her two arms on the edge of the well, then Drakestail climbed nimbly on her back, and hop! He was in the yard, where he began to sing louder than ever.

When the king, who was still at table and laughing at the good trick he had played his creditor, heard him again claiming his money, he became livid with rage. He commanded that the furnace should be heated, and this tail of a drake thrown into it, because he must be a sorcerer.

The furnace was soon hot, but this time Drakestail was not so afraid; he counted on his friend river.

> 'River, River, outward flow,
> Or to death Drakestail must go.'

My friend river hastened out, and errouf! She threw herself into the furnace, which she flooded, with all the people who had lighted it; after which she flowed growling into the hall of the palace to the height of more than four feet. And Drakestail, quite content, began to swim, singing deafeningly:

'Quack, quack, quack, when shall I get my money back?'

The king was still at table and thought himself quite sure of his game. But when he heard Drakestail singing again and they told him all that had passed, he became furious and got up from table brandishing his fists.

'Bring him here, and I'll cut his throat! Bring him here quick!' cried he.

And quickly two footmen ran to fetch Drakestail.

'At last,' said the poor chap, going up the great stairs, 'they have decided to receive me.'

Imagine his terror when on entering he saw the king as red as a turkey cock, and all his ministers attending him, sword in hand. He thought this time it was all up with him. Happily, he remembered there was still one remaining friend, and he cried with dying accents:

> *'Wasp's nest, Wasp's nest, make a sally,*
> *Or Drakestail never more may rally.'*

Hereupon the scene changed.

'Bs, bs, bayonet them!' The brave wasp's nest rushed out with all his wasps. They threw themselves on the infuriated king and his ministers and stung them so fiercely that they lost their heads and, not knowing where to hide themselves, they all jumped pell-mell from the window and broke their necks on the pavement.

Behold Drakestail much astonished, all alone in the big salon and master of the field. He could not get over it. Nevertheless, he remembered shortly why he had come to the palace, and improving the occasion, he set to work to hunt for his dear money. But in vain he rummaged in all the drawers; he found nothing. All had been spent.

Ferreting thus from room to room he came at last to the one with the throne in it and, feeling fatigued, he sat himself down on it to think over his adventure. In the meanwhile the people had found their king and his ministers with their feet in the air on the pavement, and they had gone into the palace to know how it had occurred.

On entering the throne room, when the crowd saw there was already someone on the royal seat, they broke out in cries of surprise and joy:

> *'The king is dead, long live the king!*
> *Heaven has sent us down this thing.'*

Drakestail, who was no longer surprised at anything, received the acclamations of the people as if he had never done anything else all his life.

A few of them certainly murmured that a Drakestail would make a fine king! Those who knew him replied that a knowing Drakestail was a more worthy king than a spendthrift like the one who was lying on the pavement. In short, they ran and took the crown off the head of the dead king and placed it on Drakestail, whom it fitted like wax.

Thus he became king.

'And now,' said he after the ceremony, 'ladies and gentlemen, let's go to supper. I am so hungry!'

CAROLYN HAYWOOD

# A Fourth-of-July Picnic

Not far from the Robinsons' farm was a wide river. Running along beside the river there was a narrow stream. It was separated from the river by a strip of land covered with beautiful trees. As Teddy looked at the river and the stream, he thought they looked just like a big mother river with a little baby river, but Daddy said that the little river was not a river at all. It was a canal.

"Why is it a canal?" asked Teddy.

"A canal is built," replied Daddy, "while a river is made by many little streams flowing together."

"What do they use the canal for?" asked Babs.

"They send things from one place to another up and down the canal," answered Daddy. "The boats are called barges. Perhaps if we wait a little while, we'll see a canal barge."

They walked down to a small wooden bridge that crossed the canal. The children leaned over the side of the bridge and looked at their reflections in the still water. Once Teddy dropped a pebble into the water. It made rippling circles. The children laughed when they saw their faces all full of ripples.

Just then they heard the tinkle of a bell. It didn't bongle like a cow-bell and it didn't jingle like a sleigh-bell. This was a tinkling bell.

"What is that bell, Daddy?" asked Teddy.

"A barge is coming now," said Daddy. "That is the bell on the mules that you hear."

"The mules!" exclaimed Babs. "I didn't know mules pulled boats. I thought they only pulled wagons."

The children peered ahead. They couldn't see anything, but the sound of the bell was growing louder.

"Oh, Daddy!" said Teddy, "do the mules swim in the water?"

"No," laughed Daddy, "they walk along that path beside the canal." Daddy pointed to the narrow path that ran close beside the water. "That is called the tow-path," he said.

Soon the barge appeared. The children could see it, piled high with sand. Now they could see the mules plodding along the path. They pulled the barge very slowly by a long rope. A young boy stood on the barge. As it passed under the bridge, Teddy and Babs waved their hands. The boy waved and called, "Hello."

"Oh, Daddy!" cried Teddy. "I wish I could ride on a canal barge. It goes so smooth and silky."

"Yes," said Babs, "it would be nice to ride on one."

"I'll tell you what we'll do," said Daddy. "I'll hire a canal barge on the Fourth of July and we'll go on a picnic."

"With Mother too?" asked Babs.

"And the twins?" said Teddy.

"Yes," answered Daddy, "we'll take Mother and the twins, and perhaps Mr. and Mrs. Perkins will come too."

"That will be fun!" cried Babs.

"Maybe I can ride on one of the mules," said Teddy.

"We'll see," said Daddy.

The children could hardly wait for the Fourth of July to come. Every evening Teddy stood on a chair in the kitchen and put a big black cross through the date on the calendar. Then he would say, "Only eight more days until the Fourth of July." The next day he would say, "Only seven more days until the Fourth of July." At last the evening came when he said, "Only one more day until the Fourth of July."

All that day, Teddy and Babs and the twins were busy getting ready for the picnic. Mrs. Perkins baked cookies, and Babs and Jane helped her to cut the thin dough with little tin molds. There were hearts and diamonds and circles and rings. There were halfmoons and clovers. They were sprinkled all over the top with chopped nuts.

Peter and Teddy drove into town with Mr. Perkins in the station wagon to get all the good things that Mother had ordered for the picnic supper. Teddy's mouth watered as he saw them all.

"We mustn't forget to buy some apples, Mr. Perkins," said Teddy. "We have to have an apple for each of the mules that pull the barge."

"Sure enough!" said Mr. Perkins, "some apples and some lumps of sugar for their picnic supper."

That night, after Teddy and Babs were in bed, Babs called to Teddy from her bed in the next room. "Teddy!" she said, "do you know what I am going to take on the picnic?"

"What?" asked Teddy.

"Some salt-water taffy," she replied.

"Where did you get it?" said Teddy.

"I saved it out of the box that Aunt Ethel sent us from the sea-shore."

"How many pieces have you?" Teddy asked.

"Four," replied Babs. "They're chocolate."

"Can I have one?" asked Teddy.

"Yes," said Babs. "I'll give one to Peter and one to Jane too. Aren't you glad they are chocolate?"

"Uh-huh!" murmured Teddy in a very sleepy voice.

The next morning the children were up bright and early. They ran over to see if the twins were ready, long before Mother and Daddy were down to breakfast. All morning the children kept saying, "Aren't we going soon, Daddy?" "Is it almost time to go, Mother?"

At last it was time to go. "Where is the lunch basket?" said Teddy.

"Mr. and Mrs. Perkins are bringing it in the station wagon. Mr. Perkins can't leave the farm so early," said Mother. "We will ride on the barge to the covered bridge. Mr. and Mrs. Perkins will meet us there and ride with us to the end of the canal. Then we will eat our supper and come back in the moonlight."

The four children trotted off with Mr. and Mrs. Robinson. They walked to the canal. There was the barge tied up to the landing. The mules were nibbling the grass by the side of the tow-path. The boy who had waved to Teddy and Babs the first time they had ever seen a canal barge was waiting for them. His name was James.

"How would you like to ride one of the mules a little way?" he asked Teddy.

"I'd like that," replied Teddy.

The boy lifted Teddy up on the mule's back while the others settled themselves on the barge. Soon they were off, gliding slowly up the canal. They passed little houses whose gardens came right down to the edge of the water. They could almost pick the flowers. The trees arching overhead made it cool and green. The sun shone through the leaves and made bright speckles on the water. Birds sang in the trees. Tinkle, tinkle, tinkle, went the bell. Clop, clop, clop, went the mules' feet.

After a while Teddy came on the barge and Peter rode on the mule. Then Babs and Jane each had a ride.

At last they reached the covered bridge. The children strained their eyes to be the first to catch a glimpse of Mr. and Mrs. Perkins.

"I don't see them, Mother," said Teddy.

"Well, they must be here somewhere," replied Mother. "There is a car coming down the road to the bridge now." But the car went over the bridge.

"That is strange," said Daddy; "they should have been here by this time."

"Perhaps this is the car," said Jane. Another car came down and passed by. Another and another came. They all passed on. The barge waited a long time.

At last James said to Mr. Robinson, "I'm sorry, sir, but we'll have to go on without them. We are due at the end of the canal now and I have to bring another party back."

"All right," said Mr. Robinson, "we'll go on."

"Without our supper!" cried the children. "What will we do without our supper? We can't have a picnic without our supper!"

"Don't worry," said Daddy. "Mr. and Mrs. Perkins will probably find us."

"Getty up!" said James. The mules started again. The barge glided away from the covered bridge. After what seemed a long time to the children, they reached the end of the canal. They were beginning to feel very hungry as they stepped off the barge.

Another picnic group scrambled on the barge. Soon Teddy and Babs and the twins and Mr. and Mrs. Robinson were alone, sitting on the bank of the canal. The children looked longingly after the barge. The people on the barge had such a big picnic basket and they had none. Perhaps Mr. and Mrs. Perkins wouldn't find them, they thought. Then they would have nothing to eat. Babs thought of her chocolate salt-water taffies. She hoped nothing would happen to them.

Daddy walked up to the road to see if he could see anything of Mr. and Mrs. Perkins. He watched for them a long time. At last he said, "I guess we will have to find a hot-dog stand."

"Oh, dear!" sighed Babs, "our lovely supper with cookies and everything!"

"Never mind!" said Mother, "we can have a good time eating hot-dogs. It can't spoil our fun."

The little group started to walk up to the road. The children's faces didn't look very happy.

Suddenly, Peter cried, "Oh, look! Here come Grandmother and Grandaddy now!"

"Oh, Grandaddy!" cried Jane. "We thought you were lost!"

"Have you got the supper?" asked Babs.

" 'Course he's got it," said Teddy. "Can't you see the basket?"

"We had engine trouble," said Mr. Perkins, "couldn't get the car started. We had to come in the bus."

"We thought we would find you before it got dark," said Mrs. Perkins.

Babs and Jane helped to unpack the supper basket and everyone sat down on the grass.

How the children ate! Mrs. Perkins said that she thought the sandwiches would come right out of the children's eyes.

Just at dusk the barge returned to take them home. Teddy gave the mules each an apple and Peter gave them some sugar. The mules enjoyed their picnic supper too. Then they all went on the barge. Mr. Perkins carried the empty picnic basket on board. The children were sleepy now. No one wanted to ride on the mules. They lay down on some blankets and looked up at the stars peeping through the leaves. The barge floated slowly through the darkness. Tiny lights shone fore and aft, like giant fireflies.

"It's like fairy-land," whispered Jane.

Clop! clop! clop! Tinkle! tinkle! tinkle!

# The Frog Prince

One fine evening a young princess went into a wood, and sat down by the side of a cool spring of water. She had a golden ball in her hand, which was her favorite plaything, and she amused herself with tossing it into the air and catching it again as it fell. After a time she threw it up so high that when she stretched out her hand to catch it, the ball bounded away and rolled along upon the ground, till at last it fell into the spring.

The princess looked into the spring after the ball; but it was very deep, so deep that she could not see the bottom of it. Then she began to lament her loss, and said, "Alas! if I could only get my ball again, I would give all my fine clothes and jewels, and everything that I have in the world."

Whilst she was speaking a frog put its head out of the water and said, "Princess, why do you weep so bitterly?"

"Alas!" said she, "what can you do for me, you nasty frog? My golden ball has fallen into the spring."

The frog said, "I want not your pearls and jewels and fine clothes; but if you will love me and let me live with

you, and eat from your little golden plate, and sleep upon
your little bed, I will bring you your ball again."

"What nonsense," thought the princess, "this silly frog
is talking! He can never get out of the well: however, he
may be able to get my ball for me; and therefore I will
promise him what he asks."

So she said to the frog, "Well, if you will bring me my
ball, I promise to do all you require." Then the frog put

his head down, and dived deep under the water; and after
a little while he came up again with the ball in his mouth,
and threw it on the ground.

As soon as the young princess saw her ball, she ran to
pick it up, and was so overjoyed to have it in her hand
again that she never thought of the frog, but ran home

with it as fast as she could. The frog called after her, "Stay, princess, and take me with you as you promised!" But she did not stop to hear a word.

The next day, just as the princess sat down to dinner, she heard a strange noise, tap-tap, as if somebody were coming up the marble staircase; and soon afterwards something knocked gently at the door, and said,—

*"Open the door, my princess dear,*
*Open the door to thy true love here!*
*And mind the words that thou and I said*
*By the fountain cool in the greenwood shade."*

Then the princess ran to the door and opened it, and there she saw the frog, whom she had quite forgotten; she was terribly frightened, and shutting the door as fast as she could, came back to her seat. The king, her father, asked her what had frightened her. "There is a nasty frog," said she, "at the door, who lifted my ball out of the spring this morning: I promised him that he should live with me here, thinking that he could never get out of the spring; but there he is at the door and wants to come in!"

While she was speaking the frog knocked at the door, and said,—

*"Open the door, my princess dear,*
*Open the door to thy true love here!*
*And mind the words that thou and I said*
*By the fountain cool in the greenwood shade."*

The king said to the young princess, "As you have made a promise, you must keep it; so go and let him in."

She did so, and the frog hopped into the room, and came up close to the table. "Pray lift me upon a chair," said he to the princess, "and let me sit next to you." As soon as she had done this, the frog said, "Put your plate closer to me that I may eat out of it." This she did, and when he had eaten as much as he could he said, "Now I am tired; carry me up-stairs and put me into your little bed." And the princess took him up in her hand and put him upon the pillow of her own little bed, where he slept all night long. As soon as it was light he jumped up, hopped down-stairs, and went out of the house.

"Now," thought the princess, "he is gone and I shall be troubled with him no more."

But she was mistaken; for when night came again, she heard the same tapping at the door, and when she opened it, the frog came in and slept upon her pillow as before till the morning broke: and the third night he did the same; but when the princess awoke on the following morning, she was astonished to see, instead of the frog, a handsome prince standing at the head of her bed, and gazing on her with the most beautiful eyes that ever were seen.

He told her that he had been enchanted by a malicious fairy, who had changed him into the form of a frog, in which he was fated to remain till some princess should take him out of the spring and let him sleep upon her bed for three nights. "You," said the prince, "have broken this cruel charm, and now I have nothing to wish for but that you should go with me into my father's kingdom, where I will marry you, and love you as long as you live."

The young princess, you may be sure, was not long in giving her consent; and as they spoke a splendid carriage drove up with eight beautiful horses decked with plumes of feathers and golden harness, and behind rode the prince's servant, the faithful Henry, who had bewailed the misfortune of his dear master so long and bitterly that his heart had well nigh burst. Then all set out full of joy for the prince's kingdom; where they arrived safely, and lived happily a great many years.

# The Gingerbread Boy

Now you shall hear a story that somebody's great-great-grandmother told a little girl ever so many years ago:

There was once a little old man and a little old woman, who lived in a little old house in the edge of a wood. They would have been a very happy old couple but for one thing —they had no little child, and they wished for one very much. One day, when the little old woman was baking gingerbread, she cut a cake in the shape of a little boy, and put it into the oven.

Presently, she went to the oven to see if it was baked. As soon as the oven door was opened, the little ginger-bread boy jumped out, and began to run away as fast as he could go.

The little old woman called her husband, and they both ran after him. But they could not catch him. And soon the gingerbread boy came to a barn full of threshers. He called out to them as he went by, saying:

> *"I've run away from a little old woman,*
> *A little old man,*
> *And I can run away from you, I can!"*

Then the barn full of threshers set out to run after him. But, though they ran fast, they could not catch him. And he ran on till he came to a field full of mowers. He called out to them:

> *"I've run away from a little old woman,*
> *A little old man,*
> *A barn full of threshers,*
> *And I can run away from you, I can!"*

Then the mowers began to run after him, but they couldn't catch him. And he ran on till he came to a cow. He called out to her:

> *"I've run away from a little old woman,*
> *A little old man,*
> *A barn full of threshers,*
> *A field full of mowers,*
> *And I can run away from you, I can!"*

But, though the cow started at once, she couldn't catch him. And soon he came to a pig. He called out to the pig:

> *"I've run away from a little old woman,*
> *A little old man,*
> *A barn full of threshers,*
> *A field full of mowers,*
> *A cow,*
> *And I can run away from you, I can!"*

But the pig ran, and couldn't catch him. And he ran till he came across a fox, and to him he called out:

"*I've run away from a little old woman,*
    *A little old man,*
    *A barn full of threshers,*
    *A field full of mowers,*
    *A cow and a pig,*
*And I can run away from you, I can!*"

Then the fox set out to run. Now foxes can run very fast, and so the fox soon caught the gingerbread boy and began to eat him up.

Presently the gingerbread boy said: "Oh, dear! I'm quarter gone!" and then: "Oh, I'm half gone!" And soon: "I'm three-quarters gone!" And at last: "I'm all gone!" and never spoke again.

ELEANOR FARJEON

# The Green Kitten

*Derry had just turned eight, and Jim is almost eighty. Derry loves nothing better than to listen to old Jim tell wonderful stories about his former sailing days, like this one about the green kitten.*

What would you like best on your birthday?" asked Derry.

"A sight of the sea," said Jim, "that's what I'd like better than anything else; a sight of the sea, blue, green or gray, and the smell of it in my nose."

"I hope you will live to see eighty, Jim," said Derry.

"And I hope you will!" said Jim heartily. "It's a very good age to be. What else did you have?"

"Seven birthday cards, and a letter from my Granny with ten shillings in it, and an engine from my Uncle, and a book from my Aunt, and a mouth-organ from Nanny, and a kitten from the cat. She had five yesterday, so she could spare me one."

"What color was it?" asked Jim. "Green?"

Derry burst out laughing. "It's black with white paws. There *isn't* a green kitten."

"Yes, there is," said Jim, "because I've seen one."

"Where?" asked Derry.

"Under the sea," said Jim, "when I was a sailor."

All the children in the street knew that Jim had been a sailor *on* the sea, but it surprised Derry to hear that he had been a sailor *under* it. He exclaimed, "Have you really been under the sea, Jim?"

"Of course I have! What d'ye take me for? A landlubber?"

Derry didn't know what a landlubber was, but he thought he had better not take Jim for one, so he said, "No, of course not. Tell me about the green kitten."

"I caught it in my shrimping-net," said Jim, "on the beach at Pegwell Bay." He paused.

"Do go on, Jim!" urged Derry, leaning his fairy cycle against the mail-box.

"Seeing it's your birthday," said Jim, "I will. But I've got to do some remembering first." He blew his nose thoughtfully for some time, and then began.

It happened when I was a boy. I felt the call of the sea, and ran away from the farm in Kent where I was born. Our farm was not far from the coast, and soon I came to Pegwell Bay, where the good ship *Rockinghorse* was riding at anchor.

The Captain saw me coming through his telescope, and when I was near enough he called, "Come here, boy!" He had a commanding sort of voice, so I came.

He looked me up and down, and said, "My cabin-boy has just run away to go on a farm."

"That's funny," I said, "because I've just run away from a farm to go for a cabin-boy."

The Captain looked me down and up, and said, "You'll do. What's your name?"

"Jim," I said. "What's yours?"

"Cap'n Potts," he said. "Well, Jim, we don't sail till tomorrow, and tonight I feel like shrimps."

"Like shrimps?" I said.

"Yes, like shrimps," said Cap'n Potts.

Now, when he said he was feeling like shrimps, I thought Cap'n Potts meant he was feeling sad, or seedy, or something like that. But it turned out he meant just what he said, for he handed me a big shrimping-net, and said, "Go and catch some."

That was a job any boy would enjoy, be he cabin-boy or farm-boy. I kicked off my boots in a jiffy, and went shrimping among the pools on the beach. The pools were surrounded by rocks, and the rocks were covered with thick green weed, like wet hair, very slippery to the feet.

When I'd got a nice netful of shrimps, I took them aboard the *Rockinghorse*, and Cap'n Potts said, "Well done, Jim! You'll make a first-class cabin-boy, I see. Take them below to Cookie, and tell him to boil them for tea."

I went below and found Cookie, and said, "Please, I'm Jim, the new cabin-boy, please, and please, Cap'n Potts says will you please cook these shrimps for tea?"

"Shrimps!" said Cookie. "Do you call *this* a shrimp?"

He plunged his hand into the net, and fetched up what looked like a little lump of rock smothered in green sea-weed. But the little lump wriggled in Cookie's hand, the little lump arched its weedy green back, the little lump waved a weedy green tail, the little lump pricked up two weedy green ears, the little lump wrinkled its weedy green nose, and *spat*. Next thing, it jumped out of Cookie's big hands, and clawed its way up my shoulder, where it sat rubbing its soft green head against my cheek.

That little lump was nothing less than a wee green Kitten, with eyes as pink as coral.

The next day, when *we* sailed, the Kitten sailed too, and before long it was the pet of the ship. But I was its favorite, and it always slept in my cabin. Being the cabin-boy, I had, of course, a cabin to myself.

Now, that first trip of mine we did not seem to have the best of luck. Everything a ship could have the *Rockinghorse* had, like a child who has chickenpox, measles, and mumps, one after the other. The *Rockinghorse* had hurricanes, and icebergs, and pirates, and thunderbolts. Once she was wrecked, and once she was becalmed.

It was when she was becalmed that *my* adventure happened.

Cap'n Potts was a restless man, and liked to be on the move. It gave him the fidgets when the ship got stuck like that in the middle of the sea, and one evening he came up to me and said, "Jim, I feel like lobsters!"

"Never mind, Cap'n," I said. "Perhaps we'll get a move on tomorrow."

"Perhaps we will," said Cap'n Potts, "and perhaps we won't. But whether we do or don't, tonight I feel like lobsters." Then he handed me a lobster-pot, and said, "Go and catch some."

Then I saw what he meant, and I got into a diving-suit, tucked the lobster-pot under my arm, dived over the side of the *Rockinghorse*, and sank to the bottom.

There was I, just a little nipper, all alone on the bed of the ocean. And there I saw wonders, to be sure! Coral and pearl and golden sands, colored sea-weed as big as bushes, sunfish and moonfish like red and silver jewels, anemones like brilliant beds of flowers, and a sunken ship painted with gold and vermilion, like the castle of a king. The only thing I didn't see, was lobsters.

I was just wondering how to catch what wasn't there, when I found I was caught myself. The long arm of an Octopus had shot out and whipped round me like a rope; next thing I knew, I was lifted up and dropped down into the stateroom of the gorgeous ship I mentioned.

There I found myself face to face with an angry Cat-fish. She was the biggest Catfish you ever saw, and on her head was a little coral crown. She kept opening and shutting her mouth at me, and goggling her eyes at me, as cross as two sticks, and I couldn't think why.

"You seem upset, ma'am," I said.

"Upset!" she snapped. "I should think I am upset! And on top of it all you must go and call me ma'am, as though I hadn't a royal title of my own."

"Tell me what it is, and I'll call you by it, ma'am," said I.

"There you go again!" she snapped. "Where are your

eyes, boy? Can't you see the crown on my head? I am the Queen of the Catfish, and I want my Kitten!"

"Your Kitten, ma'am-your-majesty?" said I.

"My Kitten, booby," said she, "that you caught in your shrimping-net. And till Cap'n Potts gives it me back, he sha'n't have his cabin-boy. As long as he keeps my Kitten, I'll keep *you!*"

"Who's to let him know?" I asked.

"You shall write him a letter," said she, "and I'll send it up by Octopus."

With that she set me down in the ship's saloon, a very glorious room indeed, with golden plate and jeweled goblets on the tables, and hangings of rich leather on the walls. I took off my diving-suit, pulled out my note-book and pencil, and scribbled a note to Cap'n Potts. This was it:

> *Dear Cap'n Potts:*
> *The Queen of the Catfish wants her Kittenfish, which is the green Kitten we've got aboard the* Rockinghorse, *and she's going to keep me till she gets it, so if you want me back, send down the Kitten by Octopus, but if you'd rather have the Kitten than me, don't bother. I hope you are well, as this leaves me.*
> *Yours obediently,*
> *Jim*

Just as I scribbled "Jim," the Queen of the Catfish looked in and said, "Is your letter done? The Octopus is ready to start."

"Here's the letter, ma'am-your-majesty," said I, "but I'm afraid the paper won't stand salt water."

"We'll put it in a shell to keep it dry," said the Queen of the Catfish. The saloon was littered with junk of all sorts, and she picked out a big spotted shell with a mouth like a letter-box. Then she posted my letter in the shell, gave it to the Octopus, and he went aloft.

I wondered a bit whether Cap'n Potts would rather keep the Kitten than have me back again. I would in his place, and I made ready to stay under the sea for the rest of my life. It wasn't a bad place to stay in, but I preferred the *Rockinghorse*. So when the Octopus came down again with the Kitten in its tentacle, I felt quite light-hearted.

It was a pretty sight to see that little green Kitten leap into its mother's fins, sea-mewing with pleasure; and the Queen of the Catfish was so pleased to see it, that she turned from snarly to smiley.

"Get into your diving-suit, Jim," she said, "and my respects to your Captain, and tell him the next time he catches a Kittenfish he must throw it back, or there'll be trouble."

"There *was* trouble," said I, "what with hurricanes, icebergs, pirates and all."

"Those were my doing," said the Queen of the Catfish, "but from now on you shall have fair winds and smooth sailing. Here's your lobster-pot." With that she handed me my pot, and it was full to the brim with lobsters. "Nasty vicious things!" said she. "Always nipping my kittens when they get the chance. I'm glad to be rid of a few. Good-bye, Jim."

"Good-bye, ma'am-your-majesty," said I.

"Booby!" said she.

The Octopus took me in one tentacle, and the lobster-pot in another; the Kitten waved its paw at me, and the Queen of the Catfish kissed her fin, and up we went. In another moment, I and the lobsters were put down safe and sound on the deck of the good ship *Rockinghorse*, and wasn't I glad! I'd never thought to see her more.

Cap'n Pots was sorry to lose the Kitten, but when he saw the lobsters he said, "Well done, my lad; you're an A-One Cabin-boy, *you* are!" Then the wind began to blow, the sails began to fill, and the *Rockinghorse* was well under way when we all sat down to hot lobsters for tea.

And now see here what I've got in my pocket. It's the very shell I posted my letter in. I found it lying about the deck a few days later, and I've kept it ever since. It's a good shell, and a pretty shell, and seeing it's your birthday you can keep it, as a present from Jim. Put it to your ear, and you'll hear the sea in it. But don't go putting it to your kitten's ear, or she might turn green—and then there *would* be trouble.

PEGGY BACON

# Guineapigmalion

*Juliana and Timothy are the older sister and brother of Benjy, Chug is his dog's name and Jungle his cat's. Benjy is lucky that his father is a sculptor who can work at home and be with him when the rest of the family go off on a picnic.*

There were moments when Juliana and Timothy envied Benjy his carefree life, and this feeling most often came over them at about half past eight in the morning while they were gulping down their milk, trying to find their school-books, and preparing to depart. Then Benjy would be calmly smearing honey on toast, cheeks, and forehead, with all the morning to squander on his breakfast and no pressing matters ahead of him. For Benjy had nothing much to do all day.

But on the other hand, after school was over for the day, the older children were inclined to feel rather sorry for Benjy, for it was seldom that he could take part in their games. The tables were turned and now it was Juliana and Timothy who were free—free to go where they chose, to visit their friends, to explore the countryside, to engage in adventures, providing they could think of any—while their small brother must stay around home within sight and call of grown-ups.

Thus left to himself, Benjy's occupations were various. He ran around with Chug; he fed Spooky, plucking piles of grass and clover for the rabbit and hovering about it while it ate. Sometimes he was able to coax fat Jungle to play with a paper and string. He might wheel his cars about or dig in the sand-pile, but now and then a day would come when time hung heavy on his hands and amusements like these seem dull and uninteresting. At such moments Benjy would take the orchard path that led to the studio. There Father usually welcomed him, placed him at a table in the corner, and gave him lumps of clay, from which Benjy would shape small animals.

Many were the beasts and birds he fashioned, simple toys, crudely made, but having something real about them nevertheless, so that there was never any mistake as to Benjy's intentions. If Benjy made a horse it looked like a sort of horse, although there never had been a horse exactly like it; if he made a cow, it was the queerest cow that ever was seen, but you knew at once that it was a cow. And so with the pigs, ducks, rabbits, dogs, cats, and birds; they could not be taken for anything but just what Benjy meant them to be.

While Jonathan Avon labored away on big statues, Benjy struggled and grunted over his little images. Juliana had read him all the old Greek legends, and one story had impressed him deeply: the tale of Pygmalion, the sculptor who carved a woman out of marble and named her Galatea. He fell in love with her and thought her so beautiful that he prayed she might come to life, and the kind gods answered his prayer. Benjy often chattered about Pygmalion to his father, for to tell the truth, this myth had fired him with the notion that some day, if only he modeled well enough, one of his clay animals would come alive. "Don't you think so, Father?" he would always end by asking, to which Jonathan Avon would reply cautiously, "There's no telling, Benjy"— for he knew how his son loved wonders. And so Benjy worked away earnestly, hoping for a miracle.

One Saturday Mother took Juliana, Timothy, Sammy, and Isabel on an all-day hike through the woods and fields. It was partly a picnic and partly a hunt for flowers. They took a trowel and a basket full of lunch, and their plan was to walk far into the forest, where they would eat up the lunch in some attractive place and bring home the basket filled with fringed gentians.

Gentians, as you know perhaps, are beautiful flowers that bloom here and there along the banks of streams. They are a deep, unusual blue, and they are rare and rather hard to find. The fringed gentians are rarer than the closed, so that a search for them becomes as exciting as a hunt for buried treasure. Alison Avon had learned from the neighbors that there were fringed gentians to be found in the woods behind Mayfield, and there had been a good deal of talk in the family concerning this expedition, to which every one was looking for-

ward. Every one, that is, except Benjy. Poor Benjy was
feeling very glum because he could not go.

Benjy could not walk as fast as the others. He was too
young to travel so many miles on foot. He would grow
tired and some one would have to carry him. He under-
stood all that, but though it sounded true and reasonable
enough, yet you can imagine how Benjy felt when the
morning came and he saw the others making ready to
leave.

"Never mind, Benjy, we'll bring you a fringed gen-
tian for your garden," soothed Juliana.

"You may play with my marbles today," volunteered
Timothy, "and here's my watch; you'd better take care
of it for me. I might lose it in the woods."

"Sarah told me she's going to make cookies this afternoon, and she wants you to help her cut them out," said
Mother.

"You may have this for keeps if you like, Benjy," quoth
Sammy, fishing a sponge-ball from his pocket.

"Poor Benjy will be all alone all day," said Isabel pity-
ingly.

"Certainly not!" cried Father, seizing Benjy's hand.
"Benjy and I have work to do this morning out in the
studio. Moreover, Benjy, there is a big animal book that
just came in the mail that may give you some new ideas."

So Father and Benjy watched the picnickers depart
for the woods and then made off together towards the
studio.

I shall not tell you at great length of the picnic party.

Suffice it to say that they all had a glorious time and saw many fascinating things. They came across a mother snake and her brood looking like a dish of spaghetti in a hollow between rocks. They saw a woodchuck, a quail, a snapping-turtle, and caught sight of some speckled deer grazing in a sunny glade. They ate their lunch on a slab of rock beside a tumbling brook. Sammy found a nest full of baby birds; Juliana found frog's eggs floating in a pool, and Timothy uncovered a lot of tiny lizards hatching beneath a stone. Finally, in a deep, damp, rocky dingle, when they had nearly forgotten what they came for, they discovered the precious fringed gentians, which they dug up, placed in the basket, and carried home triumphantly, late in the afternoon. And let us also return to Benjy.

He had played a bit with the marbles, the watch, and the sponge-ball. He had sat in the studio with Father looking at the big animal book. He and Father had had lunch together (there were apple dumplings for dessert), and for a short while in the afternoon Benjy had helped Sarah cut out the cookies. But the greater part of the day had been spent working in the studio, and the feeling that Benjy had now was what grown-ups call the "consciousness of work well done"—which is to say that he had made something good and knew it.

Ever since the day when the Avon children had gone as stowaways to the County Fair, Benjy had dreamed of guinea-pigs. Today as he turned the pages of the grand new animal book, he looked with pleasure at the large color-plates of nearly every animal in the world, but no picture he saw therein could crowd out of his mind that memory of soft, plump guinea-pigs. Finally, when Benjy sat down in his corner with a good big lump of clay, he simply surpassed himself; he modeled a life-sized group of two guinea-pigs eating a carrot, and Father said when he saw it that they were certainly guinea-pigs, that it was exactly what guinea-pigs would be apt to do, that it was all very life-like indeed and by far the best thing Benjy had ever done. And so it was that when the others returned, primed to tell Benjy all about their thrilling day, to their surprise and chagrin Benjy would pay very little attention to them, hardly listened to their tales of snakes, birds, and woodchucks, scarcely looked even at the wonderful fringed gentians which they had traveled so far to find—and instead was all eagerness to show them his new sculpture.

Every one came into the studio to see, and every one was properly impressed. Father praised the work again. Mother exclaimed over it. Juliana crowed, "Oh, Benjy, how cunning!"

Timothy said, "Good work, Benjy!"

Sammy said, "How do you do it, Benjy? I wish I could make things like that"—till Benjy was extremely proud and pleased.

But Isabel, who was a practical girl and had no feeling for Art, and who was rather annoyed at Benjy for his indifference to the fringed gentians, looked coldly at his handiwork and said, "Pooh, what's so wonderful? I think

real guinea-pigs are ever so much nicer than that. Adelaide Lambdin has lots. She sells them." And right away this remark of Isabel's made Benjy feel depressed.

He looked at the clay guinea-pigs and thought to himself, "Suppose their eyes twinkled. Suppose they were covered with fur." Also, he thought to himself that he did not care so much for Isabel. However, he was pleased with what he had done. And picking up the group, he carried it back to the house, where he placed it carefully in a big old candy-box which Sarah gave him. After supper was over, he carried it off to bed with him.

Father sat beside him for a while and they looked into the box together. There lay the lumps of clay, so carefully molded and smoothed, with the little tabs for ears, the little holes for eyes, and the little lozenge between them which was the carrot. Father remarked admiringly that they were certainly nice enough to come alive, so maybe —he broke off, stared thoughtfully, kissed his son good night, and went out. Benjy fetched a sigh and closed the box. Breathing one last whole-hearted prayer, he fell asleep.

"Juliana," called Father, coming downstairs, "you and Timothy come hop in the car with me. We're going over to Adelaide Lambdin's."

Next morning no sooner was Benjy awake than he peeked into the box. Thrilling to relate, the wonder of wonders had unaccountably come to pass, for within lay no lumps of sculptors' clay, but two living, breathing, munching, ravishing guinea-pigs, a sight to soothe the eye, to warm the heart, smooth and sleek—as had not Benjy's fingers made them? Moreover, item interesting to note, in their short life they had eaten already more than half the carrot!

One by one the members of the family drifted in Benjy's bedroom. One by one they heard him tell the magic tale of how his guinea-pigs had come to life.

"Little Guineapigmalion," Father dubbed him amid much laughter.

And then suddenly every one began kissing him five times and plumping packages down on the bed beside him, and Mother told him what he had forgotten and never would have remembered, that today was his birthday and he was five years old!

# Hansel and Gretel

Near a great forest there lived a poor woodcutter and his wife, and his two children; the boy's name was Hansel and the girl's, Gretel. They had very little to bite or to sup, and once, when there was great dearth in the land, the man could not even gain the daily bread.

As he lay in bed one night thinking of this, and turning and tossing, he sighed heavily, and said to his wife, who was the children's stepmother,

"What will become of us? We cannot even feed our children; there is nothing left for ourselves."

"I will tell you what, husband," answered the wife; "we will take the children early in the morning into the forest, where it is thickest; we will make them a fire, and we will give each of them a piece of bread, then we will go to our work and leave them alone. They will never find the way home again, and we shall be quit of them."

"No, wife," said the man, "I cannot do that; I cannot find it in my heart to take my children into the forest and to leave them there alone; the wild animals would soon come and devour them."

"Oh you fool," said she, "then we will all four starve; you had better get the coffins ready," and she left him no peace until he consented.

The two children had not been able to sleep for hunger, and had heard what their stepmother had said to their father. Gretel wept bitterly, and said to Hansel,

"It is all over with us."

"Do be quiet, Gretel," said Hansel, "and do not fret; I will manage something." When the parents had gone to sleep, Hansel got up, put on his little coat, opened the back door, and slipped out. The moon was shining brightly, and the white pebbles that lay in front of the house glistened like pieces of silver. Hansel stooped and filled the little pocket of his coat as full as it would hold. Then he went back again, and said to Gretel,

"Be easy, dear little sister, and go to sleep quietly; God will not forsake us," and laid himself down again in his bed.

When the day was breaking, and before the sun had risen, the wife came and awakened the two children, saying,

"Get up, you lazy bones! We are going into the forest to cut wood."

Then she gave each of them a piece of bread, and said,

"That is for dinner, and you must not eat it before then, for you will get no more."

Gretel carried the bread under her apron, for Hansel had his pockets full of pebbles. Then they set off all together on their way to the forest. When they had gone a little way Hansel stood still and looked back toward the house, and this he did again and again, till his father said to him,

"Hansel, what are you looking at? Take care not to forget your legs."

"Oh Father," said Hansel, "I am looking at my little white kitten, who is sitting up on the roof to bid me good-bye."

"You foolish boy," said the woman, "that is not your kitten, but the sunshine on the chimney pot."

Of course Hansel had not been looking at his kitten, but had been taking every now and then a pebble from his pocket and dropping it on the road.

When they reached the middle of the forest the father told the children to collect wood to make a fire to keep them warm; and Hansel and Gretel gathered brushwood enough for a little mountain; and it was set on fire, and when the flame was burning quite high the wife said,

"Now lie down by the fire and rest yourselves, you children, and we will go and cut wood; and when we are ready we will come and fetch you."

So Hansel and Gretel sat by the fire, and at noon they each ate their pieces of bread. They thought their father was in the wood all the time, as they seemed to hear the strokes of the ax, but really it was only a dry branch hanging to a withered tree that the wind moved to and fro.

So when they had stayed there a long time their eyelids closed with weariness, and they fell fast asleep. When at last they woke it was night, and Gretel began to cry, and said,

"How shall we ever get out of this wood?" But Hansel comforted her, saying,

"Wait a little while longer, until the moon rises, and then we can easily find the way home."

And when the full moon came up, Hansel took his little sister by the hand, and followed the way where the pebbles shone like silver, and showed them the road. They walked on the whole night through, and at the break of day they came to their father's house. They knocked at the door, and when their stepmother opened it and saw that it was Hansel and Gretel she said,

"You naughty children, why did you sleep so long in the wood? We thought you were never coming home again!"

But the father was glad, for it had gone to his heart to leave them both in the woods alone.

Not very long after that there was again great scarcity in those parts, and the children heard their stepmother say to their father,

"Everything is finished up; we have only half a loaf, and after that the tale comes to an end. The children must be off; we will take them farther into the wood this time, so that they shall not be able to find the way back again. There is no other way to manage."

The man felt sad at heart, and he thought,

"It would be better to share one's last morsel with one's children."

But the wife would listen to nothing that he said, but scolded and reproached him.

But the children were not asleep, and had heard all the talk. When the parents had gone to sleep, Hansel got up to go out and get more pebbles as he did before, but the stepmother had locked the door, and Hansel could not get out; but he comforted his little sister, and said,

"Don't cry, Gretel, and go to sleep quietly, and God will help us."

Early the next morning the wife came and pulled the children out of bed. She gave them each a little piece of bread—less than before; and on the way to the wood Hansel crumbled the bread in his pocket, and often stopped to throw a crumb on the ground.

"Hansel, what are you stopping behind and staring for?" said the father.

"I am looking at my little pigeon sitting on the roof, to say good-bye to me," answered Hansel.

"You foolish boy," said the wife, "that is no pigeon, but the morning sun shining on the chimney pots."

Hansel went on as before, and strewed bread crumbs all along the road.

The woman led the children far into the wood, where they had never been before in all their lives. And again there was a large fire made, and the stepmother said,

"Sit still there, you children, and when you are tired you can go to sleep; we are going into the forest to cut wood, and in the evening, when we are ready to go home, we will come and fetch you."

So when noon came Gretel shared her bread with Hansel, who had strewed his along the road.

Then they went to sleep, and the evening passed, and no one came for the poor children. When they awoke it was dark night, and Hansel comforted his little sister, and said,

"Wait a little, Gretel, until the moon gets up, then we shall be able to see our way home by the crumbs of bread that I have scattered along the road."

So when the moon rose they got up, but they could find no crumbs of bread, for the birds of the woods and of the fields had come and picked them up. Hansel thought they might find the way all the same, but they could not.

They went on all that night, and the next day from the morning until the evening, but they could not find the way out of the wood, and they were very hungry, for they had nothing to eat but the few berries they could pick up. And when they were so tired that they could no longer drag themselves along, they lay down under a tree and fell asleep.

It was now the third morning since they had left their father's house. They were always trying to get back to it, but instead of that they only found themselves farther in the wood, and if help had not soon come they would have been starved. About noon they saw a pretty snow-white bird sitting on a bough, and singing so sweetly that they stopped to listen. And when he had finished, the bird spread his wings and flew before them, and they followed after him until they came to a little house, and the bird perched on the roof, and when they came nearer they saw that the house was built of gingerbread, and roofed with cakes; and the window was of transparent sugar.

"We will have some of this," said Hansel, "and make a fine meal. I will eat a piece of the roof, Gretel, and you can have some of the window—that will taste sweet."

So Hansel reached up and broke off a bit of the roof, just to see how it tasted, and Gretel stood by the window and gnawed at it. Then they heard a thin voice call out from inside,

> "Nibble, nibble, like a mouse,
> Who is nibbling at my house?"

And the children answered,

> "Never mind,
> It is the wind."

And they went on eating, never disturbing themselves. Hansel, who found that the roof tasted very nice, took down a great piece of it, and Gretel pulled out a large round windowpane, and sat her down and began upon it. Then the door opened, and an aged woman came out, leaning upon a crutch. Hansel and Gretel felt very frightened, and let fall what they had in their hands. The old woman, however, nodded her head, and said,

"Ah, my dear children, how come you here? You must come indoors and stay with me, you will be no trouble."

So she took them each by the hand, and led them into her little house. And there they found a good meal laid out, of milk and pancakes, with sugar, apples, and nuts.

After that she showed them two little white beds, and Hansel and Gretel laid themselves down on them, and thought they were in heaven.

The old woman, although her behavior was so kind, was a wicked witch, who lay in wait for children, and had built the little house on purpose to entice them. When they were once inside she used to kill them, cook them, and eat them, and then it was a feast-day with her. The witch's eyes were red, and she could not see very far, but she had a keen scent, like the beasts, and knew very well when human creatures were near. When she knew that Hansel and Gretel were coming, she gave a spiteful laugh, and said triumphantly,

"I have them, and they shall not escape me!"

Early in the morning, before the children were awake, she got up to look at them, and as they lay sleeping so peacefully with round rosy cheeks, she said to herself,

"What a fine feast I shall have!"

She grasped Hansel with her withered hand, and led him into a little stable, and shut him up behind a grating; and call and scream as he might, it was no good. Then she went back to Gretel and shook her, crying,

"Get up, lazy bones! Fetch water, and cook something nice for your brother; he is outside in the stable, and must be fattened up. And when he is fat enough, I will eat him."

Gretel began to weep bitterly, but it was of no use, she had to do what the wicked witch bade her.

And so the best kind of victuals was cooked for poor

Hansel, while Gretel got nothing but crab shells. Each morning the old woman visited the little stable, and cried,

"Hansel, stretch out your finger, that I may tell if you will soon be fat enough."

Hansel, however, held out a little bone, and the old woman, who had weak eyes, could not see what it was, and supposing it to be Hansel's finger, wondered very much that it was not getting fatter. When four weeks had passed and Hansel seemed to remain so thin, she lost patience and could wait no longer.

"Now then, Gretel," cried she to the little girl, "be quick and draw water. Be Hansel fat or be he lean, to-morrow I must kill and cook him."

Oh, what a grief for the poor little sister to have to fetch water, and how the tears flowed down over her cheeks!

"Dear God, pray help us!" cried she. "If we had been devoured by wild beasts in the wood, at least we should have died together."

"Spare me your lamentations," said the old woman. "They are of no avail."

Early next morning Gretel had to get up, make the fire, and fill the kettle.

"First we will do the baking," said the old woman. "I have heated the oven already, and kneaded the dough."

She pushed poor Gretel towards the oven, out of which the flames were already shining.

"Creep in," said the witch, "and see if it is properly hot so that the bread may be baked."

And Gretel once in, she meant to shut the door upon her and let her be baked, and then she would have eaten her. But Gretel perceived her intention, and said,

"I don't know how to do it. How shall I get in?"

"Stupid goose," said the old woman, "the opening is big enough, do you see? I could get in myself!" and she stooped down and put her head in the oven's mouth. Then Gretel gave her a push, so that she went in farther, and she shut the iron door upon her, and put up the bar. Oh, how frightfully she howled! But Gretel ran away, and left her in the oven. Then Gretel went straight to Hansel, opened the stable door and cried,

"Hansel, we are free! The old witch is dead!"

Then out flew Hansel like a bird from its cage as soon as the door is opened. How rejoiced they both were! How they fell each on the other's neck! And danced about, and kissed each other! And as they had nothing more to fear, they went over all the old witch's house, and in every corner there stood chests of pearls and precious stones.

"This is something better than pebbles," said Hansel, as he filled his pockets. And Gretel, thinking she also would like to carry something home with her, filled her apron full.

"Now, away we go," said Hansel, "if we only can get out of the witch's wood!"

When they had journeyed a few hours they came to a great piece of water.

"We can never get across this," said Hansel. "I see no stepping-stones  and no bridge."

"And there is no boat either," said Gretel. "But here comes a white duck; if I ask her, she will help us over." So she cried,

> *"Duck, duck, here we stand,*
> *Hansel and Gretel, on the land,*
> *Stepping-stones and bridge we lack,*
> *Carry us over on your nice white back."*

And the duck came accordingly, and Hansel got upon her and told his sister to come too.

"No," answered Gretel, "that would be too hard upon the duck; we can go separately, one after the other."

And that was how it was managed, and after that they went on happily, until they came to the wood, and the way grew more and more familiar, till at last they saw in the distance their father's house. Then they ran till they came up to it, rushed in at the door, and fell on their father's neck. The man had not had a quiet hour since he left his children in the wood; but his wife was dead. And when Gretel opened her apron, the pearls and precious stones were scattered all over the room, and Hansel took one handful after another out of his pocket. Then was all care at an end, and they lived in great joy together.

MARIE SHEDLOCK

# The Hare
# That Ran Away

Once upon a time there was a wise lion who did much to help his fellow-animals, and there was a great deal to be done. For instance, there was a little nervous Hare who was always afraid that something dreadful was going to happen to her. She was always saying: "Suppose the Earth were to fall in, what would happen to me?" And she said this so often that at last she thought it really was about to happen.

One day, when she had been saying over and over again, "Suppose the Earth were to fall in, what would happen to me?" she heard a slight noise: it really was only a heavy fruit which had fallen upon a rustling leaf, but the little Hare was so nervous she was ready to believe anything, and she said in a frightened tone: "The Earth *is* falling in!"

She ran away as fast as she could go, and presently she met an old brother Hare, who said: "Where are you running to, Mistress Hare?"

And the little Hare said: "I have no time to stop and tell you anything. The Earth is falling in, and I am running away."

"The Earth is falling in, is it?" said the old brother Hare, in a tone of much astonishment; and he repeated that to *his* brother hare, and *he* to *his* brother hare, and *he* to *his* brother hare, until at last there were a hundred thousand brother hares, all shouting: "The Earth is falling in."

Now presently the bigger animals began to take the cry up. First the deer, and then the sheep, and then the wild boar, and then the buffalo, and then the camel, and then the tiger, and then the elephant.

Now the wise Lion heard all this noise and wondered at it. "There are no signs," he said, "of the Earth falling in. They must have heard something." And then he stopped them all short and said: "What is this you are saying?"

And the Elephant said: "I remarked that the Earth was falling in."

"How do you know this?" asked the Lion.

"Why, now I come to think of it, it was the Tiger that remarked it to me."

And the Tiger said: "*I* had it from the Camel," and the Camel said: "*I* had it from the Buffalo." And the buffalo from the wild boar, and the wild boar from the sheep, and the sheep from the deer, and the deer from the hares, and the Hares said: "Oh! *we* heard it from *that* little Hare."

And the Lion said: "Little Hare, *what* made you say that the Earth was falling in?"

And the little Hare said: "I *saw* it."

"You saw it?" said the Lion. "Where?"

"Yonder by the tree."

"Well," said the Lion, "come with me and I will show you how——"

"No, no," said the Hare, "I would not go near that tree for anything, I'm *so* nervous."

"But," said the Lion, "I am going to take you on my back." And he took her on his back, and begged the animals to stay where they were until they returned. Then he showed the little Hare how the fruit had fallen upon the leaf, making the noise that had frightened her, and she said: "Yes, I see—the Earth is *not* falling in." And the Lion said: "Shall we go back and tell the other animals?"

And they went back. The little Hare stood before the animals and said: "The Earth is *not* falling in." And all the animals began to repeat this to one another, and they dispersed gradually, and you heard the words more and more softly:

"The Earth is *not* falling in," "the Earth is *not* falling in," until the sound died away altogether.

# The House in the Wood

A poor wood-cutter lived with his wife and three daughters in a little hut on the borders of a lonely forest. One morning, when he was going to work, he said to his wife: "Send my eldest daughter out into the wood with my dinner at noon, or else I shall not get through with my day's work; and that she may not lose her way, I will take a bag of millet with me, and strew the seeds along the path."

As soon as the sun was at its height, and directly over the wood, the maiden started on her road with a large jug of soup and some bread for her father's dinner. But the field and hedge sparrows, the larks, the finches, and other birds, had long before picked up the seeds, so that the girl could not find the track.

She went straight ahead, however, and the sun went down, and night came on before she could find shelter. The trees rustled in the darkness, the night owl screamed, and the poor girl was in great fear, when all at once she saw a light twinkling in the distance through the trees. "There must be people living yonder," she thought, "and no doubt they will give me a night's lodging."

Following the light from the window, she soon came to the house. She knocked at the door, and a rough voice cried from within, "Come in." She stepped into a dark passage, and tapped at the room door. The same voice cried out again, "Come in." When the door opened she saw a very old man sitting at a table; his chin rested on his hands, and his white beard fell over it nearly to the ground. Near the stove lay three animals, a cock, a hen, and a speckled cow. The maiden told the old man of her trouble, and asked if she could have a night's lodging. Instead of answering her the old man turned to the animals and said:

> *"Little chicks and spotted cow,*
> *Shall we keep her here or no?"*

The animals made certain sounds which meant that she was to stay. So the old man said: "You will find plenty of everything here, so go into the kitchen and cook us some supper."

The maiden found an abundance of all she wanted, and after cooking a dish full of good food she placed it on the table, and seating herself with the old man ate a hearty meal, but she never thought of the animals. When she was satisfied, she said: "I am very tired, where is a bed on which I can sleep?" In reply came a voice:

*"You can eat and drink,*
*But you cannot think*
*Of poor animals such as we;*
*You shall have a bed,*
*Just to rest your head,*
*But you don't know where it will be."*

Then the old man told her to go upstairs, where she would find a room with two beds in it; she was to shake the beds well, and make them both. The young maiden went quickly upstairs, made her own bed, and forgetting about making one for the old man, she lay down and went fast asleep. After awhile the old man came up to his room, and, finding his bed not made, and the maiden asleep, he shook his head. Then he opened a trap-door in the floor, and let down the bed into the cellar beneath.

Meanwhile, the wood-cutter returned home in the evening very late, and reproached his wife for having let him go hungry the whole day. "It is not my fault," she said, "I sent our daughter with your dinner at noon, and I suppose she must have lost her way. But she will be back again tomorrow, no doubt."

Before daybreak, however, the wood-cutter was obliged to be off to the forest, and he asked his wife to send their second daughter with his dinner. "I will carry a bag of lentils with me this time," he said, "as the seeds are larger than the millet she will see them more easily, and will not be likely to lose her way."

But at noon, when the maiden went with her father's dinner, the lentils had disappeared; the birds of the forest, as on the day before, had picked them all up, so that there was not a single one left. She too wandered all day, and at last found a good supper and a night's lodging in the old man's cottage. But she also never thought of feeding the animals, or of making the old man's bed, so at night while she slept, he opened the trap-door and let her down into the cellar below as he had done her sister.

On the third morning, the wood-cutter told his wife, "You must send our youngest child with my dinner to-day, she is always good and obedient, and will not lose her way like her sisters who wander about like wild bees when they swarm."

The mother, however, would not listen. "No," she said, "why should I lose my dearest child now that the others are gone?"

"Don't fear," he said, "this girl will never wander, she is too clever and sensible; besides, I will take a quantity of peas with me and strew them in the way to show her the right path. They are so much larger than lentils, and will be sure to remain."

So the next day the mother, with much advice and caution, sent her youngest daughter to the forest with a basket on her arm. But there were no peas to guide her; they were all eaten up by the pigeons, and therefore, she knew not which path to take. She was very unhappy, and thought how hungry her poor father would be, and how her mother would fret if she remained away all night. At last, in her wanderings after dark, she also saw the light, and came, as her sisters had done, to the house in the wood. She went in and begged for a night's lodging so gently that the man with the white beard said to his animals:

> *"Little chicks and spotted cow,*
> *Shall we keep her here or no?"*

The voice answered, "Yes," and presently the maiden went over to the stove where the animals lay, stroked the

smooth feathers of the cock and hen with her hand, and rubbed the spotted cow between the horns. When the old man told her to go and cook some supper she got it ready very quickly. But when she placed the dishes on the table, she said: "I am not going to feast with all these good things while the poor animals have nothing. There will be plenty left for me, and I shall take care of them first."

Then she went and fetched some barley, which she scattered before the chickens, and a whole armful of sweet hay for the cow. "Eat that up, you dear animals," she said, "and perhaps you are thirsty; I will bring you some fresh water."

Then she brought in a large basin of water, and the cock and hen sprung on the brink, dipped in their beaks, and lifted their heads in the manner that birds always drink, while the spotted cow took a long draught. After the animals were fed the maiden seated herself at the table, and ate what the old man had left her. In a very little while the fowls had their heads behind their wings, and the cow began to blink her eyes, so the maiden said, "Shall we now go to rest?"

And the old man cried:

> *"Little chicks and spotted cow,*
> *Shall we let her sleep here now?"*

And they replied quickly:

> *"Yes, for she is very good,*
> *She has brought us drink and food."*

Then the maiden went upstairs, shook both beds, and made them up, and presently the old man came to his room, and when he laid himself on the bed his white beard nearly reached to his feet.

The maiden said her prayers, and lying down slept peacefully till midnight, when a number of strange noises awoke her. The corners of the house were creaking and cracking, the doors sprang open and struck against the walls. The rafters groaned, as if their joints were broken and separated; the stairs were turning upside down, and at last there was a crash, as if the roof and the walls had fallen in together. Then all was still.

The maiden had been too frightened to move, and all had happened so quickly that she would have had scarcely time to do so. But now, finding she was not hurt, and still in her comfortable bed, she lay quiet and went to sleep again.

But in the morning, when the bright sunshine awoke her, what a sight met her eyes! She was lying in a noble room, and everything around her as splendid as the furniture of a royal palace. The walls were covered with golden flowers on a silken ground. The bed was of ivory, and the covering of red velvet, and on a chair near it stood a pair of slippers embroidered with pearls.

The maiden fancied herself in a dream; but while she wondered three neatly-dressed servants came in, and asked her what they could do for her.

"Nothing," she replied, "only go away, and I will get up and cook the old man's breakfast for him, and give those dear animals their food."

She dressed herself quickly, and went to the old man's room; but what was her astonishment to see lying on the bed a strange man, asleep. While she stood, and saw with surprise that he was young and handsome, he woke, raised himself and said, "Don't go away; I am a king's son, and a wicked witch changed me into a bearded, grey old man.

My castle was changed into the wooden house, and my servants into a cock, a hen, and a spotted cow. The spell was never to be broken unless a maiden came to visit us who had a kind heart, and who was as careful to feed poor animals as human beings, and you are that maiden. And at midnight, while we slept, we were all through you set free; the little house in the wood is again my royal castle, and the animals are restored to their former shape. I will now send my servants to fetch your father and mother, that they may be present at our marriage, for you are to be my wife."

"But where are my sisters?" she asked.

"I have shut them up in the cellar," he replied, "but tomorrow I will send them to work as servants, until they have learnt to be thoughtful and kind to poor animals."

HOPE NEWELL

# How She Kept
# Her Geese Warm

One cold winter night, the Little Old Woman was out in the barn putting her geese to bed. She gave them some corn and took off their little red coats. Then she brushed each little coat with a whisk-broom and carefully shook out the wrinkles.

As she was folding the coats in a neat pile, she thought:

"My poor geese must be very cold at night. I have my cozy fire and my feather bed. But they have not even a blanket to keep them warm."

After the geese had eaten their corn, they began to go to roost.

"Honk, honk!" said the big gander, and he hopped up on the roost.

"Honk, honk!" said the grey goose, and she hopped up on the roost.

"Honk, honk!" said all the other geese, and they hopped up on the roost.

Then the Little Old Woman closed the barn door and went into the house. When she went to bed, she lay awake worrying about the geese. After a while she said to herself:

"I cannot sleep a wink for thinking how cold the geese must be. I had better bring them in the house where it is warm."

So the Little Old Woman dressed herself and went out to the barn to fetch the geese. She shooed them off the roost and put on their little red coats. She picked up two geese, and tucking one under each arm, she carried them into the house.

Then she went out to the barn and picked up two more geese. She tucked one goose under each arm and carried them into the house.

When the Little Old Woman had brought all the geese into the house, she said to herself:

"Now I must get them ready for bed again."

She took off their little red coats and gave the geese some corn. Then she brushed each little coat with a whisk-broom and carefully shook out all the wrinkles.

As she was folding the coats in a neat pile, she thought:

"It was very clever of me to bring the geese into the house. Now they will be warm, and I shall be able to sleep."

Then the Little Old Woman undressed herself again and went to bed.

After the geese had eaten their corn, they began to roost.

"Honk, honk!" said the gander, and he hopped up on the foot of the Little Old Woman's bed.

"Honk, honk!" said the grey goose, and she hopped up on the foot of the Little Old Woman's bed.

"Honk, honk!" said all the other geese, and they tried to hop up on the foot of the Little Old Woman's bed.

But it was not a very big bed, and there was not enough room for all the geese to roost. They began to fight. They pushed and shoved each other. They hissed and squawked and flapped their wings.

All night long the geese pushed and shoved each other. All night long they hissed and squawked and flapped their wings.

They made so much noise that the Little Old Woman did not sleep a wink.

"This will never do," she said. "When they were in the barn, I did not sleep for thinking how cold they must be. When they are in the house, I cannot sleep because they make so much noise. Perhaps if I use my head, I shall know what to do."

The Little Old Woman tied a wet towel around her forehead. Then she sat down with her forefinger against her nose and shut her eyes.

She used her head and used her head, and after a while she knew what to do.

"I will move the roost into the house," she said. "The geese will have the cozy fire to keep them warm. Then I will move my bed out into the barn. My feather bed will keep me warm, and I will not be worrying about the geese.

They will not keep me awake with their noise. I shall sleep very comfortably in the barn."

The Little Old Woman moved the roost into the house, and she moved her bed out into the barn.

When night came again, she brought the geese into the house. After she had fed them some corn, she took off their little red coats. Then they all hopped up on the roost, and the Little Old Woman went out to the barn to sleep.

Her feather bed kept her as warm as toast. She was not worried about the geese, because she knew that they were warm too. So she slept as sound as a top all night long.

HOPE NEWELL

# How She Made the Baby Elephant Happy

When the Little Old Woman came in sight of her house, she saw something gray and round and fat running around her garden.

As she came near enough to get a good look at it, she saw that it was a baby elephant.

"Mercy on me!" she said. "This is a great day indeed. First, I see the circus come to town and now I find a baby elephant in my garden."

As she watched the baby elephant running about the garden, and pulling up carrots and cabbages and turnips with his trunk, she thought: "It is not often that I find an elephant eating my vegetables. Indeed, so far as I can recall, I have never seen one in my garden before.

"I wonder where he came from. I could use my head and find out, of course. But this is no time to use my head. The main thing is that he is here, and I must make him happy so that he will not run away."

The baby elephant kept running about the garden pull-

ing up cabbages and carrots and turnips with his trunk
and eating them.

"I do not need to worry about feeding him," said the
Little Old Woman. "He is feeding himself very well.
However, I must find him a house, so that he can have a
roof over his head."

"He could live in my house," she thought. "Then he
could have my roof over his head. But his feet are so big
he might step on the rats.

"Or, he might live in the barn," she said. "Then he
could have the barn roof over his head. But, if I put him
in the barn, he might step on the geese. I had better build
him a little shed and then he will have his own roof over
his head."

As soon as she had fed the geese and the rats, the Little
Old Woman set to work building a shed for the baby elephant. When the shed was finished she coaxed him into
it by feeding him peanuts. She nailed a board across the
front of it so that he would stay inside. Then she began
to weed her garden.

The baby elephant started running after her and dragging the shed with him.

"What a funny elephant," said the Little Old Woman.
"He likes to move his shed around with him."

But the shed was not easy to move. The posts dragged
on the ground and made the baby elephant stumble. He
did not like this so he lifted up his trunk and squealed.
He squealed and squealed.

"Dear me!" said the Little Old Woman. "It is very sad
to hear a baby elephant squeal. I must use my head and

try to figure out how he can move his shed around without stumbling."

The Little Old Woman went into the house, and tied a wet towel around her head. Then she sat down with her forefinger against her nose and shut her eyes.

She used her head and used her head. Before long she had figured out how the baby elephant could move his shed around without stumbling.

"I will put a wheel on the bottom of each post," she said. "Then he can move his shed around very easily."

The Little Old Woman took the wheels off the little wagon that she used for hauling firewood in the winter. She put a wheel on the bottom of each post of the baby elephant's shed.

Then she went on weeding her garden. The baby elephant started running after her. The posts did not drag on the ground and he moved the shed very easily.

"It was very clever of me to think of putting wheels on his shed," said the Little Old Woman. "Now he can move it wherever he wants to and he will not stumble."

All day the Little Old Woman pulled weeds out of her garden. All day, the baby elephant followed her and pulled up carrots and cabbages and turnips with his trunk and ate them.

When the geese went for their evening swim in the nearby pond, the baby elephant went with them. He waded into the pond and filled his trunk with water. He blew water over the top of his shed, and he blew water on the geese.

He was very happy.

After supper the Little Old Woman took her mending and sat down in her rocking-chair on the porch.

The baby elephant had come back from the pond. He was running about the garden, pulling up carrots and cabbages and turnips with his trunk and eating them.

"I like this baby elephant very much," said the Little Old Woman. "However, I hope no more baby elephants come to live with me. I have no more wood to make sheds and they would have no roofs over their heads.

"Moreover, I would not have enough vegetables to feed them. As it is, this baby elephant will have eaten everything in the garden by morning. Then I shall have to use my head to find out how to feed him."

Just then the Little Old Woman heard a great noise in the distance. Wagon wheels were rumbling, men were shouting, and horses' hoofs were going "plack-plack" over the cobblestones.

"Dear me," said the Little Old Woman. "That must be the circus leaving town."

The baby elephant heard the noise, too. When the Little Old Woman went around to the back of her house where she could watch the circus going over the distant hill, the baby elephant went with her.

They watched the big animal wagons go over the hill. They watched the camels and they watched the big white circus horses, and the little Shetland ponies.

When the baby elephant saw the big elephants walking slowly over the hill, he dropped the carrot he was eating and his big ears started waving back and forth. Then he

lifted up his trunk and squealed. He squealed and squealed and squealed.

One of the big elephants dropped the tail of the elephant in front of her. She lifted up her trunk, and rumbled as loud as thunder.

Before the Little Old Woman could wink her eye, the baby elephant started running in his little shed. When he reached the fence he did not stop. He broke right through the fence and kept on running. He reached the hill just as the big cook-wagon went over its top.

The baby elephant ran up the hill and in a few seconds he too disappeared over the top.

"Dear me," said the Little Old Woman, "I do believe the baby elephant belonged to the circus. The big elephant who rumbled so loudly must have been his mother. Now he has gone back to her and I have no baby elephant."

She went back to the porch and sat down in her rocking chair.

"I shall miss the baby elephant very much," she thought.

"However, perhaps it is just as well that he has gone back to his mother. If he ate as much every day as he did today, I would have to use my head very hard to find out how to feed him.

"I am glad that I made him a little shed so that he will always have a roof over his head. It is a very useful thing to know how to make a shed for an elephant. If ever I find another elephant in my garden, I will know just how to go about it. I am a very wise old woman indeed."

# Jack and the Beanstalk

There was once upon a time a poor widow who had an only son named Jack and a cow named Milky-White. And all they had to live on was the milk the cow gave every morning, which they carried to the market and sold. But one morning Milky-White gave no milk, and they didn't know what to do.

"What shall we do, what shall we do?" said the widow, wringing her hands.

"Cheer up, Mother, I'll go and get work somewhere," said Jack.

"We've tried that before, and nobody would take you," said his mother; "we must sell Milky-White and with the money start a shop or something."

"All right, Mother," said Jack; "it's market day today, and I'll soon sell Milky-White, and then we'll see what we can do."

So he took the cow's halter in his hand, and off he started. He hadn't gone far when he met a funny-looking old man, who said to him: "Good morning, Jack."

"Good morning to you," said Jack, and wondered how he knew his name.

"Well, Jack, and where are you off to?" said the man.

"I'm going to market to sell our cow here."

"Oh, you look the proper sort of chap to sell cows," said the man; "I wonder if you know how many beans make five."

"Two in each hand and one in your mouth," said Jack, as sharp as a needle.

"Right you are," said the man, "and here they are, the very beans themselves," he went on, pulling out of his pocket a number of strange-looking beans. "As you are so sharp," said he, "I don't mind doing a swop with you— your cow for these beans."

"Go along," said Jack; "wouldn't you like it?"

"Ah! you don't know what these beans are," said the man; "if you plant them overnight, by morning they grow right up to the sky."

"Really?" said Jack; "you don't say so."

"Yes, that is so, and if it doesn't turn out to be true you can have your cow back."

"Right," said Jack, and handed him over Milky-White's halter and pocketed the beans.

Back goes Jack home, and as he hadn't gone very far, it wasn't dusk by the time he got to his door.

"Back already, Jack?" said his mother; "I see you haven't got Milky-White, so you've sold her. How much did you get for her?"

"You'll never guess, Mother," said Jack.

"No, you don't say so. Good boy! Five pounds, ten, fifteen, no, it can't be twenty."

"I told you you couldn't guess. What do you say to

these beans; they're magical, plant them overnight and——"

"What!" said Jack's mother, "have you been such a fool, such a dolt, such an idiot, as to give away my Milky-White, the best milker in the parish, and prime beef to boot, for a set of paltry beans? Take that! Take that! Take that! And as for your precious beans, here they go out of the window. And now off with you to bed. Not a sup shall you drink, and not a bit shall you swallow this very night."

So Jack went upstairs to his little room in the attic, and sad and sorry he was, to be sure, as much for his mother's sake as for the loss of his supper.

At last he dropped off to sleep.

When he woke up, the room looked so funny. The sun was shining into part of it, and yet all the rest was quite dark and shady. So Jack jumped up and dressed himself and went to the window. And what do you think he saw? Why, the beans his mother had thrown out of the window into the garden had sprung up into a big beanstalk, which went up and up and up till it reached the sky. So the man spoke truth, after all.

The beanstalk grew up quite close past Jack's window; so all he had to do was to open it and give a jump on to the beanstalk which ran up just like a big ladder. So Jack climbed, and he climbed, and he climbed, and he climbed, and he climbed, and he climbed, and he climbed till at last he reached the sky. And when he got there he found a long, broad road going as straight as a dart. So he walked along, and he walked along, and he walked along till he came to a great big tall house, and on the doorstep there was a great big tall woman.

"Good morning, mum," said Jack, quite polite-like. "Could you be so kind as to give me some breakfast?" For he hadn't had anything to eat, you know, the night before, and was as hungry as a hunter.

"It's breakfast you want, is it?" said the great big tall woman. "It's breakfast you'll be if you don't move off from here. My man is an ogre and there's nothing he likes better than boys broiled on toast. You'd better be moving on or he'll soon be coming."

"Oh! please, mum, do give me something to eat, mum. I've had nothing to eat since yesterday morning, really and truly, mum," said Jack. "I may as well be broiled as die of hunger."

Well, the ogre's wife was not half so bad after all. So she took Jack into the kitchen and gave him a chunk of bread and cheese and a jug of milk. But Jack hadn't half finished these when thump! thump! thump! the whole house began to tremble with the noise of someone coming.

"Goodness gracious me! It's my old man," said the ogre's wife. "What on earth shall I do? Come along quick and jump in here." And she bundled Jack into the oven just as the ogre came in.

He was a big one, to be sure. At his belt he had three calves strung up by the heels, and he unhooked them and threw them down on the table and said: "Here, wife, broil me a couple of these for breakfast. Ah, what's this I smell?"

*"Fee, fi, fo, fum,*
*I smell the blood of an Englishman,*
*Be he alive, or be he dead*
*I'll grind his bones to make my bread."*

"Nonsense, dear," said his wife, "you're dreaming. Or perhaps you smell the scraps of that little boy you liked so much for yesterday's dinner. Here, you go and have a wash and tidy up, and by the time you come back your breakfast'll be ready for you."

So off the ogre went, and Jack was just going to jump out of the oven and run away when the woman told him not to. "Wait till he's asleep," said she; "he always has a doze after breakfast."

Well, the ogre had his breakfast, and after that he went to a big chest and took out of it a couple of bags of gold, and down he sat and counted till at last his head began to nod, and he began to snore till the whole house shook again.

Then Jack crept out on tiptoe from his oven, and as he was passing the ogre he took one of the bags of gold under his arm, and off he peltered till he came to the beanstalk, and then he threw down the bag of gold, which of course fell into his mother's garden, and then he climbed down, and climbed down till at last he got home and told his mother and showed her the gold and said, "Well, Mother, wasn't I right about the beans? They are really magical, you see."

So they lived on the bag of gold for some time, but at last they came to the end of it, and Jack made up his mind to try his luck once more up at the top of the beanstalk. So one fine morning he rose up early, and got on to the beanstalk, and he climbed, and he climbed, and he climbed, and he climbed, and he climbed, and he climbed till at last he came out onto the road again and up to the great big tall house he had been to before. There, sure enough, was the great big tall woman a-standing on the doorstep.

"Good morning, mum," said Jack, as bold as brass, "could you be so good as to give me something to eat?"

"Go away, my boy," said the big tall woman, "or else my man will eat you up for breakfast. But aren't you the youngster who came here once before? Do you know, that very day, my man missed one of his bags of gold."

"That's strange, mum," said Jack, "I dare say I could tell you something about that; but I'm so hungry I can't speak till I've had something to eat."

Well, the big tall woman was so curious that she took him in and gave him something to eat. But he had scarcely begun munching it as slowly as he could when thump! thump! thump! they heard the giant's footstep, and his wife hid Jack away in the oven.

All happened as it did before. In came the ogre as he did before, said: "Fee-fi-fo-fum," and had his breakfast off three broiled oxen. Then he said: "Wife, bring me the hen that lays the golden eggs." So she brought it, and the ogre said: "Lay," and it laid an egg all of gold. And then the ogre began to nod his head and to snore till the house shook.

Then Jack crept out of the oven on tiptoe and caught hold of the golden hen and was off before you could say "Jack Robinson." But this time the hen gave a cackle which woke the ogre, and just as Jack got out of the house he heard him calling: "Wife, wife, what have you done with my golden hen?"

And the wife said: "Why, my dear?"

But that was all Jack heard, for he rushed off to the beanstalk and climbed down like a house on fire. And when he got home he showed his mother the wonderful hen, and said "Lay" to it; and it laid a golden egg every time he said "Lay."

Well, Jack was not content, and it wasn't very long before he determined to have another try at his luck up there at the top of the beanstalk. So one fine morning he rose up early and got on to the beanstalk, and he climbed, and he climbed, and he climbed, and he climbed till he got to the top. But this time he knew better than to go straight to the ogre's house. And when he got near it, he waited behind a bush till he saw the ogre's wife come out with a pail to get some water, and then he crept into the house and got into the copper boiler. He hadn't been there long when he heard thump! thump! thump! as before, and in came the ogre and his wife.

"Fee-fi-fo-fum, I smell the blood of an Englishman," cried out the ogre. "I smell him, wife, I smell him."

"Do you, my dearie?" said the ogre's wife. "Then, if it's that little rogue that stole your gold and the hen that laid the golden eggs he's sure to have got into the oven."

And they both rushed to the oven. But Jack wasn't there, luckily, and the ogre's wife said: "There you are again with your fee-fi-fo-fum. Why of course it's the boy you caught last night that I've just broiled for your breakfast. How forgetful I am, and how careless you are not to know the difference between live and dead after all these years."

So the ogre sat down to the breakfast and ate it, but every now and then he would mutter: "Well, I could have sworn——" and he'd get up and search the larder and the cupboards and everything, only, luckily, he didn't think of the copper boiler.

After breakfast was over, the ogre called out, "Wife, wife, bring me my golden harp." So she brought it and put it on the table before him. Then he said: "Sing!" and the golden harp sang most beautifully. And it went on singing till the ogre fell asleep and commenced to snore like thunder.

Then Jack lifted up the copper-lid very quietly and got down like a mouse and crept on hands and knees till he came to the table, when up he crawled, caught hold of the golden harp and dashed with it towards the door. But the harp called out quite loud: "Master! Master!" and the ogre woke up just in time to see Jack running off with his harp.

Jack ran as fast as he could, and the ogre came running after and would soon have caught him only Jack had a start and dodged him a bit and knew where he was going. When he got to the beanstalk the ogre was not more than twenty yards away when suddenly he saw Jack disappear,

and when he came to the end of the road he saw Jack underneath climbing down for dear life. Well, the ogre didn't like trusting himself to such a ladder, and he stood and waited; so Jack got another start. But just then the harp cried out: "Master! Master!" and the ogre swung himself down on to the beanstalk, which shook with his weight. Down climbed Jack, and after him climbed the ogre. By this time Jack had climbed down, and climbed down, and climbed down till he was very nearly home. So he called out: "Mother! Mother! bring me an ax, bring me an ax." And his mother came rushing out with the ax in her hand; but when she came to the beanstalk she stood stock-still with fright, for there she saw the ogre with his legs just through the clouds.

But Jack jumped down and got hold of the ax and gave a chop at the beanstalk which cut it half in two. The ogre felt the beanstalk shake and quiver, so he stopped to see what was the matter. Then Jack gave another chop with the ax, and the beanstalk was cut in two and began to topple over. Then the ogre fell down and broke his crown, and the beanstalk came toppling after.

Then Jack showed his mother his golden harp, and what with showing that and selling the golden eggs Jack and his mother became very rich, and he married a great princess, and they lived happily ever after.

From *English Fairy Tales*, edited by Joseph Jacobs.

JAMES BALDWIN

# King John and the Three Questions

There was once a king of England whose name was John. He was a bad king; for he was harsh and cruel to his people, and so long as he could have his own way, he did not care what became of other folks.

Now, there was in the town of Canterbury a rich old abbot who lived in grand style in a great house called the Abbey. Every day a hundred noble men sat down with him to dine, and fifty brave knights, in fine velvet coats and gold chains, waited upon him at his table.

When King John heard of the way in which the abbot lived, he was jealous and made up his mind to put a stop to it. So he sent for the old man to come and see him.

"How now, my good abbot?" he said, "I hear that you keep a far better house than I. How dare you do such a thing? Don't you know that no man in the land ought to live better than the king? And I tell you that no man shall."

"O king!" said the abbot, "I beg to say that I am spend-

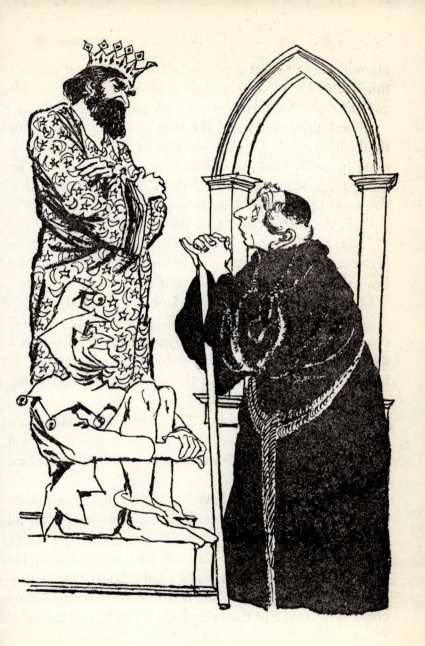

ing nothing but what is my own. I hope that you will not think ill of me for making things pleasant for my friends and the brave knights who are with me."

"Think ill of you?" said the king. "How can I help but think ill of you? All that there is in this broad land is mine by right. How do you dare to put me to shame by living in grander style than I do? One would think that you were trying to be king in my place."

"Oh, do not say so!" said the abbot. "For I"—

"Not another word!" cried the king. "Your fault is plain, and unless you can answer me three questions, your head shall be cut off, and all your riches shall be mine."

"I will try to answer them, O king!" said the abbot.

"Well, then," said King John, "as I sit here with my crown of gold on my head, you must tell me to within a day just how long I shall live. Secondly, you must tell me how soon I shall ride round the whole world; and lastly, you shall tell me what I think."

"O king!" said the abbot, "these are deep, hard questions, and I cannot answer them just now. But if you will give me two weeks to think about them, I will do the best that I can."

"Two weeks you shall have," said the king; "but if then you fail to answer me, you shall lose your head, and all your lands shall be mine."

The abbot went away very sad and in great fear. He rode first to Oxford. Here was a great school, called a university, and he wanted to see if any of the wise professors could help him. But they shook their heads, and said that there was nothing about King John in any of their books.

Then the abbot rode down to Cambridge, where there was another university. But not one of the teachers in that great school could help him either.

At last, sad and sorrowful, he rode toward home to bid his friends and his brave knights good-by. For now he had not a week to live.

## THE THREE ANSWERS

As the abbot was riding up the lane which led to his grand house, he met his shepherd going to the fields.

"Welcome home, good master," cried the shepherd. "What news do you bring us from great King John?"

"Sad news, sad news," said the abbot. And then he told him all that had happened.

"Cheer up, cheer up, good master," said the shepherd. "Have you never yet heard that a fool may teach a wise man wit? I think I can help you out of your trouble."

"You help me!" cried the abbot. "How? how?"

"Well," answered the shepherd, "you know that everybody says that I look just like you, and that I have sometimes been mistaken for you. So, lend me your servants and your horse and your gown, and I will go up to London and see the king. If nothing else can be done, I can at least die in your place."

"My good shepherd," said the abbot, "you are very, very kind; and I have a mind to let you try your plan. But

if the worst comes to the worst, you shall not die for me.
I will die for myself."

So the shepherd got ready to go at once. He dressed
himself with great care. Over his shepherd's coat he threw
the abbot's long gown, and he borrowed the abbot's cap
and golden staff. When all was ready, no one in the world
would have thought that he was not the great man himself. Then he mounted his horse, and with a great train
of servants set out for London.

Of course the king did not know him.

"Welcome, Sir Abbot!" he said. "It is a good thing
that you have come back when you promised. But, prompt
as you are, if you fail to answer my three questions, you
shall lose your head."

"I am ready to answer them, O king!" said the shepherd.

"Indeed, indeed!" said the king, and he laughed to
himself. "Well, then, answer my first question: How long
shall I live? Come, you must tell me to the very day."

"You shall live," said the shepherd, "until the day that
you die, and not one day longer. And you shall die when
you take your last breath, and not one moment before."

The king laughed.

"You are witty, I see," he said. "But we will let that
pass, and say that your answer is right. And now tell me
how soon I may ride round the world."

"You must rise with the sun," said the shepherd, "and
you must ride with the sun until it rises again the next
morning. As soon as you do that, you will find that you

have ridden round the world in twenty-four hours."

The king laughed again. "Indeed," he said, "I did not think that it could be done so soon. You are not only witty, but you are wise, and we will let this answer pass. And now comes my third and last question: What do I think?"

"That is an easy question," said the shepherd. "You think that I am the Abbot of Canterbury. But, to tell you the truth, I am only his poor shepherd, and I have come to beg your pardon for him and for me." And with that, he threw off his long gown.

The king laughed loud and long.

"A merry fellow you are," said he, "and you shall be the Abbot of Canterbury in your master's place."

"O king! that cannot be," said the shepherd, "for I can neither read nor write."

"Very well, then," said the king, "I will give you something else to pay you for this merry joke. I will give you four pieces of silver every week as long as you live. And when you get home, you may tell the old abbot that you have brought him a pardon from King John."

ELEANOR *and* ADA SKINNER

# The King's Rabbit Keeper

Once upon a time a king wanted a good rabbit keeper. He made it known throughout the country that he would give not only good pay, but also the hand of the princess, to any youth who could take good care of his wonderful rabbits.

Now it happened that an old farmer had three very lazy sons, Jan, Hans, and Olaf. They disliked the work on the farm and spent most of their time amusing themselves, or doing as they pleased. When Jan heard that the king wanted a rabbit keeper, he told his father he would go to the palace and try to get the place.

"What!" cried the old man. "The king does not want an idler. The rabbits are brisk and lively and need care every moment. A lazybones like you could never be His Majesty's rabbit keeper."

"Well, I am determined to go. I should like the work better than the farm drudgery," replied Jan. He filled a bag with things to eat, and a few clothes, and started to the palace of the king. After he had traveled a few miles he heard a voice calling him: "Help! Help!" Jan hurried toward the sound and came to a deep pit. He looked down into it, and there was a shriveled old woman. She spoke very sharply to him. "Pull me up! Pull me up!" she cried. "I have been here for one year, and have had no food in all that time. Pull me up!"

"Not I," replied Jan. "Only a witch could live a year in such a place without food. I'll have nothing to do with you," and on he went.

At length he came to the palace of the king and asked to serve as rabbit keeper. The delighted king said, "He who guards the rabbits well and lets none escape shall have fine food, good pay, and perhaps the hand of a beautiful princess."

The next day Jan took the rabbits into a large field to browse. During the daytime they nibbled the tender grass and stayed together, but when the sun began to set, they darted toward a wood which bordered a meadow and they soon became lost in the shadows of the trees. Jan called to them and ran after them until he was out of breath, but he could not bring them together. He rested awhile and tried again. It was of no use; they had scattered in every direction. Surely they were playing hide and seek, and Jan was not in the game. When he reached the palace, he told his story to the king, who burst into a rage and banished Jan from the country.

In a short time the king got another warren of rabbits and again made it known that he wanted a keeper. Jan's brother, Hans, now determined that he would try to serve the king and perhaps gain the rich reward. Off he started. He passed the pit and heard the old woman calling for help, but he hurried on without even stopping to see what was the matter with her.

The king made him keeper of the rabbits, but the first time he took them out to browse he failed in his work. All was well during the day, but when the sun sank, the rabbits scurried away to the woods, and no matter what he did, Hans could not gather them together again. When he returned to the palace without a single rabbit, the furious king banished him, too, from the country.

A third time the king got beautiful rabbits and made it known that he wanted a keeper. "Father," said Olaf, the youngest of the three brothers, "it is my turn to try. I am sure I could guard the king's rabbits."

"It will be the same old story," said the farmer. "If you take no better care of the rabbits than you do of the calves, you will share your brothers' fate."

"At any rate I mean to try," replied Olaf. Throwing his bag over his shoulder, he set out for the palace of the king.

"Help! Help!" called a voice from the field near the road. Olaf ran in the direction of the sound and saw the old woman in the pit.

"What can I do for you, my good woman?" he asked.

"Please reach me your hand and help me out. I've had nothing to eat for a year and I can't get out without help."

Olaf willingly reached down and pulled the old woman up. Then he gave her food from his bag and brought her water from a spring. She ate a large share of Olaf's store while he good-naturedly looked on. When she had finished, she drew from her pocket a magic horn.

"Take this for your pains," said she. "It is a wonderful horn and will help you in many ways. If you blow into the small end of it, you will scatter to the four winds whatever you wish away from you. If you blow into the large end of it, you will bring near you whatever you wish. If you should lose it, or if by chance it should be stolen from you, a wish will bring it back again."

"A wonderful help it will be to me," said Olaf, as he took it eagerly from the old woman's hand.

He sauntered on again, and after some time he came to the palace of the king. The rabbits were put into his charge, and Olaf's heart beat high when he thought of the princess he might win.

The next morning he took the rabbits out into the meadow. They danced about in high glee for several hours. But about noon, Olaf noticed two of them scamper away to the woods. These two were soon followed by others. "Very well," said Olaf, "go away from me if you like." He blew into the small end of the magic horn, and then cried out, "Be off, every one of you!" and away they scattered in every direction.

Olaf then ate his noonday lunch and stretched himself out for a nap on the soft green bank. When he awoke, the sun was low in the west. He took up the magic horn and blew into the large end of it. From every direction came the frisky rabbits dancing and hopping about him. Olaf

counted them and was well pleased to find exactly the right number. When he reached the palace with the rabbits, he saw that the king, the queen, and the princess were on the lookout for him. Also he noticed that each one counted the rabbits and then glanced at the others in wonder.

"Alas!" sighed the princess, "how I wish he were of noble birth! But a farmer's lad! Dear me!"

Day after day Olaf took the rabbits out to browse in the meadow. At noon he scattered them in the deep wood, and when the sun began to sink behind a distant hill, he gathered them together and led them back to the palace.

The king was very much puzzled and determined to send a servant to spy upon Olaf. With greatest care the servant slipped into the field and noticed Olaf asleep on the soft green bank near the edge of the wood. The servant hid himself in the low underbrush of the wood and waited until evening. At sunset, Olaf awoke, drew out his magic horn, gathered together the rabbits, and led them back to the palace. The servant explained to the king what he had seen, and the king told his queen and the princess. "I shall steal his horn while he is asleep in the meadow," said the princess, "for I am determined not to marry a common farmer's son."

The next day she stole carefully to Olaf's side while he lay asleep and took the magic horn from his pocket. She had not reached the palace before Olaf awoke and thought of his rabbits. But where was his horn? He searched about the banks in vain. "Oh, how I wish I had my magic horn!"

he cried. No sooner had he made his wish than he found the horn in his hands. He blew into the larger end of it and again the rabbits danced and frisked about him ready to return.

Now the queen thought she would try her skill in getting Olaf's horn. She had no trouble in getting it from his pocket, but as she neared the palace, the horn slipped away from her. In the evening, Olaf returned with his flock as usual.

"I see that I must do the thing myself," muttered the king. "That farmer's lad shall not outwit me. I'll tie the horn in one of my hunting bags to make sure of it."

Anxiously the queen and princess awaited the king's return. At last he came, untied the bag, and reached in for the horn. Alas! it had disappeared. And there in the distance came Olaf and the rabbits. The king sent word for Olaf to appear before the royal family. "Tell me about that horn of yours. Where did you get it? Hasn't it magic power?" said the king, impatiently.

"Sire, it is a magic horn," began Olaf.

"Prove it," said the king.

"I would rather not," said Olaf.

"Do as I bid you, without a word!" roared the king, becoming red with anger.

Olaf raised the little end of his horn to his lips and blew a strong blast, while secretly he made a wish. In a moment the royal family scattered in all directions.

"Bring us back! Bring us back! How dare you? I'll have

you punished for this!" roared the king, as he tumbled into the distance.

Olaf blew into the big end of his horn and instantly the royal family were back at the palace. The king, in a rage, tried to seize Olaf, but just then the rabbit keeper raised the small end of the horn to his lips.

"Hold, hold!" cried the king. "I will do you no harm if you will keep that wicked horn from your lips. I would rather give up half my kingdom than take another flighty trip. You are a wonderful lad and the best of rabbit keepers. The reward is yours."

In a short time there was a beautiful wedding at the palace. Olaf had won the princess.

# The Lad Who Went to the North Wind

Once on a time there was an old widow who had one son, and as she was poorly and weak, her son had to go into the storehouse to fetch meal for cooking; but when he got outside the storehouse, and was just going down the steps, there came the North Wind, puffing and blowing, caught up the meal, and so away with it through the air. Then the lad went back into the storehouse for more; but when he came out again on the steps, if the North Wind didn't come again and carry off the meal with a puff; and more than that, he did so a third time. At this the lad got very angry; and as he thought it hard that the North Wind should behave so, he thought he'd just look him up and ask him to give up his meal.

So off he went, but the way was long, and he walked and walked; but at last he came to the North Wind's house.

"Good day," said the lad, and "thank you for coming to see us yesterday."

"GOOD DAY," answered the North Wind, for his

voice was loud and gruff, "AND THANKS FOR COM-ING TO SEE ME. WHAT DO YOU WANT?"

"Oh," answered the lad, "I only wished to ask you to be so good as to let me have back the meal you took from me on the storehouse steps, for we haven't much to live on; and if you're to go snapping up the morsel we have there'll be nothing for it but to starve."

"I haven't got your meal," said the North Wind; "but if you are in such need, I'll give you a cloth which will get you everything you want, if you only say, 'Cloth, spread yourself, and serve up all kinds of good dishes.'"

With this the lad was well content. But, as the way was so long he couldn't get home in one day, he turned into an inn on the way; and when they were going to sit down to supper, he laid the cloth on a table which stood in the corner and said—

"Cloth, spread yourself, and serve up all kinds of good dishes." He had scarce said it, before the cloth did as it was bid; and all who stood by thought it a fine thing, but most of all the landlord. So, when all were fast asleep, at the dead of night, he took the lad's cloth, and put another in its stead, just like the one he had got from the North Wind, but which couldn't so much as serve up a bit of dry bread.

When the lad woke, he took his cloth and went off with it, and that day he got home to his mother.

"Now," said he, "I've been to the North Wind's house, and a good fellow he is, for he gave me this cloth, and when I only say to it, 'Cloth, spread yourself, and serve up all kinds of good dishes,' I get any sort of food I please."

"All very true, I dare say," said his mother; "but seeing is believing; and I shan't believe it till I see it."

So the lad made haste, drew out a table, laid the cloth on it and said—

"Cloth, spread yourself, and serve up all kinds of good dishes."

But never a bit of dry bread did the cloth serve up.

"Well," said the lad, "there's no help for it but to go to the North Wind again"; and away he went.

So he came to where the North Wind lived late in the afternoon.

"Good evening!" said the lad.

"Good evening!" said the North Wind.

"I want my rights for that meal of ours which you took," said the lad; "for as for the cloth I got, it isn't worth a penny."

"I've got no meal," said the North Wind; "but yonder you have a ram which coins nothing but golden ducats as soon as you say to it—

" 'Ram, ram! make money!' "

So the lad thought this a fine thing; but as it was too far to get home that day, he turned in for the night at the same inn where he had slept before.

Before he called for anything, he tried the truth of what the North Wind had said of the ram; and found it all right; but when the landlord saw that, he thought it was a famous ram, and when the lad had fallen asleep, he took another which couldn't coin gold ducats, and changed the two.

Next morning off went the lad; and when he got home to his mother, he said,

"After all, the North Wind is a jolly fellow; for now he has given me a ram which can coin gold ducats if I only say, 'Ram, ram! make money!'"

"All very true, I dare say," said his mother; "but I shan't believe any such stuff until I see the ducats made."

"Ram, ram! make money!" said the lad; but, if the ram made anything it wasn't money.

So the lad went back to the North Wind, and blew him up, and said the ram was worth nothing, and he must have his rights for the meal.

"Well," said the North Wind; "I've nothing else to give you but that old stick in the corner yonder; but it's a stick of that kind that if you say,

" 'Stick, stick! lay on!' it lays on till you say,

" 'Stick, stick! now stop!'"

So, as the way was long, the lad turned in this night again, to the landlord; but as he could pretty well guess how things stood as to the cloth and the ram, he lay down at once on the bench and began to snore, as if he were asleep.

Now the landlord, who easily saw that the stick must be worth something hunted up one which was like it. When he heard the lad snore, he was going to change the two; but just as he was about to take it the lad bawled out,

"Stick! stick! lay on!"

So the stick began to beat the landlord, till he jumped over the chairs and tables and benches and yelled and roared,

"Oh, my! oh, my! bid the stick be still, else it will beat me to death, and you shall have back both your cloth and your ram."

When the lad thought the landlord had got enough, he said,

"Stick, stick! now stop!"

Then he took the cloth and put it into his pocket, and went home with his stick in his hand, leading the ram by a cord round its horns; and so he got his rights for the meal he had lost.

From *Popular Tales From the Norse,* edited by P. C. Asbjörnsen and Jörgen Moe.

# Little Red Riding Hood

Once upon a time there was a sweet little girl who was loved by everybody who knew her, but most of all by her grandmother, who could never make enough of the child. Once she gave her a little red velvet cloak with a hood, and this was so becoming to her that she would never wear anything else. So she was always called Red Riding Hood.

One day her mother said to her, "Come, little Red Riding Hood, here is a cake and a bottle of wine for you to take to Grandmother. She is weak and ill and they will do her good. Start quickly, before it gets too hot, and on your way walk properly and don't run off the path, or you may fall and break the bottle, and then there would be no wine left for Grandmother. And when you go into her room, don't forget to say, 'Good morning' nicely, instead of staring about you."

"I will be sure to do as you say," Red Riding Hood promised her mother.

Now the grandmother lived out in the woods, about a half hour's walk from the village, and just as Red Riding

Hood entered the woods, she met a wolf. But as she did not know what a wicked animal he was, she was not at all afraid of him.

"Good day, little Red Riding Hood," said he.

"Thank you kindly, Wolf," she answered.

"Where are you going so early, little Red Riding Hood?"

"To my grandmother's."

"What are you carrying in your basket?"

"Some cake and wine. Yesterday was baking day, so Grandmother is to have something good to make her stronger."

"Where does your grandmother live, little Red Riding Hood?"

"About a quarter of an hour farther on in the woods. Her house stands just under the three big oak trees, and the nut tree just below. You surely must know it," said Red Riding Hood.

The wolf thought to himself, "That tender young thing would be a delicious morsel—much better to eat than the old woman. I must act craftily and catch both of them."

He walked along by the side of Red Riding Hood for a little while and then said, "Just look at the pretty flowers all about here. Why don't you look around? And I don't think you are listening to how sweetly the birds are singing. You just walk along as if you were going to school, while everything in the woods is so merry."

Red Riding Hood raised her eyes, and when she saw

the sunbeams dancing through the trees, and the lovely flowers everywhere, she thought, "If I were to take Grandmother a bouquet of fresh flowers, I am sure she would be very pleased. It is still so early in the day, I shall get there in plenty of time."

So she left the path and ran into the woods looking for flowers. Every time she picked one, she imagined she saw a still prettier one farther on. And so she got deeper and deeper into the woods.

Meanwhile the wolf ran straight to the grandmother's house and knocked at the door.

"Who is there?" cried the grandmother.

"Red Riding Hood," replied the wolf, "and I've brought you some cake and some wine. Please open the door."

"Lift the latch," called out the grandmother. "I am too weak to get up."

So the wolf lifted the latch and the door sprang open. He went straight up to the grandmother's bed without saying a word, and ate her up. Then he put on her night-dress and her cap, lay down in her bed, and drew the curtains.

Red Riding Hood had been running about picking flowers, and when she could hold no more, she remembered her grandmother and set out on the way. When she came to the house she was surprised to find the door standing open, and when she went into the room, she had such a strange feeling that she said to herself, "Oh dear, how uncomfortable I feel! And usually I like being with Grandmother so much."

Red Riding Hood called out, "Good morning!" But there was no answer. So she went to the bed and drew back the curtains. There lay her grandmother with her cap pulled down over her face and looking very strange.

"Oh, Grandmother," she said, "what big ears you have!"

"The better to hear you with, my dear."

"Grandmother, what big eyes you have!"

"The better to see you with, my dear."

"Grandmother, what big hands you have!"

"The better to hug you with, my dear."

"But Grandmother, what big teeth you have!"

"The better to eat you with, my dear."

No sooner had the wolf said this than he made one bound out of bed and swallowed up little Red Riding Hood. Having satisfied his hunger, he lay down again on the bed and was soon snoring loudly.

A huntsman who was passing the house heard him and thought, "How loudly the old woman snores—I had better see if there is anything the matter with her."

So he went into the room, and when he came to the bed he saw the wolf lying there. "At last I find you, you old sinner!" said he. "I have been seeking you for a long, long time!"

Then just as he was about to shoot, it occurred to him that the wolf might have swallowed the grandmother whole, and that she might still be saved. So he took a pair of scissors and began to cut open the sleeping wolf. When he had made two snips, he saw the little red hood shining;

and after two more snips, the little girl sprang out crying, "Oh, how frightened I was! How dark it was inside the wolf." Then out came the old grandmother, alive, too, though scarcely able to breathe.

Red Riding Hood quickly brought some big stones with which they filled the wolf's body. When he awoke and tried to run away, the stones were so heavy that he collapsed and fell down dead.

They were all three delighted. The huntsman took off the wolf's skin and carried it home. The grandmother ate the cake and drank the wine and felt much better. And Red Riding Hood said to herself that she would never again wander off into the woods alone, but would mind what her mother told her.

JANE TAYLOR

# The Star

> Twinkle, twinkle, little star;
> How I wonder what you are!
> Up above the world so high,
> Like a diamond in the sky.

RICHARD HUGHES

# Living in W'ales

Once there was a man who said he didn't like the sort of houses people lived in, so he built a model village. It was not really like a model village at all, because the houses were all big enough for real people to live in, and he went about telling people to come and live in W'ales.

There was also living in Liverpool a little girl who was very nice. So when all the people went off with the man to live in W'ales, she went with them. But the man walked so fast that presently some of them got left behind. The ones who were left behind were the little girl, and an Alsatian dog, and a very cross old lady in a bonnet and black beads, who was all stiff, but had a nice husband, who was left behind too.

So they went along till they came to the sea; and in the sea was a whale. The little girl said, "That was what he meant, I suppose, when he talked about living in W'ales. I expect the others are inside: or, if not, they are in another one. We had better get in this one."

So they shouted to know if they might come in, but the whale didn't hear them. The nice husband said that if that was what living in W'ales meant, he would rather go back to Liverpool; but the horrid old lady said, "Nonsense! I will go and whisper in its ear."

But she was very silly, and so instead of whispering in its ear she went and tried to whisper in its blowhole. Still the whale didn't hear; so she got very cross and said, "None of this nonsense, now! Let us in at once! I won't have it, do you hear? I simply won't stand it!" and she began to stir in his blowhole with her umbrella.

So the whale blew, like an enormous sneeze, and blew her right away up into the sky on top of the water he blew out of his hole, and she was never seen again. So then the nice husband went quietly back to Liverpool.

But the little girl went to the whale's real ear, which was very small and not a bit like his blowhole, and whispered into it, "Please, nice whale, we would so like to come in, if we may, and live inside." Then the whale opened his mouth, and the little girl and the Alsatian dog went in.

When they got right down inside, of course, there was no furniture. "He was quite right," said the little girl. "It is certainly not a bit like living in a house."

The only thing in there was a giant's wig that the whale had once eaten. So the little girl said, "This will do for a doormat." So she made it into a doormat, and the Alsatian dog went to sleep on it.

When he woke up again he started to dig holes; and, of course, it gave the whale most terrible pains to have holes dug by such a big dog in his inside, so he went up

to the top of the water and shouted to the Captain of a
ship to give him a pill. On board the ship there was a cold
dressed leg of mutton that the Captain was tired of, so he
thought, "That will make a splendid pill to give the
whale." So he threw it to the whale, and the whale swallowed it; and when it came tobogganing down the whale's
throat the Alsatian dog, who was very hungry, ate it, and
stopped digging holes; and when the dog stopped digging
holes the whale's pain went away. So he said "Thank you"
to the Captain. "That was an excellent pill."

The Captain was very surprised that his pill had made
the whale well again so soon; he had really done it only
to get rid of the cold mutton.

But the poor little girl wasn't so lucky as the Alsatian
dog. *He* had a doormat to sleep on, and something to eat.
But there was no bed, and the little girl couldn't possibly
sleep without a bed to sleep on; and she had nothing to
eat—and this went on for days and days.

Meanwhile the whale began to get rather worried about
them. He had swallowed them without thinking much
about it; but he soon began to wonder what was happening to them, and whether they were comfortable. He
knew nothing at all about little girls. He thought she
would probably want something to eat by now, but he
didn't know at all what. So he tried to talk down into his
own inside, to ask her. But that is very difficult; at any
rate, *he* couldn't do it. The words all came out instead of
going in.

So he swam off to the tropics, where he knew a parrot,

and asked him what to do. The parrot said it was quite simple, and flew off to an island where there was a big snake. He bit off its head and bit off its tail, and then flew back to the whale with the rest of it. He put most of the snake down the whale's throat, so that one end just came up out of its mouth.

"There," he said, "now you have a speaking tube. You speak into one end of the snake, and the words will go down it inside you."

So the whale said "Hello" into one end of the snake, and the little girl heard "Hello" come out of the other. "What do you want?" said the whale. "I want something to eat," said the little girl. The whale told the parrot, "She wants something to eat. What do little girls eat?"

"Little girls eat rice pudding," said the parrot. He had one, in a big glass bowl; so he poured it down the snake too, and it came down the other end and the little girl ate it.

When she had eaten it she caught hold of her end of the snake, and called "Hello!" up it.

"Hello!" said the whale.

"May I have a bed?" said the little girl.

"She wants a bed," the whale said to the parrot.

"You go to Harrod's for that," said the parrot, "which is the biggest shop in London," and flew away.

When the whale got to Harrod's, he went inside. One of the shopwalkers came up to him and said, "What can I do for *you*, please?" which sounded very silly.

"I want a bed," said the whale.

"Mr. Binks, BEDS!" The shopwalker called out very loud, and then ran away. He was terribly frightened, because there had never been a whale in the shop before.

Mr. Binks the Bed Man came up and looked rather worried.

"I don't know that we have got a bed that will exactly fit you, sir," he said.

"Why not, silly?" said the whale. "I only want an ordinary one."

"Yes, sir," said the Bed Man, "but it will have to be rather a large ordinary one, won't it?"

"Of course not, silly," said the whale. "On the contrary, it will have to be rather a small one."

He saw a very nice little one standing in a corner.

"I think that one will just about fit me," he said.

"You can have it if you like," said the Bed Man. "But I think it's you who are the silly to think a little bed like that will fit you!"

"I want it to fit me *inside*, of course," said the whale, "not *outside!* . . . Push!" and he opened his mouth.

So they all came and pushed, and sure enough it just did fit him. Then he ate all the pillows and blankets he could find, which was far more than was needed really, and when it all got down inside, the little girl made the bed and went to sleep on it.

So the whale went back to the sea. Now that the little girl and the Alsatian dog both had had something to eat and somewhere to sleep, they said:

"The man was right, it really is much more fun living in W'ales than living in houses."

So they stayed on.

P.S. The parrot went on feeding them, not always on rice pudding.

ELEANOR FARJEON

# Mrs. Peck-Pigeon

Mrs. Peck-Pigeon
Is picking for bread,
Bob-bob-bob
Goes her little round head.
Tame as a pussy-cat
In the street,
Step-step-step
Go her little red feet.
With her little red feet
And her little round head,
Mrs. Peck-Pigeon
Goes picking for bread.

MARGARET BAKER

# The Lost Merbaby

Once upon a time there were a fisherman and his wife who lived in a little stone house by the sea. It was only a tiny house, but that was no matter, for it was so neat and pretty that no one could wish it to be different. There was a creeper climbing on the wall, and a pot of flowers in each little window; and in the little kitchen there was a tall old clock, and a dresser with rows of blue platters, and there were two chairs and a round table and a carved oak settle, and by the fireside was a wooden cradle.

But the cradle was empty.

"A baby would be so troublesome," said the fisherman's wife. How should I keep my little house neat and clean with a baby to mind?"

"A baby may be very well in its way," said the fisherman, "but we are happier as we are."

Every day the fisherman set the sails of his boat and went out to sea, and every day his wife went busily about and about the little house. And when her work was done she took her knitting and sat beside the door. She would watch the clouds wandering across the sky, and the waves breaking on the sand, and the sea-gulls wheeling above the cliffs, and then at last she would see the little boat come sailing into the bay, and she would run down to the beach to wave a welcome to the fisherman as soon as he should be near enough to see it.

"Who could be happier than we?" said they.

Now not so very far away there was another little home, but it could not be seen from the fisherman's house however hard one looked, for it lay under the sea. It was only a sandy hollow among the rocks, but it was set about so prettily with sea-weeds that it could not be bettered; and in the hollow lived four little mermaids and a merbaby.

The little mermaids loved the merbaby dearly, but for all that they often found her a great deal of trouble.

"Oh dear!" they would sigh, "how glad we shall be when she is grown up! She is sure to want us if we swim far away; and see how she plays with our sea-weeds and spoils them, and how she disturbs the sand in our little hollow when we have taken care to make it smooth. She is the most beautiful merbaby that could be," said they, "but she is rather a nuisance sometimes."

Now it happened one day that they found a round basket, such as the fishermen use, floating on the waves.

"Here is a cradle for our baby!" cried they. "When we want to play we can lay her inside and the waves will rock her to sleep."

So they took the basket and stopped up the holes and

lined it with sea-weed, and then they put the baby inside. The baby laughed and crowed with delight, and the mermaids swam to their home in the hollow among the rocks. They tidied the sea-weed and smoothed the sand upon the floor, and when they swam back to the cradle and peeped inside the baby was fast asleep.

"See how useful a cradle can be!" they cried. "Now we can swim away to play, for she will not need us for a long, long time."

But the little mermaids had forgotten all about the wind and the tide, and while they were gone the basket was carried far away. It was carried so far that at last it came to the foot of the cliffs near the fisherman's house, and there it rolled over and the merbaby slipped into a rock pool among the anemones.

When the fisherman came sailing home he saw something shining at the foot of the cliffs, and as soon as he had brought his boat to land he went to find out what it could be. And it was the merbaby's hair shining like polished gold in the sun.

"Good lack!" cried the fisherman. "What have we here?"

The merbaby was very tired of being all alone and it held out its little arms and cried to be taken up.

What was there left for the fisherman to do but to lift the baby from the pool and hurry home with it as fast as he could?

The fisherman's wife was just as surprised as he. She took the baby in her arms and hushed it and sang to it and coaxed the smile back into its face.

"How it laughs and crows!" cried she. "Look! its eyes are the color of the sea, and what a dear little tail it has! It is nearly as beautiful as a real baby."

Then they pulled out the wooden cradle and put the baby inside, and there it lay crooning happily to itself. The fisherman's wife kept running to look at it and sing to it, and the baby laughed to see her and tangled its tiny hands in her hair; and the fisherman brought it shells for toys and threaded them in a chain.

That was all well enough, but away under the sea things were not going well at all. The little mermaids had come back from their playing and were looking everywhere for the baby.

"Have you seen our baby?" they asked the plaice who were lying almost buried in the sand.

The largest plaice flicked the sand off itself, for it is not polite to speak to anyone with only your eyes showing. "I have not seen any merbabies for quite a long time," it said, "but that may be because I only see things that are above me on account of my eyes. Perhaps you have noticed my eyes are both on one side of my head," he said proudly; "we are not like other fishes."

"Our baby was in a cradle," explained the little mermaids. "It was only a round basket, but it rocked up and down on the waves and sent her to sleep as well as a real cradle could have done."

"Something that might have been your cradle floated overhead a little while ago," said the plaice. "That is

the way it went. Now, if my eyes had been one on each side of my head I should never have seen it."

Away swam the little mermaids, but no sign of the merbaby could they find.

Presently they met a porpoise. "Have you seen our baby?" they asked, and told him all the tale.

"This is very sad business," said the porpoise. "Come with me and we will see what can be done."

So they swam away together and asked all the fishes they met for news of the merbaby. Not one of them had seen her, but they were so sorry for the little mermaids that they all joined in the search.

The fisherman stood at the door of his house. "There is no wind," said he. "But look how strangely the sea is tossing!"

How could he know the waves were made by the mermaids and fishes as they looked for the lost baby?

"Let us look for her in the rock pools under the cliffs," said the little mermaids.

The lobsters came out of their holes to see what was wanted.

"We have lost our baby," said the mermaids. "We used to think she was only a nuisance, but now she is lost we are sure we can never be happy until she is found." And they told them all about it.

The lobsters waved their legs in surprise. "How strange to mind losing a baby!" said they. "We never take any notice of our own."

The eldest lobster drew his claws thoughtfully among

his feelers. "There is a nasty wicker thing over there that might be your baby's cradle," said he. "It looks too much like a lobster trap for my taste, but as you are not lobsters perhaps you will not mind going near it."

Away went the little mermaids, and among the rocks they found the basket they had used for a cradle. But there was no baby in it.

A big crab came sidling toward them.

"You look as unhappy as though you had just cast your shells," he said. "What can be the matter?"

Then the mermaids told their sorrowful tale all over again and the crab was very sad for them. He went up and down the rock pools explaining what had happened to everything he met, to the fishes and the shrimps and the sea-horses and the whelks, but not one of them could tell him anything.

At last he came to the anemones. "Have you seen the merbaby?" he asked.

"How could we see it?" asked the anemones. "We have no eyes."

"How dreadful to have no eyes!" exclaimed the crab, popping his own in and out with horror at the thought.

"It is not dreadful at all," said the anemones. "We have dozens of feelers and they are much more sensible than eyes, we think."

"But I can't help being sorry for you," said the crab. "Why, even if the mermaids' baby was here you could not see her, and she is worth seeing, they say. Her hair is golden yellow and her eyes are the color of the sea."

"What does it matter what color hair may be as long as it is hair?" said the biggest anemone crossly. "There is a piece twisted around one of my feelers now and it is most uncomfortable."

The crab brought the mermaids to look. He twiddled his eyes in great excitement. "See what I have found!" cried he.

One of the mermaids gently untangled the hair, and it was so fine and so shining that it could have belonged to no one but a merbaby.

"Our baby has been here," said they, "but where can she be now?"

The puffins came waddling along to see what was the matter. They looked very wise indeed when they heard all there was to be told.

"Now we come to think of it . . ." began one.

"We don't think often, you know," said the others, "but when we do we think to some purpose."

"When we come to think of it," said the first puffin again, "we saw the fisherman pick a merbaby from that very pool where you were talking to the anemones."

"Oh, tell us what he did with her!" cried the little mermaids.

"He took it home, of course," said the puffins. "Your baby is not lost now because we have told you where she is."

And they waddled away.

"Alas!" cried the mermaids. "We are scarcely any better off than when we did not know where to find her.

The fisherman's house lies far beyond the reach of the waves and we can only go where the waves can carry us."

Then the mermaids lifted themselves out of the water. "Sea-gulls! Sea-gulls!" they cried. "Fly to the fisherman's house and tell us what has become of our baby."

So the sea-gulls flew across the sand and round and round the fisherman's house.

"Surely there is a storm coming," said the fisherman, "else why should the gulls fly so near and cry so loudly?"

How could he know they had come to see what was done with the merbaby?

"The fisherman has put the baby in the cradle and his wife is tending it as though it was their own," said the sea-gulls when they came back. Then the little mermaids began to weep and sigh. "If they grow to love our baby they will never give her to us again," they sobbed.

"How the sea moans tonight!" said the fisherman. "There is surely a storm coming."

But when the merbaby heard it she began to wail and would not be comforted. "Hush, hush!" soothed the fisherman's wife and ran to pick the baby out of the cradle, but the baby only wailed the more pitifully.

"It is the moaning of the sea that distresses her," said the fisherman's wife. "I could almost weep myself for the sorrowful sound of it." And she shut her window.

How could she know the baby cried because she knew the sound was the mermaid's weeping?

Now, as was only to be expected, the news of the merbaby spread among the fisherfolk, and they one and all made some excuse to come tapping at the fisherman's door.

The fisherman's wife showed the baby proudly. "Look what beautiful eyes she has!" she would say. "And see her tiny hands and the shining of her hair!"

"Yes! yes!" said the fisherfolk, "but it is a great pity that she has a tail."

"It is a very beautiful tail," said the fisherman's wife. "And there are so many people with feet that to have a tail is to be quite distinguished."

"A tail will be very awkward when she grows up," said the fisherfolk shaking their heads. "Why don't you put her back in the sea?"

"How cruel that would be!" cried the fisherman's wife. "She is far too tiny to care for herself. Besides, we love her too much to part with her now."

So the merbaby lay from day to day in the wooden cradle and cooed and crooned to itself. The fisherman would leave the mending of his nets to play with it, and his wife sang it gay little songs as she went about her work and ran to kiss its tiny hands and cover it with caresses.

"How could we think a baby was too much trouble!" cried they. "A baby is the loveliest thing in the world."

But the little mermaids in their home among the rocks had no heart to tend the sea-weeds, nor to smooth the sand upon the floor and make all neat and tidy; they had no heart to talk to the fishes, nor to play as they had done before.

"How could we think our baby a trouble?" cried they.

"Perhaps some day the fisherman's wife may tire of her," said the eldest.

So every day they swam to the foot of the cliffs. "Sea-gulls! Sea-gulls!" they cried. "Fly away and bring news of our baby!"

And every day the sea-gulls told how the fisherman's wife was fondling the baby as though it were her own.

"Alas! Alas!" wept the little mermaids. "We shall never see our baby again."

And every day when the merbaby heard the sound of their crying it began to wail and would not be comforted.

Then the fisherman would shake his head and ponder. "'Tis strange," said he, "the moaning of the sea is as the sound of someone weeping."

His wife, too, would ponder on the strangeness as she tried to hush the baby's crying, and she pondered so long that in the end she could not help but find the truth.

"Hark!" cried she. "The baby weeps in answer to the sound. It is no moaning of the waves we hear, but the sorrowing of those who have lost her."

Then she lifted the baby from the cradle and kissed it on this cheek and that, and ran with it to the shore. There sat the little mermaids weeping, and when they saw the fisherman's wife they held out their arms.

"Give us our baby!" cried they. "We cannot play nor sing nor be happy till we have her again."

"Sorrow no more. Here is your baby," said the fisherman's wife, and she kissed it over and over and gave it to them.

But when she came back to the little house and saw the empty cradle she fell to weeping as sadly as ever the little mermaids had done.

"It is my turn to sorrow now," said she.

And the fisherman could find no words to comfort her, for he was as sad as she.

But the little mermaids were happier than they had ever been before, and they swam up and down with the baby to tell all the sea-creatures of their good fortune and to thank them for their help.

"You look much happier than you did," said the crabs, but, "It is rather hard to understand family life," said the puffins. "We think a great deal of our babies, but of course they are much nicer than merbabies because they have down and feathers."

"And wings," added the sea-gulls. "We cannot imagine what use arms can be."

The anemones shut up as soon as the mermaids came near. "We are glad you have found the baby, since it pleases you so much," said they. "But do take her away or we shall get hair all over us again."

The fishes looked at the merbaby very curiously. "Her tail is very fine," they said, "but a fin or two would improve her."

"Or having both her eyes on one side of her head," said the plaice.

"But of course if you are satisfied with her there is

nothing more to be said," added the porpoise, and waved his flipper as he swam away.

The little mermaids hugged and kissed their baby. "'Fancy thinking she is not perfect!" they cried. "Only the fisherman and his wife know how to love her as we do, and now they are sorrowful because we have taken her back again."

So sometimes they swam to the little bay and called, and the fisherman's wife would hear them and come running to the edge of the sea. Then the mermaids would give her the baby, and she would sit on the rocks to play with it and fondle it.

"It is so lonely now that the cradle is empty," she would sigh for sympathy. "We will come again soon," said they.

But one day when they swam to the bay, though they called and called, the fisherman's wife did not come running out to greet them.

"What can have befallen her?" they asked one another. Then they lifted themselves out of the water. "Sea-gulls! Sea-gulls!" they cried. "Fly away across the sand and tell us why the fisherman's wife does not hear us calling."

So the sea-gulls flew round and round the little house as they had done before.

"You need not sorrow longer for the loneliness of the fisherman's wife," said they. "There is another baby in the cradle; it has feet instead of a tail and its eyes are the color of the sky, but she does not seem to mind, nor does the fisherman. They have not heard you call because they are too happy to hear anything but their own joy."

Then the little mermaids swam back to the hollow among the rocks.

"Now we can be happy all day long," said they, "for there is no one left lonely and sorrowing. And some day we will go again to the bay and the fisherman's wife will show us her baby and we will love it next to our own."

PEGGY BACON

# The Mischievous Monkey

Once there was a monkey who spent quite a lot of time sitting in the top of a tall nut tree cracking nuts. He would sit there all day munching and throwing the shells on the ground below. This constant fall of shells much annoyed the little squirrel who lived in a hole at the base of the tree. The squirrel was a tidy animal and did not like the piles of shells about his door.

"What do you mean by making all this nasty mess around my house?" he chattered angrily to the monkey, who replied by throwing down another handful of shells. "Besides," added the squirrel, "I sometimes mistake the empty shells for good nuts and thus waste a lot of my valuable time collecting them."

"You should not make such silly mistakes," the monkey replied. "Moreover, if you do not like a mess around your door you may sweep it up as much as you choose. I like a neat home myself," he added, "but I am willing to take some trouble to keep it so."

This was really maddening of the monkey, and the squirrel fairly danced with rage. But there was nothing he could do so he darted back into his hole, muttering to himself.

The squirrel had been born and raised in the nut tree, so although he disliked the monkey he was determined to remain. When the monkey had come to live in the tree the squirrel had moved down out of his hole high up in the trunk of the tree to another hole nearer the ground in order to be as far away from the monkey as possible. He wished very much to get rid of the monkey but knew not how.

On the following day he went to a neighboring tree to tell his troubles to another squirrel, an intimate friend of his. While he was gone the mischievous monkey climbed down the tree and thrust his hand into the squirrel's hole. Finding the pile of nuts the squirrel had gathered he scooped them all out, and carried them to the top of the tree. There he perched on a branch and began to crunch them, chuckling to himself.

By and by the squirrel returned to his home and it was not long before he discovered the loss of the nuts. Nor did it take him long to decide who had been the thief. This time he was beside himself with fury. Out of his hole he scurried and shrieked up at the monkey:

"How dare you steal my food out of my house! How dare you! You shall pay for this, you miserable, mean, low-down, mangy, brown, rat-tailed simian!!"—for the squirrel was quite a master of invective, which means that

he knew how to say a lot of saucy things when he felt like it. But the monkey only laughed and chattered back. He did not seem to mind the squirrel's remarks and was in fact without proper pride.

"Sticks and stones will break my bones but words will never hurt me," he sang out boldly. And this gave the squirrel an idea.

The thought that had occurred to him soothed his temper. The knowledge that he would have his revenge gave him patience to wait. He went quietly into his hole.

Next day he was up very early. He went to the pine woods and gathered a lot of sticky brown resin that oozes from the pine trees. Wrapping this in a leaf he carried it to his home. Then he went to the wide, stony brook and trotted about picking up small, round pebbles, which he also carried home. This took him a long while, for he could only carry one at a time in his mouth. When he had collected quite a pile of these pebbles he covered them with dry leaves so that no one would find them. Finally he went outside his house, and picking up all the broken shells which the monkey had dropped, he bore them inside as though tidying up his dooryard.

The monkey observed how busy the squirrel was but did not notice exactly what the little beast was doing. From time to time, however, as he threw down a handful of nut shells he would call out derisively:

"Here are some more bits to clear away, master squirrel. Be sure to pick them all up." Such remarks as these would have irritated the squirrel extremely at any other time, but just now he was so busy that he hardly even heard the monkey's teasing laughter.

For three whole days now the squirrel was very busy indeed inside his hole. About each pebble he carefully pieced the broken shells, gluing them together securely with the rosin from the pine trees, till when all was done you would have thought it a pile of perfect nuts, so cleverly had he matched and fitted the bits.

On the fourth day he pretended to leave home, but after he had gone a short distance he returned on tiptoe and hid himself in the next tree to see what might happen.

The monkey saw him depart and when the squirrel seemed well out of sight down he climbed, thrust his hand into the hole, and discovered the pile of nuts. Gleefully he conveyed them all to the treetop and set the first one between his teeth.

Crack! crack! went the nut, and crack! crack! went two of the monkey's teeth as they struck the hard pebble inside. The monkey's teeth were strong, but they were not made to crush stone, so he threw away the nut and tried another. He set the second nut between two different teeth as the first two were still aching from the shock. Crack! crack! again went nut and teeth. After the third nut the monkey had cracked six of his teeth and was groaning with pain.

"I never saw such nuts as these!" scolded the monkey as he examined the remainder. So neatly had the squirrel joined the pieces that the monkey's eyes failed to detect the fraud. They looked for all the world like the other nuts on the tree around him.

"The nuts on this tree are evidently growing too stale and hard," mused the monkey who was quite ignorant. "They are no longer good to eat," he decided, scratching his head. So fearing to try any more of them lest he lose the rest of his teeth, he moved on to another part of the forest, leaving the triumphant squirrel in possession of the tree.

FRANK ROSENGREN

# Miss Crumpet's Great Day

The people of London were preparing to crown their new King. Preparations for the great event had gone on for months. Streets were gay with banners and flags, and no expense was spared to make the event the greatest of its kind in history. And in the midst of it all stood the tiny little candy shop of Miss Crumpet.

Miss Crumpet was a lively little lady, plump, rather short, and always amiable and cheerful. As the Great Day drew nearer, Miss Crumpet seemed to lose some of her usual cheerfulness. At first she had watched the activity with great joy, but as days passed, she noticed that London grew more and more crowded. She suddenly realized that she would be at a serious disadvantage among the huge crowds. First of all her plumpness prevented her from walking very far; and, secondly, her shortness kept her from seeing over other people's heads. She knew how much these difficulties would interfere, and she was so anxious to see EVERYTHING. And then—Professor Beep came to town!

Did you never hear of Professor Beep, the great inventor?— Professor Beep, inventor, explorer, and sometimes strong man in the circus? Why, he could invent anything. Once when the King of Siam wanted to know who was coming around the corner before he got there, Professor Beep invented the Around-the-Corner-Squinter and gave it to the King. The King was so grateful that he gave the Professor a huge reward—an elephant that weighed tons.

One day, shortly after his arrival in London, he wandered into Miss Crumpet's candy shop.

"And, my dear lady," said the Professor to Miss Crumpet, "I suppose that on Coronation Day your shop will be closed, while you watch the great affair?"

"Alas!" said Miss Crumpet. "Well could I spare my shop the presence of myself, but how is one so short as I to see anything over the heads of the crowds that will line the way of the procession?"

" 'Tis true she is a bit on the short side, and she tends to be rather a bit overdone on the sturdy side, as well," thought Professor Beep. "However, something will have to be done. She seems a sweet lady deserving of my help." He bowed low.

"Madam," said Professor Beep, "I am a great inventor. I must place my brain at your disposal and invent something that will help you to see the Coronation Parade."

"Ah! if you only could," sighed Miss Crumpet. "But, kind sir, I fear I could not afford the services of one so great."

It pleased the Professor to have Miss Crumpet recognize his greatness so quickly, and he assured her, with a grand gesture, that there would be no charge. With that he cried, "Good day, fair lady, I am off to serve you."

But day followed day, and Professor Beep, rack his brains as he would, could discover no solution to the problem. He visited Miss Crumpet at her shop and there reviewed the situation and also reviewed Miss Crumpet. "Even if she could be stretched, she could not be stretched enough," thought the Professor, and he would come away completely disheartened. And the day of the Coronation drew *nearer* and *nearer*.

While the Professor was strolling through the Zoo the next morning, he saw a kangaroo give a mighty jump, and as soon as he saw that jump, he shouted, "Ha! I've got it!" Away he rushed madly to his home. When he arrived there, he hurried to his trunk and brought out a pair of boots. Hugging the boots closely, he started for Miss Crumpet's.

When he arrived there, he found her sitting on her doorstep weeping. "And why are you weeping, my Little Pet?" said he. The Professor felt he had known Miss Crumpet long enough to shorten her name, but for some reason he preferred to call her "my Little Pet" rather than "my Little Crum."

"I weep because I shall not see the parade," said she.

"Tomorrow is the great day, and you have failed me."

"Not so, my Little Crum, I mean—Pet," cried the Professor, and with a flourish he brought the boots from behind his back. "Behold!"

"Worrying about me has driven the poor man distracted," thought Miss Crumpet. "What use can those boots be?"

But the Professor was busy and while the children stood about goggle-eyed, listening and watching, he put on the boots. Then he jumped lightly and bounded into the air.

"Come back," cried the children, but before the words were well out of their mouths, the Professor had disappeared around the corner. The children ran swiftly after him but had scarcely gone ten steps when they heard a voice behind them saying, "Where to, my little friends?"

They turned around and there was Professor Beep! He had bounded clear around the block almost as quick as a wink.

"But how will the Bouncing Boots help Miss Crumpet?" asked the children.

"Heavens, I never thought of that," said the Professor. "I must invent something at once, for the Coronation takes place tomorrow." As the Professor bounded away, Miss Crumpet thought, "He is a dear man, but he seems a bit silly at times. I know I shall never see the parade." And she fell to weeping again.

Professor Beep bounded away toward his home. These Bouncing Boots were his greatest invention. He well remembered the needy occasion when they had been invented. He had been exploring in the upper reaches of the Amazon River in South America. No, he must have been in Africa. He couldn't remember where it was. Anyway, they were after him foot and sleigh, tooth and nail. He had to escape them. They were coming closer and closer, and then he came to a deserted blockhouse. Or was it a castle? He couldn't remember. All he could remember was that he needed to escape. He hurried into the—whichever it was—and almost immediately stumbled into a pot of some strange-smelling mixture that was simmering over a fire. The pot overturned and its contents spilled on the floor. He stepped into the mixture and then stepped out of it. The fluid hardened on his boots and he found himself bouncing a bit each time he stepped. He stepped into the mixture again and then out to let it harden. He did this many times and each time a layer was added to the soles of his boots he found that he bounded higher into the air on making the slightest effort. One time he stepped down too hard and his head went right through the thatched roof of the blockhouse. Or was it the castle? He couldn't remember. Anyway, he was saved.

By this time his enemies had almost reached him. He heard their mad yells through the forest. He carefully left wherever he was, and once in the open air he gave a mighty jump. Up he flew over the tree tops but he came right straight down again in the same spot. He tried again, but this time he bounded forward. It worked.

He came back years later to measure the distance he

had bounded forward and found it something less than five hundred feet . . . but it had been enough. He had bounded all that day until he reached civilization. By that time he was tired of the boots and never wore them again until this day.

When the Professor reached his home, he spent a few hours in thought and then he went to the market place and bought various things, including a rocking chair. That evening he gave a huge sigh of relief and went to bed. He knew he would not fail Miss Crumpet on the morrow.

The day of the Coronation arrived and, for what seemed a dreadfully long time, Miss Crumpet sat on her doorstep, completely disheartened. She had given up all hope of seeing the parade. Suddenly, while looking off down the road, a strange sight met her eyes. Could it be? It seemed impossible! Yes, it was—it *was* Professor Beep. But what in the world was that on his shoulders? It looked like a rocking chair. And so it was! When the Professor arrived at her doorstep, he reached down and catching Miss Crumpet about the waist he lifted her high into the air and into the chair. Miss Crumpet screamed with fright at first, but Professor Beep soon reassured her.

"And now, I suggest that you tighten across your lap that strap I have fastened to the side of the chair," said the Professor. "We're going traveling."

Miss Crumpet did as she was told, and then the Professor called, "Here we go," and gave a gentle bound into the air. Up they flew, and Miss Crumpet was so amazed that she forgot to be frightened. However, there was nothing to be frightened about. Professor Beep bounced away so gently that it was like sitting at home in one's rocking chair, with one remarkable difference.

"I can see everything for blocks and blocks," cried Miss Crumpet. And that, of course, was the Professor's plan.

Now, Miss Crumpet could see over the heads of everybody. People turned to stare as the Professor bounded along—stared with envy, when they realized how easily both Miss Crumpet and the Professor saw everything without straining and craning their necks. Miss Crumpet, fascinated by the Parade itself, was oblivious of them all. Her eyes feasted on gorgeous color, beautiful uniforms, regal clothing, gayly decorated horses, and magnificent coaches until she became weary. Suddenly, she looked down at the crowds and discovered something was missing. She had nothing to wave—why, she didn't even have a camera.

"Professor Beep," she called, "you must let me down a moment."

And then, as the Professor worriedly lifted her to the ground, she said, "Professor, I must have a banner to wave. I must have a camera so that I can take pictures."

He felt better immediately. Why, she was enjoying herself so much she felt she must wave something, and shout, and tell the world about it. Very well, she should have it. But it suddenly dawned upon him that he had no money.

"Gladly would I purchase you the trifles you request," he said ever so grandly to Miss Crumpet, accompanying his fine words with a bow, "but I have no money."

"No money?" said Miss Crumpet.

"No money," said the Professor.

They looked at each other in dismay.

"No money," again said Miss Crumpet.

"No money," repeated the Professor.

"That is too bad," said Miss Crumpet.

"Precisely," said the Professor. "But being a man of many talents, I suggest that you allow me to commune with myself for a moment and the difficulty I am sure will vanish."

Miss Crumpet sat down while the Professor communed. Suddenly the Professor stirred. Then he shook himself. Then he jumped up with glee and looked as though he were going to shake Miss Crumpet—just a jolly, cheerful shake. But he didn't. Instead he said, "The answer is simple. These goodly folk have been watching us with envy. Many of those in the back rows can see scarcely a thing. I shall sell them bounces so that they can see the sights, and for this slight service they shall pay me." With these words the Professor bounded away, and soon she heard him singing as he moved behind the crowd:

"The Price is not sixpence, nor fivepence, nor four,
It's tuppence a bounce, and you'll see so much more;
You will see your new King and your Queen on their way
To be crowned at Westminster on this very day.
You pay by the bounce
And not by the ounce.
Come large and come small,

Come one and come all."

The Professor was besieged by people wanting to ride, and soon he had earned enough to buy a handful of banners and flags and balloons for Miss Crumpet. And last of all he bought a small camera.

Returning to Miss Crumpet he soon had her perched

in her chair. How merrily she waved her banners and flags! How gaily she let loose her balloons! How carefully did she click her camera! She cheered the King and she cheered the Queen and she carefully snapped their pictures.

And then the parade was over. Miss Crumpet was tired, but not too tired to give one final cheer for Professor Beep who had made her glorious day possible.

Finally, the Professor stopped bouncing and, glancing up at Miss Crumpet, discovered that she was fast asleep. She was all tired out, but she had a most contented smile on her face. The Professor brought her to her own door and there awakened her and gently let her down. Then he said, "Miss Crumpet, has it been a happy day?"

"O Professor!" said Miss Crumpet. "The most glorious day of my life. If only—if only the King had sat still and stopped his bobbing up and down."

ROBERT LOUIS STEVENSON

# Singing

Of speckled eggs the birdie sings
    And nests among the trees;
The sailor sings of ropes and things
    In ships upon the seas.

The children sing in far Japan,
    The children sing in Spain;
The organ with the organ man
    Is singing in the rain.

MARGERY WILLIAMS BIANCO

# Mr. Murdle's Large Heart

In nearly every town you will find one store which keeps all those foolish little things that the other stores forget, or are so apt to be out of.

Mr. Murdle's is just such a store. Many years ago, when Mr. Murdle was a round-faced little boy, he must have said to his mother: "When I grow up I'm going to keep a store!"

He had no idea at all of what he wanted to sell in his store; it was just going to be a store. And so it turned out. He started by buying a little bit here and a little bit there, just as he fancied, and all sorts of funny cardboard boxes began to pile up on his shelves. He thought of ginger ale and slate pencils and newspapers and paper clips, and of course candy; of little celluloid dolls and hairpins and pencil sharpeners, and ash trays with scalloped gilt edges and pictures on them, and lots and lots of cigars.

Mr. Murdle himself doesn't really know all that he has in his store, and certainly no one else does. But if ever it happens that you want to buy something that you cannot find in any of the other stores along the street, sooner or later someone will scratch his head and say:

"Well, you *might* try Mr. Murdle, across the way!"

So across the way you go, and sure enough, after Mr. Murdle has stood for a moment thinking, he will rummage among his cardboard boxes and pull one of them out, and nine times out of ten there it is, the very thing you were looking for!

All this is wonderful enough, but it isn't the most remarkable thing about Mr. Murdle, by any means.

The most remarkable thing about Mr. Murdle is his Large Heart.

Everyone who knows Mr. Murdle will tell you what a Large Heart he has. And it is really true. I have seen it myself, hanging up at the back of Mr. Murdle's store. It is pink and purple, with yellow around the edges, and in the middle, which is white, there are rows of little elastic loops, which once upon a time held tiny bottles of pink and purple and yellow lozenges. Fairy lozenges, they must have been, but that is so long ago that no one knows what they really were like. But the Heart is still there.

It is a fine thing for anyone to have such a Large Heart. But there are disadvantages also, especially for anyone like Mr. Murdle, who is in business, and who really ought to be thinking of money every minute, as all the other storekeepers do. It makes it very nice of course for Mr. Murdle's customers, but it must be difficult for Mr. Murdle. That Large Heart of his is always getting in the way.

When a little girl comes into his store, for instance, and wants an ice-cream cone and has only three cents, or when some little boy wants candy and Mr. Murdle knows perfectly well that he should only give him five chocolates for a nickel, then that Large Heart begins to whisper to him, and before Mr. Murdle knows it he has

handed out the cone with an extra lump of strawberry ice cream on, or he has slipped seven chocolates into the bag instead of five.

And if you want some particular-sized envelopes, or some special kind of paper clip such as you bought three years ago and have never been able to find since, and Mr. Murdle has hunted through and through his cardboard boxes and finally found it, then as likely as not he will say:

"Oh, I've had that in stock so long I wouldn't know what to charge you for it. We'll make it up next time!" And next time, of course, never comes.

Then there are the cats.

It began with one cat. She was a tortoise-shell cat, and she found that the pleasantest place to spend the morning was curled up in the sun, on top of Mr. Murdle's stack of daily papers, just inside the store. She spent every morning there, and usually the afternoon as well. Mr. Murdle used to give her the melted ice cream that was left over at night.

Presently she married and had a family, and they all came to live in Mr. Murdle's store. Several of her cousins came, too. Now there were eleven cats, and not nearly enough melted ice cream to go round. So Mr. Murdle—having such a Large Heart—took to melting the ice cream on purpose. He found that the cats liked vanilla best, so he always ordered more of the vanilla than of any other kind, and with it he gave them crumbled-up wafers and peppermint creams.

Early every morning when Mr. Murdle came to open the store, there were the cats waiting for him, and the very first thing he did was to look in the ice-cream can and see if there was anything left over from the day before. Usually there wasn't, and then Mr. Murdle would take eight pennies from the till behind the counter and go over to the grocery to buy milk for the cats' breakfast.

Everyone liked Mr. Murdle, including the cats, and Mr. Murdle himself was one of the happiest people in the world, and all on account of his Large Heart.

But there was one person who did not at all approve of Mr. Murdle's Large Heart. This was Mr. Murdle's aunt. It may seem funny for anyone like Mr. Murdle, who is at least forty and quite bald on the top of his head, to have an aunt; but he had, and one fine day she came all the way from Vermont to keep house for him. She was a busy, active sort of woman, and not content with managing Mr. Murdle's house for him, she soon began to think of managing his store as well.

She didn't approve of the cats and she didn't approve of the little boys and girls. In fact, she didn't approve of anything at all that Mr. Murdle liked and least of all of the way he did business. She decided that all that sort of thing must be changed.

At first she didn't have much success. Mr. Murdle had been going along very comfortably in his own way for so long that it wasn't easy, even for a determined person like Mr. Murdle's aunt, to change him. But she did her best, and as luck would have it, while she was rummaging about and tidying the store up one day, she came upon Mr. Murdle's Large Heart. She didn't at all know what it was, but she certainly didn't like the look of it. She leaned on her broom and stared.

"Now that's a foolish sort of thing," she said. "Cluttering the store up and taking space where it isn't wanted. I'm going to throw it out!"

And she did.

From that moment, a very dreadful change came over Mr. Murdle.

The aunt thought it was all due to her lecturing and her good advice. But it wasn't at all. It was just because Mr. Murdle had lost his Large Heart.

In two days you wouldn't have known Mr. Murdle's store.

Everything was tidy, and Mr. Murdle himself just as business-like as he could be. He knew the price of everything. When little boys came in and asked for a nickel's worth of candy, believe me they *got* a nickel's worth of candy, and not one speck more, and if the little girls hadn't enough money for their ice-cream cones they might just turn right around and walk out again.

It was terrible, and as for the cats, they all left in a body and went to live with the fat lady at the delicatessen store across the way. Mr. Murdle said he couldn't afford to feed a lot of lazy cats that did nothing but sleep all day, and that moreover they mussed up his newspapers.

Can you *imagine* that!

All the little boys and girls were very upset. But luckily there was one little boy who had more sense than the rest.

He was loitering in the store one day. Mr. Murdle's aunt happened to be away shopping, or you may be very sure she would have chased him out. But there he was staring about him and trying to make out just why it was that everything should look so different. And all at once he realized that something was missing.

It was Mr. Murdle's Large Heart.

It wasn't there in its usual place above the counter, and it wasn't anywhere in the store, though he searched

high and low. Being a clever little boy he soon put two
and two together.

"I bet you," he said, "that mean old woman has thrown
it out!"

He went straightway into the yard behind the store,
where Mr. Murdle kept all his old boxes and empty crates,
and began to hunt. And sure enough, after a little while
there he found it, thrown out with a pile of rubbish and
broken pasteboard boxes, waiting to be burned.

It was torn at one side and a bit crumpled, but
he smoothed it out and carried it back to its old place on
the wall behind the counter, and to make sure this time,
he fetched a hammer and nails and he *nailed* it, all around
the edge.

Not even Mr. Murdle's aunt could have torn it down
again!

What's more, she never got a chance. For as soon as
Mr. Murdle set foot in the store, now that his Large
Heart was back in its right place again, he became just
the same Mr. Murdle that he had been before.

The very first thing that he did was to send his aunt
packing.

Then he telephoned for fresh ice cream—every kind
he could think of—and he opened all the candy boxes
and told the little boys and girls, who by this time had
heard the news and had all come trooping round, that
they might help themselves, and if they didn't have any
money they could pay him next year.

And he dragged his old armchair out, and lit a big cigar,

and settled down by the doorway, as happy as could be.

When the cats saw that, they all came trooping back again, too.

So today things are just as they used to be, and there is very little danger they will ever change again. Not as long as Mr. Murdle's Large Heart stays there, right in its place, and that, you may be very sure, will be for a long time to come.

As for Mr. Murdle's aunt, she gave him up as a bad job and went back to Vermont, broom and all.

And if you don't believe me, all you need do is to walk into Mr. Murdle's store some fine morning, past the curled-up cats and the newspapers and ask for a nickel's worth of candy.

You will see how much you get!

MIRIAM CLARK POTTER

# Mrs. Goose's Rubbers

One day Mrs. Goose could not find her rubbers. She looked in the same old place in the dark hall closet, and she looked under the bed, and she looked on the back porch; but she could not see them. So she went to Mrs. Pig's house and knocked at the door. When Mrs. Pig came to see who was knocking, Mrs. Goose said: "Have you seen my rubbers?"

"Of course I haven't seen your rubbers, Mrs. Goose," Mrs. Pig told her. "They wouldn't be at my house, would they?"

"I don't know," said Mrs. Goose. "I just thought they might be."

Then she went to Mrs. Squirrel's house and knocked at the door. When Mrs. Squirrel came to let her in, Mrs. Goose said, "I just came to see if you had seen my rubbers."

Mrs. Squirrel was making a nut-patty pudding. "No, I haven't seen them," she said. "Did you think they were *here*?"

"I didn't know," sighed Mrs. Goose. "I just thought they might be."

Then Mrs. Goose went home. She looked under the stove, she looked behind the door, she looked up on the clock shelf, she looked in the wastepaper basket, she looked in the icebox, but she could not find her rubbers.

Just then Mrs. Sheep went by.

"Oh, Mrs. Sheep," called Mrs. Goose; "have you seen my rubbers?"

Mrs. Sheep stopped by the fence. "Why, no, I haven't seen your rubbers," she said. "Where do you usually keep them?"

"In their same old place in the dark hall closet," said Mrs. Goose. "But they are not there."

Mrs. Sheep thought for a minute, and then she said, "Why do you want your rubbers, anyway, Mrs. Goose? It's sunny!"

"Well, it might rain tomorrow," Mrs. Goose replied, "and then I'd want them."

"That's right," said Mrs. Sheep. "Come to think of it, I don't know where *my* rubbers are, either. I'd better go home and look them up." And she hurried on.

Still Mrs. Goose could *not* find her rubbers. She looked in the teakettle, she looked on the back stairs, she looked in the bread box, she looked under her pillow, and then she got a ladder and climbed up on the roof and stared all around; but her black eyes did not spy them anywhere.

"Dear me, dear me," she sighed, "where can my rubbers *be?*"

Then she ate her supper and went to bed. Next morning when she woke up, rain was coming down—*drip,*

*drip, drip,* on the roof. "Oh, it *is* raining today," said Mrs. Goose, "and I've got to go to market, and I haven't found my rubbers, and I'll get my poor feet all wet!"

She got up and made her bed and ate her breakfast. She dusted her house; and then she just *had* to go to market. The rain was coming down in big bursts and splashes and there were puddles all over the sidewalk.

"I *must* find my rubbers!" thought Mrs. Goose. And she looked and looked in all the same places, but they did not turn up. "Well," she sighed, "I shall have to go without them. That's *what!*" And she put on her coat and bonnet, took her big green umbrella from its place in the dark hall closet, and started out. She shut the door behind her, locked it with the tiny key, and stepped out on her porch. Then she put her big green umbrella up.

"Plop! Plop!" Two big somethings hit her on the head and almost knocked her bonnet off. They fell down on the porch behind her. "What can they be?" thought Mrs. Goose. She turned around and looked at them. They were her rubbers!

"I must have put them inside my umbrella," said Mrs. Goose. "Oh, now I remember! I put them there so they would not be lost. But it would have been a good deal better if I had put them back in their same place, in the dark hall closet."

Then she put her rubbers on and went splashing along through the puddles on her way to market.

# Nail Broth

There was once a tramp who was plodding his way through a forest. The distance between the houses was so great that he had little hope of finding shelter before the night set in. But all of a sudden he saw some lights between the trees. He then discovered a cottage, where there was a fire burning on the hearth. How nice it would be to roast oneself before that fire and to get a bite of something, he thought; and so he dragged himself towards the cottage.

Just then an old woman came towards him.

"Good evening, and well met!" said the tramp.

"Good evening," said the woman. "Where do you come from?"

"South of the sun, and east of the moon," said the tramp; "and now I am on the way home again, for I have been all over the world with the exception of this parish," he said.

"You must be a great traveler, then," said the woman. "What may be your business here?"

"Oh, I want a shelter for the night," he said.

"I thought as much," said the woman; "but you may as well get away from here at once, for my husband is not at home, and my place is not an inn," she said.

"My good woman," said the tramp, "you must not be so cross and hard-hearted, for we are both human beings, and should help one another, it is written."

"Help one another?" said the woman. "Help? Did you ever hear such a thing? Who'll help me, do you think? I haven't got a morsel in the house! No, you'll have to look for quarters elsewhere," she said.

But the tramp was like the rest of his kind; he did not consider himself beaten at the first rebuff. Although the old woman grumbled and complained as much as she could, he was just as persistent as ever and went on begging and praying like a starved dog, until at last she gave in, and he got permission to lie on the floor for the night.

That was very kind, he thought, and he thanked her for it.

"Better on the floor without sleep, than suffer cold in the forest deep," he said; for he was a merry fellow, this tramp, and was always ready with a rhyme.

When he came into the room he could see that the woman was not so badly off as she had pretended; but she was a greedy and stingy woman of the worst sort, and was always complaining and grumbling.

He now made himself very agreeable, of course, and asked her in his most insinuating manner for something to eat.

"Where am I to get it from?" said the woman. "I haven't tasted a morsel myself the whole day."

But the tramp was a cunning fellow, he was.

"Poor old granny, you must be starving," he said. "Well, well, I suppose I shall have to ask you to have something with me, then."

"Have something with you!" said the woman. "You don't look as if you could ask any one to have anything! What have you got to offer one, I should like to know?"

"He who far and wide does roam sees many things not known at home; and he who many things has seen has wits about him and senses keen," said the tramp. "Better dead than lose one's head! Lend me a pot, grannie!"

The old woman now became very inquisitive, as you may guess, and so she let him have a pot.

He filled it with water and put it on the fire, and then he blew with all his might till the fire was burning fiercely all round it. Then he took a four-inch nail from his pocket, turned it three times in his hand and put it into the pot.

The woman stared with all her might.

"What's this going to be?" she asked.

"Nail broth," said the tramp, and began to stir the water with the porridge stick.

"Nail broth?" asked the woman.

"Yes, nail broth," said the tramp.

The old woman had seen and heard a good deal in her time, but that anybody could have made broth with a nail, well, she had never heard the like before.

"That's something for poor people to know," she said, "and I should like to learn how to make it."

"That which is not worth having, will always go a-begging," said the tramp.

But if she wanted to learn how to make it she had only to watch him, he said, and went on stirring the broth.

The old woman squatted on the ground, her hands clasping her knees, and her eyes following his hand as he stirred the broth.

"This generally makes good broth," he said; "but this time it will very likely be rather thin, for I have been making broth the whole week with the same nail. If one only had a handful of sifted oatmeal to put in, that would make it all right," he said. "But what one has to go without, it's no use thinking more about," and so he stirred the broth again.

"Well, I think I have a scrap of flour somewhere," said the old woman, and went out to fetch some, and it was both good and fine.

The tramp began putting the flour into the broth, and went on stirring, while the woman sat staring now at him and then at the pot until her eyes nearly burst their sockets.

"This broth would be good enough for company," he said, putting in one handful of flour after another. "If I had only a bit of salted beef and a few potatoes to put in, it would be fit for gentlefolks, however particular they might be," he said. "But what one has to go without, it's no use thinking more about."

When the old woman really began to think it over, she thought she had some potatoes, and perhaps a bit of beef

as well; and these she gave the tramp, who went on stirring, while she sat and stared as hard as ever.

"This will be grand enough for the best in the land," he said.

"Well, I never!" said the woman; "and just fancy—all with a nail!"

He was really a wonderful man, that tramp! He could do more than drink a sup and turn the tankard up, he could.

"If one had only a little barley and a drop of milk, we could ask the king himself to have some of it," he said; "for this is what he has every blessed evening—that I know, for I have been in service under the king's cook," he said.

"Dear me! Ask the king to have some! Well, I never!" exclaimed the woman, slapping her knees. She was quite awestruck at the tramp and his grand connections.

"But what one has to go without, it's no use thinking more about," said the tramp.

And then she remembered she had a little barley; and as for milk, well, she wasn't quite out of that, she said, for her best cow had just calved. And then she went to fetch both the one and the other.

The tramp went on stirring, and the woman sat staring, one moment at him and the next at the pot.

Then all at once the tramp took out the nail.

"Now it's ready, and now we'll have a real good feast," he said. "But to this kind of soup the king and the queen always take a dram or two, and one sandwich at least. And then they always have a cloth on the table when they eat," he said. "But what one has to go without, it's no use thinking more about."

But by this time the old woman herself had begun to feel quite grand and fine, I can tell you; and if that was all that was wanted to make it just as the king had it, she thought it would be nice to have it just the same way for once, and play at being king and queen with the tramp. She went straight to a cupboard and brought out the brandy bottle, dram glasses, butter and cheese, smoked beef and veal, until at last the table looked as if it were decked out for company.

Never in her life had the old woman had such a grand feast, and never had she tasted such broth, and just fancy, made only with a nail!

She was in such a good and merry humor at having learnt such an economical way of making broth that she did not know how to make enough of the tramp who had taught her such a useful thing.

So they ate and drank, and drank and ate, until they became both tired and sleepy.

The tramp was now going to lie down on the floor. But that would never do, thought the old woman. "Such a grand person must have a bed to lie in," she said.

He did not need much pressing. "It's just like the sweet Christmastime," he said, "and a nicer woman I never came across. Ah, well! Happy are they who meet with such good people," said he; and he lay down on the bed and went asleep.

And next morning when he woke the first thing he got was coffee and a dram.

When he was going the old woman gave him a bright dollar piece.

"And thanks, many thanks, for what you have taught me," she said. "Now I shall live in comfort, since I have learnt how to make broth with a nail."

"Well, it isn't very difficult, if one only has something good to add to it," said the tramp as he went his way.

The woman stood at the door staring after him.

"Such people don't grow on every bush," she said.

From *Fairy Tales From the Swedish*, edited by Nils Djurklov.

from LUCRETIA P. HALE'S

# The Peterkin Papers

*The Peterkin family is always making silly mistakes and getting into situations they can't solve. But they can usually rely on their wise and kind friend, the lady from Philadelphia, to fix things up for them.*

## THE LADY WHO PUT SALT IN HER COFFEE

This was Mrs. Peterkin. It was a mistake. She had poured out a delicious cup of coffee, and, just as she was helping herself to cream, she found she had put in salt instead of sugar! It tasted bad. What should she do? Of course she couldn't drink the coffee; so she called in the family, for she was sitting at a late breakfast all alone. The family came in; they all tasted, and looked, and wondered what should be done, and all sat down to think.

At last Agamemnon, who had been to college, said, "Why don't we go over and ask the advice of the chemist?" (For the chemist lived over the way, and was a very wise man.)

Mrs. Peterkin said, "Yes," and Mr. Peterkin said, "Very well," and all the children said they would go too.

So the little boys put on their india-rubber boots, and over they went.

Now the chemist was just trying to find out something which should turn everything it touched into gold; and he had a large glass bottle into which he put all kinds of gold and silver, and many other valuable things, and melted them all up over the fire, till he had almost found what he wanted. He could turn things into almost gold. But just now he had used up all the gold that he had round the house, and gold was high. He had used up his wife's gold thimble and his great-grandfather's gold-bowed spectacles; and he had melted up the gold head of his great-great-grandfather's cane; and, just as the Peterkin family came in, he was down on his knees before his wife, asking her to let him have her wedding-ring to melt up with all the rest, because this time he knew he should succeed, and should be able to turn everything into gold; and then she could have a new wedding-ring of diamonds, all set in emeralds and rubies and topazes, and all the furniture could be turned into the finest of gold.

Now his wife was just consenting when the Peterkin family burst in. You can imagine how mad the chemist was! He came near throwing his crucible—that was the name of his melting-pot—at their heads. But he didn't. He listened as calmly as he could to the story of how Mrs. Peterkin had put salt in her coffee.

At first he said he couldn't do anything about it; but when Agamemnon said they would pay in gold if he would only go, he packed up his bottles in a leather case, and went back with them all. First he looked at the coffee, and then stirred it. Then he put in a little chlorate of potassium, and the family tried it all round; but it tasted no better. Then he stirred in a little bichlorate of magnesia. But Mrs. Peterkin didn't like that. Then he added some tartaric acid and some hypersulphate of lime. But no; it was no better. "I have it!" exclaimed the chemist— "a little ammonia is just the thing!" No, it wasn't the thing at all.

Then he tried, each in turn, some oxalic, cyanic, acetic, phosphoric, chloric, hyperchloric, sulphuric, boracic, silicic, nitric, formic, nitrous nitric, and carbonic acids. Mrs. Peterkin tasted each and said the flavor was pleasant, but not precisely that of coffee. So then he tried a little calcium, aluminum, barium, and strontium, a little clear bitumen, and a half of a third of a sixteenth of a grain of arsenic. This gave rather a pretty color; but still Mrs. Peterkin ungratefully said it tasted of anything but coffee. The chemist was not discouraged. He put in a little belladonna and atropine, some granulated hydrogen, some potash, and a very little antimony, finishing off with a little pure carbon. But still Mrs. Peterkin was not satisfied.

The chemist said that all he had done ought to have taken out the salt. The theory remained the same, although the experiment had failed. Perhaps a little starch would have some effect. If not, that was all the time he could give. He should like to be paid, and go. They were all much obliged to him, and willing to give him $1.37½ in gold. Gold was now 2.69 3/4, so Mr. Peterkin found in the newspaper. This gave Agamemnon a pretty little sum. He sat himself down to do it. But there was the coffee! All sat and thought awhile, till Elizabeth Eliza said, "Why don't we go to the herb-woman?" Elizabeth Eliza was the only daughter. She was named after her two aunts, —Elizabeth, from the sister of her father; Eliza, from her mother's sister. Now, the herb-woman was an old woman who came round to sell herbs, and knew a great deal. They all shouted with joy at the idea of asking her, and Solomon John and the younger children agreed to go and find her too. The herb-woman lived down at the very end of the street; so the boys put on their india-rubber boots again, and they set off. It was a long walk through the village, but they came at last to the herb-woman's house, at the foot of a high hill. They went through her little garden. Here she had marigolds and hollyhocks, and old maids and tall sunflowers, and all kinds of sweet-smelling herbs, so that the air was full of tansy-tea and elderblow. Over the porch grew a hop-vine, and a brandy-cherry tree shaded the door, and a luxuriant cranberry-vine flung its delicious fruit across the window. They went into a small parlor, which smelt very spicy. All around hung little bags full of catnip, and peppermint, and all kinds of herbs; and dried stalks hung from the ceiling; and on the shelves were jars of rhubarb, senna, manna, and the like.

But there was no little old woman. She had gone up into the woods to get some more wild herbs, so they all thought they would follow her—Elizabeth Eliza, Solomon John, and the little boys. They had to climb up over high rocks, and in among huckleberry-bushes and black-berry-vines. But the little boys had their india-rubber boots. At last they discovered the little old woman. They knew her by her hat. It was steeple-crowned, without any vane. They saw her digging with her trowel round a sassa-

fras bush. They told her their story—how their mother had put salt in her coffee, and how the chemist had made it worse instead of better, and how their mother couldn't drink it, and wouldn't she come and see what she could do? And she said she would, and took up her little old apron, with pockets all round, all filled with everlasting and pennyroyal, and went back to her house.

There she stopped, and stuffed her huge pockets with

some of all the kinds of herbs. She took some tansy and peppermint, and caraway-seed and dill, spearmint and cloves, pennyroyal and sweet marjoram, basil and rosemary, wild thyme and some of the other time—such as you have in clocks—sappermint and oppermint, catnip, valerian, and hop; indeed, there isn't a kind of herb you can think of that the little old woman didn't have done up in her little paper bags, that had all been dried in her little Dutch-oven. She packed these all up, and then went back with the children, taking her stick.

Meanwhile Mrs. Peterkin was getting quite impatient for her coffee.

As soon as the little old woman came she had it set over the fire, and began to stir in the different herbs. First she put in a little hop for the bitter. Mrs. Peterkin said it tasted like hop-tea, and not at all like coffee. Then she tried a little flagroot and snakeroot, then some spruce gum, and some caraway and some dill, some rue and rosemary, some sweet marjoram and sour, some oppermint and sappermint, a little spearmint and peppermint, some wild thyme, and some of the other tame time, some tansy and basil, and catnip and valerian, and sassafras, ginger, and pennyroyal. The children tasted after each mixture, but made up dreadful faces. Mrs. Peterkin tasted, and did the same. The more the old woman stirred, and the more she put in, the worse it all seemed to taste.

So the old woman shook her head, and muttered a few words, and said she must go. She believed the coffee was bewitched. She bundled up her packets of herbs, and took her trowel, and her basket, and her stick, and went back to her root of sassafras, that she had left half in the air and half out. And all she would take for pay was five cents in currency.

Then the family were in despair, and all sat and thought a great while. It was growing late in the day, and Mrs. Peterkin hadn't had her cup of coffee. At last Elizabeth Eliza said, "They say that the lady from Philadelphia, who is staying in town, is very wise. Suppose I go and ask her what is best to be done." To this they all agreed, it was a great thought, and off Elizabeth Eliza went.

She told the lady from Philadelphia the whole story—how her mother had put salt in the coffee; how the chemist had been called in; how he tried everything but could make it no better; and how they went for the little old herb-woman, and how she had tried in vain, for her mother couldn't drink the coffee. The lady from Philadelphia listened very attentively, and then said, "Why doesn't your mother make a fresh cup of coffee?" Elizabeth Eliza started with surprise. Solomon John shouted with joy; so did Agamemnon, who had just finished his sum; so did the little boys who had followed on. "Why didn't we think of that?" said Elizabeth Eliza; and they all went back to their mother, and she had her cup of coffee.

THE PETERKINS' PICNIC

There was some doubt about the weather, Solomon John looked at the "Probabilities"; there were to be "areas of rain" in the New England States.

Agamemnon thought if they could only know where the areas of rain were to be they might go to the others. Mr. Peterkin proposed walking round the house in a procession, to examine the sky. As they returned they met Ann Maria Bromwick, who was to go, much surprised not to find them ready.

Mr. and Mrs. Peterkin were to go in the carryall, and take up the lady from Philadelphia, and Ann Maria, with the rest, was to follow in a wagon, and to stop for the daughters of the lady from Philadelphia. The wagon arrived, and so Mr. Peterkin had the horse put into the carryall.

A basket had been kept on the back piazza for some days, where anybody could put anything that would be needed for the picnic as soon as it was thought of. Agamemnon had already decided to take a thermometer; somebody was always complaining of being too hot or too cold at a picnic, and it would be a great convenience to see if she really were so. He thought how he might take a barometer, as "Probabilities" was so uncertain. Then, if it went down in a threatening way, they could all come back.

The little boys had tied their kites to the basket. They had never tried them at home; it might be a good chance on the hills. Solomon John had put in some fishing-poles; Elizabeth Eliza, a book of poetry. Mr. Peterkin did not like sitting on the ground, and proposed taking two chairs, one for himself and one for anybody else. The little boys were perfectly happy; they jumped in and out of the wagon a dozen times, with new india-rubber boots, bought for the occasion.

Before they started, Mrs. Peterkin began to think she had already had enough of the picnic, what with going and coming, and trying to remember things. So many mistakes were made. The things that were to go in the wagon were put in the carryall, and the things in the carryall had to be taken out for the wagon! Elizabeth Eliza forgot her water-proof, and had to go back for her veil, and Mr. Peterkin came near forgetting his umbrella.

Mrs. Peterkin sat on the piazza and tried to think. She felt as if she must have forgotten something; she knew she must. Why could not she think of it now, before it was too late? It seems hard any day to think what to have for dinner, but how much easier now it would be to stay at home quietly and order the dinner—and there was the butcher's cart! But now they must think of everything.

At last she was put into the carryall, and Mr. Peterkin in front to drive. Twice they started, and twice they found something was left behind—the loaf of fresh brown bread on the back piazza, and a basket of sandwiches on the front porch. And, just as the wagon was leaving, the little boys shrieked, "The basket of things was left behind!"

Everybody got out of the wagon. Agamemnon went
back into the house, to see if anything else were left. He
looked into the closets; he shut the front door, and was
so busy that he forgot to get into the wagon himself. It
started off and went down the street without him!

He was wondering what he should do if he were left
behind (why had they not thought to arrange a telegraph
wire to the back wheel of the wagon, so that he might

have sent a message in such a case!), when the Brom-
wicks drove out of their yard, in their buggy and took him
in.

They joined the rest of the party at Tatham Corners
where they were all to meet and consult where they were
to go. Mrs. Peterkin called to Agamemnon, as soon as

he appeared. She had been holding the barometer and the thermometer, and they waggled so that it troubled her. It was hard keeping the thermometer out of the sun, which would make it so warm. It really took away her pleasure, holding the things. Agamemnon decided to get into the carryall, on the seat with his father, and take the barometer and thermometer.

The consultation went on. Should they go to Cherry Swamp, or Lonetown Hill? You had the view if you went to Lonetown Hill, but maybe the drive to Cherry Swamp was prettier.

Somebody suggested asking the lady from Philadelphia, as the picnic was got up for her.

But where was she?

"I declare," said Mr. Peterkin, "I forgot to stop for her!" The whole picnic there, and no lady from Philadelphia!

It seemed the horse had twitched his head in a threatening manner as they passed the house, and Mr. Peterkin had forgotten to stop, and Mrs. Peterkin had been so busy managing the thermometers that she had not noticed, and the wagon had followed on behind.

Mrs. Peterkin was in despair. She knew they had forgotten something! She did not like to have Mr. Peterkin make a short turn, and it was getting late, and what would the lady from Philadelphia think of it, and had they not better give it all up?

But everybody said "No!" and Mr. Peterkin said he could make a wide turn round the Lovejoy barn. So they made the turn, and took up the lady from Philadelphia, and the wagon followed behind and took up her daughters, for there was a driver in the wagon besides Solomon John.

Ann Maria Bromwick said it was so late by this time they might as well stop and have the picnic on the Common! But the question was put again, Where should they go?

The lady from Philadelphia decided for Strawberry Nook—it sounded inviting. There were no strawberries, and there was no nook, it was said, but there was a good place to tie the horses.

Mrs. Peterkin was feeling a little nervous, for she did not know what the lady from Philadelphia would think of their having forgotten her, and the more she tried to explain it the worse it seemed to make it. She supposed they never did such things in Philadelphia; she knew they had invited all the world to a party, but she was sure she would never want to invite anybody again. There was no fun about it till it was all over. Such a mistake—to have a party for a person, and then go without her; but she knew they would forget something! She wished they had not called it their picnic.

There was another bother! Mr. Peterkin stopped. "Was anything broke?" exclaimed Mrs. Peterkin. "Was something forgotten?" asked the lady from Philadelphia.

No! But Mr. Peterkin didn't know the way; and here he was leading all the party, and a long row of carriages following.

They all stopped, and it seemed nobody knew the way to Strawberry Nook, unless it was the Gibbons boys, who were far behind. They were made to drive up, and said that Strawberry Nook was in quite a different direction, but they could bring the party round to it through the meadows.

The lady from Philadelphia thought they might stop anywhere, such a pleasant day; but Mr. Peterkin said they were started for Strawberry Nook, and had better keep on.

So they kept on. It proved to be an excellent place where they could tie the horses to a fence. Mrs. Peterkin did not like their all heading different ways; it seemed as if any of them might come at her, and tear up the fence, especially as the little boys had their kites flapping round. The Tremletts insisted upon the whole party going up on the hill; it was too damp below. So the Gibbons boys, and the little boys, and Agamemnon, and Solomon John, and all the party, had to carry everything up to the rocks. The large basket of "things" was very heavy. It had been difficult to lift it into the wagon, and it was harder to take it out. But, with the help of the driver, and Mr. Peterkin, and old Mr. Bromwick, it was got up the hill.

And at last all was arranged. Mr. Peterkin was seated in his chair. The other was offered to the lady from Philadelphia, but she preferred the carriage cushions; so did old Mr. Bromwick. And the table-cloth was spread—for they did bring a table-cloth—and the baskets were opened, and the picnic really began. The pickles had

tumbled into the butter, and the spoons had been forgotten, and the Tremletts' basket had been left on their
front door-step. But nobody seemed to mind. Everybody
was hungry, and everything they ate seemed of the best.
The little boys were perfectly happy, and ate of all the
kinds of cake. Two of the Tremletts would stand while
they were eating, because they were afraid of the ants and
the spiders that seemed to be crawling round. And Elizabeth Eliza had to keep poking with a fern-leaf to drive
the insects out of the plates. The lady from Philadelphia
was made comfortable with the cushions and shawls,
leaning against a rock. Mrs. Peterkin wondered if she
forgot she had been forgotten.

John Osborne said it was time for conundrums, and
asked, "Why is a pastoral musical play better than the
music we have here? Because one is a grasshopper, and
the other is a grass-opera!"

Elizabeth Eliza said she knew a conundrum, a very
funny one, one of her friends in Boston had told her. It
was, "Why is——" It began, "Why is something
like——" —no, "Why are they different?" It was something about an old woman, or else it was something about
a young one. It was very funny, if she could only think
what it was about, or whether it was alike or different.

The lady from Philadelphia was proposing they should
guess Elizabeth Eliza's conundrum, first the question,
and then the answer, when one of the Tremletts came
running down the hill, and declared she had just discovered a very threatening cloud, and she was sure it was

going to rain down directly. Everybody started up, though no cloud was to be seen.

There was a great looking for umbrellas and water-proofs. Then it appeared that Elizabeth Eliza had left hers, after all, though she had gone back for it twice. Mr. Peterkin knew he had not forgotten his umbrella, because he had put the whole umbrella-stand into the wagon, and it had been brought up the hill, but it proved to hold only the family canes!

There was a great cry for the "emergency basket," that had not been opened yet. Mrs. Peterkin explained how for days the family had been putting into it what might be needed, as soon as anything was thought of. Every-body stopped to see its contents. It was carefully covered with newspapers. First came out a backgammon-board. "That would be useful," said Ann Maria, "if we have to spend the afternoon in anybody's barn." Next, a pair of andirons. "What were they for?" "In case of needing a fire in the woods," explained Solomon John. Then came a volume of the Encyclopædia. But it was the first vol-ume, Agamemnon now regretted, and contained only A and a part of B, and nothing about rain or showers. Next, a bag of peanuts, put in by the little boys, and Elizabeth Eliza's book of poetry, and a change of boots for Mr. Peterkin; a small foot-rug in case the ground should be damp; some paint-boxes of the little boys'; a box of fish-hooks for Solomon John; an ink-bottle, carefully done up in a great deal of newspaper, which was fortunate, as the ink was oozing out; some old magazines, and a blacking-bottle; and at the bottom a sun-dial. It was all very enter-taining, and there seemed to be something for every oc-casion but the present. Old Mr. Bromwick did not won-der the basket was so heavy. It was all so interesting that nobody but the Tremletts went down to the carriages.

The sun was shining brighter than ever, and Ann Maria insisted on setting up the sun-dial. Certainly there was no danger of a shower, and they might as well go on with the picnic. But when Solomon John and Ann Maria had arranged the sun-dial they asked everybody to look at their watches, so that they might see if it was right. And then came a great exclamation at the hour: "It was time they were all going home!"

The lady from Philadelphia had been wrapping her shawl about her, as she felt the sun was low. But nobody had any idea it was so late! Well, they had left late, and went back a great many times, had stopped sometimes to consult, and had been long on the road, and it had taken a long time to fetch up the things; so it was no wonder it was time to go away. But it had been a delightful picnic, after all.

# The Picnic Basket

One cool summer morning Andrewshek's Auntie Katushka said, "Andrewshek, I think I will put some sandwiches and some cottage cheese and some poppy seed cakes and two eggs in our picnic basket. Then we will go to the park and eat our lunch there, near the water."

"May I go with you, Auntie Katushka?" said Andrewshek.

"Of course you may go to the park with me," said Auntie Katushka. "But first we have a great many things to do, before we can start to the park. I must go into the garden and catch the white goat. I will tie her up so she will not run away. Please find the kitten, Andrewshek, and put her in the cellar, so she will not worry the chickens while we are gone."

"Yes, indeed, I will find the kitten and put her in the cellar," said Andrewshek, "so she will not worry the chickens while we are gone."

But all Andrewshek really did was to lift up the red and white napkin which Auntie Katushka had laid over the picnic basket and look at the eggs and the poppy seed cakes and touch the sandwiches and taste the cottage cheese.

The goat was not easy to catch. The goat wanted to go to the park, too. She galloped round and round the garden.

At last Auntie Katushka caught her and tied her firmly to a post.

Then Auntie Katushka went into the house to get Andrewshek and the lunch basket. She saw Andrewshek peeping under the red and white napkin and tasting the cottage cheese. He had forgotten all about the kitten.

The kitten was nowhere to be found. "I think she must be paying a visit to the Mouse family," said Auntie Katushka.

Then Auntie Katushka put on her bright shawl and took her umbrella with the long crooked handle under one arm. Then she picked up the lunch basket with the red and white napkin on top and she and Andrewshek started for the park.

They went down the hill and across the tracks and past the market and down a long street until they came to the park by the water.

Andrewshek sat down on the grass beside a little stream. Andrewshek's Auntie Katushka laid her umbrella with the long crooked handle and the basket of lunch on the grass beside Andrewshek.

"Andrewshek," said Auntie Katushka, "I must go to the spring and get some water for us to drink. Please watch the basket with the eggs and the sandwiches and

poppy seed cakes and cottage cheese while I am gone."

"Yes, indeed, I will watch the basket of lunch," said Andrewshek.

But what Andrewshek really did was to say to himself, "I would like to take off my shoes and my stockings and wade in the little stream. I believe I will!"

Andrewshek took off his shoes and his stockings and went wading in the little stream.

A big white swan came floating calmly down the stream. He saw the picnic basket lying on the grass. He stopped and stretched and stretched his long neck, till he could touch the basket. "Honk! honk! honk!" said he. "I wonder what is under the red and white napkin."

The big white swan lifted the napkin with his red bill and looked in the basket. "Oh, oh, oh! Won't Mother Swan be pleased with this nice lunch!" said he. "Sandwich bread makes fine food for baby swans."

He picked up the basket in his strong red bill and floated it ahead of him down the stream.

Andrewshek could not wade after the big white swan. The water was too deep.

"Stop! Stop! White Swan!" cried Andrewshek. "That is my Auntie Katushka's picnic basket and it has our lunch in it. Please put it back on the grass."

"No, indeed! I will not put the basket back," honked the big white swan. "Sandwich bread makes fine food for baby swans and I have ten baby swans to feed."

The big white swan gave the picnic basket a little push with his red bill. The basket floated on down the little stream. The big white swan floated calmly behind it.

Just then Andrewshek's Auntie Katushka came hurrying up with the spring water. She saw the big white swan floating down the stream, with the lunch basket floating ahead of him.

Andrewshek stood in the middle of the stream, crying.

Auntie Katushka picked up her umbrella with the long crooked handle. Auntie Katushka ran along the shore until she overtook the big white swan, with the lunch basket floating ahead of him.

She caught the handle of the picnic basket in the crook of her long handled umbrella. She drew the basket safely to shore.

"Well! well!" said Auntie Katushka, as she spread the red and white napkin on the grass, and laid the sandwiches and the poppy seed cakes and the cottage cheese and the eggs upon it. "It always pays to carry an umbrella to a picnic."

*from* C. S. FORESTER'S

# Poo-Poo and the Dragons

*One morning as Poo-Poo (his other name was Harold Heavyside Brown) was walking down the street he met a very friendly and attractive dragon. They had some fun together, swishing down the length of a water pipe, and then the dragon followed the boy home. Poo-Poo wondered what his mother would say.*

## AN OBLIGING VISITOR

Poo-Poo's mother was in the kitchen beside the back door when Poo-Poo came in, and she said, "Oh, there you are," the way she often did say, and then she saw the dragon, and she said—

"What have you brought that dragon home for?"

And Poo-Poo said, "I like him," and the dragon wagged his tail and squirmed and wriggled and started coming in through the door.

Poo-Poo's mother said: "We don't want dragons in this house."

And Poo-Poo said: "But he's a very nice dragon."

And Poo-Poo's mother said, "All the same, I don't want him in this house."

Then Poo-Poo's father came out, and he stopped and looked at the dragon as he squirmed and wriggled halfway through the door.

"Poo-Poo's brought a dragon home with him," said Poo-Poo's mother.

"That's what it looks like," said Poo-Poo's father. "Where did you find him, son?"

"He was on a vacant lot beside the house of the man who mends chimney pots," said Poo-Poo, "Mr.——Mr.——"

But Poo-Poo could not remember the name of the man who constructed chimney pots.

"Well," said Poo-Poo's father, "I think you'd better take him back where he came from."

"Oh," said Poo-Poo disappointed, "but I don't think he could possibly get up the pipe."

"Up the pipe?" said Poo-Poo's father.

"Well that was the way we came," said Poo-Poo.

This time it was Poo-Poo's father who said "Oh!" And he felt in his pockets and brought out a cigarette and then he began to look for a match, and he felt first in his trouser pockets and then in his coat pockets and then he began to look around the room, and as he did that the dragon opened his mouth with a click like a cigarette lighter and a long flame came out of his mouth the way it does with dragons.

"That's very convenient," said Poo-Poo's father, lighting his cigarette.

And the dragon shut his mouth and put the flame out and wagged his tail with pleasure.

"There—you see?" said Poo-Poo. "Can't I keep him?"

"Not if your mother—" said Poo-Poo's father—"And don't you expect me to go into any argument about it because I've got all that lawn to mow, and I'm not in a fit state to argue."

And then Poo-Poo's father looked out of the kitchen window and he stopped suddenly and he took his cigarette out of his mouth and he said, "My golly!" And Poo-Poo's mother looked out of the window and Poo-Poo peeked round the door, and they saw that the dragon's long wriggling tail had mowed that lawn as close as a billiard table.

"Now there's something to be said for a dragon that can mow lawns," said Poo-Poo's father looking at Poo-Poo's mother. "I've always said I'd rather go to the dentist three times a week than mow lawns."

"But all the same we don't want any dragons here," said Poo-Poo's mother. "He'd only mean a lot of work and bother."

And while she said this the front half of the dragon that was in the kitchen door went on squirming and wriggling first this way and then the other.

"You see," said Poo-Poo's mother, "I just couldn't have a dragon in the house who did that."

But then she looked and she saw that the floor that

the dragon had been wriggling on was polished up by the dragon's wriggles so brightly that you could see your face in it without stooping.

"Well," said Poo-Poo's mother, "that's very nice, but—"

"I'm sure he'll work very hard," said Poo-Poo. "Please let me keep him."

"Oh, very well," said Poo-Poo's mother.

And Poo-Poo began to jump about the floor and the dragon began to wriggle harder than ever until Poo-Poo's mother had to say, "Now stop it, this minute!"

"What shall we call him?" asked Poo-Poo.

"Well," said Poo-Poo's father (do you remember that he was a very clever man?), "he looks as if his name was HORATIO."

And he had no sooner said the name when the dragon nodded and smiled and was just going to start wriggling all over again, when he remembered Poo-Poo's mother and left off hurriedly.

"Yes," said Poo-Poo's father, "that's it. HORATIO HEAVYSIDE DRAGON. It's quite a good name."

(If I were you I should try to remember what the dragon's name is.)

"It's dinnertime," said Poo-Poo's mother, "and I don't know what dragons eat."

But of course Poo-Poo's father knew what dragons had for dinner.

"Oh—this and that," said Poo-Poo's father. "On Tuesdays they have to have the other thing, and on Fridays they have to have something else; and on Sundays, it's just as well to give them something different; and you must think up something new for Mondays and Wednesdays. On Saturdays it doesn't matter much, and on Thursdays they'll eat anything that's going."

"Well, that's all right then," said Poo-Poo's mother. "We'd better have dinner right away."

So they had dinner, and the dragon ate first one thing and then the other, and he had a second helping of something else, and he finished up with whatever there was, and his manners were as good as gold as he sat on the floor with his chin on the table and his tail stretching out through the door out into the street. And every time they called him Horatio (I hope you remember what his other names were) he nodded and smiled. Whenever Poo-Poo's father made a joke he laughed politely, and whenever Poo-Poo's mother wanted anything out of the kitchen he turned his head around and shot out his long neck and brought it in quicker than lightning.

## THE DRAGON GOES TO THE MOVIES

Now Mr. Brown had a rule about Poo-Poo going to the movies. He did not think that Poo-Poo should go there very often, and so the rule was that Poo-Poo could go on the fifth Saturday of every month as long as it fell on a Friday. But today Mr. Brown said that as it had very nearly happened because Friday was only one day back, they could all go to the movies that afternoon. So Poo-

Poo and Mr. Brown and Poo-Poo's mother all got into the car and drove down the hill with the dragon going clippety-clop after them and Poo-Poo looking out of the window and waving to him, and Poo-Poo's father parked the car and they walked across to the theater and Mr. Brown bought three tickets.

"And what about that dragon?" said the lady at the window. (Her name was AMELIA MONTGOMERY.)

"I won't have to pay for him," said Mr. Brown, "because he won't be occupying a seat."

"I don't know about that," said the lady at the window (what was her name?), "he'll be going inside the theater, won't he?"

"But you don't charge for dragons," said Mr. Brown, "anyone can see that."

And he pointed to the notice which said MATINEE PRICES.

"You've got a charge for adults," said Mr. Brown, "and you've got a charge for children, and because you don't say anything about dragons it's obvious that you don't make any charge for them."

"I hadn't looked at it that way," said the lady at the window (I expect you have forgotten her name already). "But that doesn't mean to say that we'd let dragons in."

"Oh yes it does," said Poo-Poo's father, still pointing at the notice. "You say, 'The Management reserves the right to refuse admission to any person for any reason whatever,' but a dragon isn't a person, and so you can't refuse him admission, now can you?"

**By** this time there were a lot of people waiting behind Mr. Brown to buy tickets, so Miss Amelia Montgomery said, "Oh, very well then," just like Poo-Poo's mother sometimes. And they went along into the theater. Poo-Poo and his father and mother sat down in the seat and Horatio stretched himself out along the aisle with his head beside Poo-Poo's knee, and Horatio was very good indeed and did not mind at all even when people fell over him in the darkness. Very soon the picture began.

Poo-Poo enjoyed the picture very much and was very excited when the cowboys started riding off after the rustlers; but then some Indians came on the screen and Poo-Poo's father (you know what his name was by now, but you must never forget that he was a very clever man) sat up and became very nervous.

"There may be trouble," said Poo-Poo's father. "Dragons don't like Indians. There's been a feud between them since Columbus discovered America. Horatio, be quiet."

He said it just in time for this once, because Horatio was already sitting up and moving restlessly about in the aisle when Poo-Poo's father spoke to him. He sat down again, but it could not last very long because very soon the Indians brought out their guns. He got up, and before Poo-Poo's father could stop him again he made one jump and went straight through the screen!

"My golly," said Poo-Poo's father. "There's going to be trouble about this."

And the lady beside him (she was called ARAMINTA

WIGGINS) said very crossly: "People who bring drag-ons to the movies ought to keep them under proper con-trol."

So Poo-Poo's father (you have heard that Poo-Poo was very polite, and that was because his father was, as well as being a very clever man) said, "I'm very sorry, madam."

What with Horatio being half through the screen and his tail waving about outside it, nobody in the theater could see anything of the picture at all, and there were a great many other complaints as well as from the lady sit-ting beside Mr. Brown (I expect you've forgotten her name already), and Mr. Brown stood up and said—

"It looks to me as if we had better get out of this, *quick*."

So they stood up with Poo-Poo very excited, and Poo-Poo said, "Come along, Horatio!"—and they scuttled out of one of the side doors as quick as they could and ran across the road, and Poo-Poo and his father and mother jumped into the car and Poo-Poo's father drove like mad up the hill, so fast that Horatio, instead of going clippety-clop behind them, was going clippety-*clippety*-clop, and sometimes even clippety-*clippety-clippety*-clop. They got home, and they had hardly put the car into the garage when they heard the police sirens coming up the hill.

"There, you see?" said Poo-Poo's father. "They're after us already."

"Will they do anything to Horatio?" asked Poo-Poo.

"They'll want to put him in prison, I expect," said Mr. Brown, "and we can't have that, can we?"

"Oh, no, we can't," said Poo-Poo's mother, and Horatio laid his nose on the ground and looked very frightened indeed.

"We'll have to hide him," said Poo-Poo's father. He looked round him and went on, "But it's not going to be so easy to hide a dragon around here."

Of course Poo-Poo's father had a good idea. Beside the road outside the garage there was a long drain for carrying off storm water, and Mr. Brown said, "Here, Horatio, make yourself as small as you can and crawl up there."

So Horatio made himself as small as he could and wriggled up the drain, but when he was in it his nose still stuck out at one end while his tail stuck out at the other.

"Can't you make yourself smaller than that?" said Poo-Poo's father. But when Horatio tried, the drain bulged up in the middle and Poo-Poo's father had to tell him to stop, while the noise of the siren was getting nearer and nearer.

"Quick," said Poo-Poo's father to Poo-Poo. "Sit on Horatio's nose and you, my dear, please sit on his tail."

So Poo-Poo sat on Horatio's nose and Mrs. Brown sat on Horatio's tail, just in time as the policeman on his motorcycle came round the corner and stopped.

"I'm looking for a dragon," said the policeman (his

name was PATRICK MACGILLICUDDY).

"That's very interesting," said Poo-Poo's father.

"I want to arrest him," said the policeman (if you can't remember what his name was it isn't much use going on with the story), "for malicious damage to property."

"That's more interesting than ever," said Poo-Poo's father, "and it's very kind of you to tell us about it, but I don't see why you should."

"I have information," said Policeman Macgillicuddy, "that the dragon is domiciled here."

"Now look," said Poo-Poo's father, "can you see any dragons here?"

And the policeman (I hope you've remembered his name this time) looked round him and of course there were no dragons in sight at all.

"Perhaps you have been misinformed," said Poo-Poo's father; "what a pity that you have come all this way for nothing."

"I wonder why the lady and the little boy are sitting in the road like that?" asked the policeman.

"I can think of all sorts of possible reasons," said Poo-Poo's father (who was a very clever man); "perhaps they are sitting there because they think there are chairs there, although there aren't any; or perhaps their feet hurt them, or perhaps they're playing at trains, or perhaps they're waiting for someone to come along, or perhaps that's where they sit when they're not sitting anywhere else. Or perhaps their legs won't hold them up. Or perhaps it's because they like it."

"It might be something like that," agreed the policeman, a little bewildered.

"It's very nice talking to you like this," said Poo-Poo's father, "but I don't think I ought to keep you here when you have to go out and hunt for dragons. I wouldn't interfere with your doing your duty for anything. Good afternoon, Officer, and thank you very much for our very pleasant conversation."

"Good afternoon," said the policeman, more bewildered than ever. And he got on his motorcycle and went away.

"Now," said Poo-Poo's father to Horatio, "you can come out." And Horatio wriggled and he wriggled and he wriggled, and he couldn't manage to get another inch farther down the pipe.

"Come out backwards, then," said Poo-Poo, and Horatio wriggled and wriggled and wriggled and he couldn't manage to go backwards up the pipe either. He was stuck quite tight.

"My gracious," said Poo-Poo's mother. "What are we going to do now? Come along, Horatio, try again."

And Horatio wriggled and he wriggled and he wriggled but he was stuck quite tight.

"This is just terrible," said Poo-Poo's mother.

"Of course," said Poo-Poo's father (do you remember anything special about him?), "we don't have to worry very much because Horatio has only got to stay there with nothing to eat for a few days and then he'll be thin enough to come out again."

"But we don't want to do that," said Poo-Poo's mother.

"No, we don't want to do that at all," said Poo-Poo, and the dragon shook his head very mournfully and looked as if he were just going to cry.

"Can't you think of anything else?" asked Poo-Poo's mother, because she knew that Poo-Poo's father was a very clever man.

"Well, yes," said Poo-Poo's father. "Some people would use dynamite and some people would use pneumatic drills and some people would get a lot of men with spades to dig him out, and some people would dig a tunnel underneath, but all I want is just a feather. Poo-Poo, find me a feather."

So Poo-Poo found a feather and his father stooped down where the tip of Horatio's tail was sticking out of the pipe.

"It's a good thing," said Poo-Poo's father, "that dragons are very ticklish." He took hold of the spiky part shaped like an arrowhead at the end of Horatio's tail, and began to tickle Horatio on the joint just above it. And as he tickled, Horatio began to squirm, and he squirmed and he wriggled more and more frantically and more and more frantically until at last there was a tremendous crash and the drainpipe split all the way along its length and Horatio came out through the top very pleased with himself.

"That isn't quite what I intended," said Poo-Poo's father, rather disappointed because the noise had been very loud indeed and now there was this great big long hole right across the road from one side to the other.

"It will take a very clever man to explain what has happened here," said Poo-Poo's father. (So you see that it was just as well that Poo-Poo's father was a very clever man.)

And he had no sooner said this than they heard the policeman's siren going again.

"Quick," said Poo-Poo's father to Poo-Poo's mother. "Take this dragon away. Take him away, I don't mind where you take him as long as he's out of sight quicker than lightning."

So Poo-Poo's mother ran up the garden with Horatio scuttling along behind her, and they had just got round the side of the house when up came the policeman (whose name of course you remember).

"My goodness gracious me," said the policeman, getting off his motorcycle, "whatever has happened here?"

"Well," said Poo-Poo's father, "of course it might have been an earthquake, or on the other hand it might be just a landslide. And then again some heavy truck might have come along the road and squashed it in, and there is always the possibility that it was rats. Or maybe some little boy was flying a kite in the next block and that made the pipe fall in."

"That doesn't sound very likely to me," said Policeman Macgillicuddy.

"It doesn't sound very likely to me either," said Poo-Poo's father. "But I was only trying to make a helpful suggestion."

"I think we'd better call it an earthquake," said the policeman, taking out his notebook and licking his pencil the way his mother always told him not to.

And so now you know the true history of the earthquake at Poo-Poo's house. All the newspaper reporters for a hundred miles round came to see that hole, and they asked Poo-Poo's father all sorts of questions, and the newsreel people brought their cameras and took a lot of photographs, and geologists came from all the universities and measured the hole with long tapes. And then in the end the city workmen came and made a new storm drain, and eventually the whole affair was forgotten.

# The Princess and the Pea

### (THE REAL PRINCESS)

There was once a prince, and he wanted a princess, but then she must be a *real* princess. He traveled right round the world to find one, but there was always something wrong. There were plenty of princesses, but whether they were real princesses he had great difficulty in discovering; there was always something which was not quite right about them. So at last he had to come home again, and he was very sad because he wanted a real princess so badly.

One evening there was a terrible storm; it thundered and lightened and the rain poured down in torrents; indeed it was a fearful night.

In the middle of the storm somebody knocked at the town gate, and the old king himself went to open it.

It was a princess who stood outside, but she was in a terrible state from the rain and the storm. The water streamed out of her hair and her clothes, it ran in at the

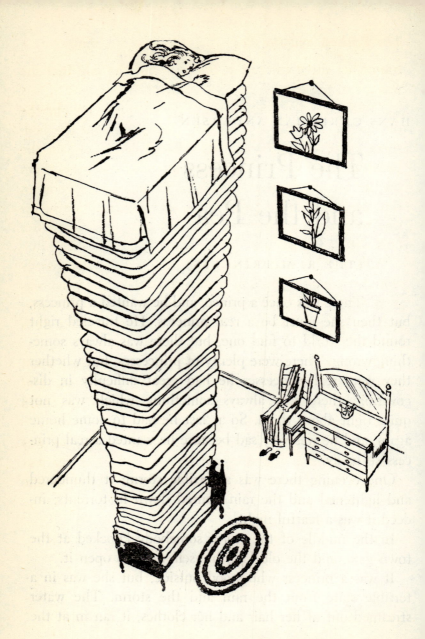

top of her shoes and out at the heel, but she said that she was a real princess.

"Well, we shall soon see if that is true," thought the old queen, but she said nothing. She went into the bedroom, took all the bedclothes off and laid a pea on the bedstead; then she took twenty mattresses and piled them on the top of the pea, and then twenty feather beds on the top of the mattresses. This was where the princess was to sleep that night. In the morning they asked her how she had slept.

"Oh, terribly badly!" said the princess. "I have hardly closed my eyes the whole night! Heaven knows what was in the bed. I seemed to be lying upon some hard thing, and my whole body is black and blue this morning. It is terrible!"

They saw at once that she must be a real princess when she had felt the pea through twenty mattresses and twenty feather beds. Nobody but a real princess could have such a delicate skin.

So the prince took her to be his wife, for now he was sure that he had found a real princess, and the pea was put into the Museum, where it may still be seen if no one has stolen it.

Now this is a true story.

# Puss in Boots

There was once a miller, who, at his death, had
nothing to leave to his three children but his mill, his
ass, and his cat; so he called in no lawyer, and made no
will. The eldest son took the mill; the second the ass;
while the youngest had nothing but the cat, who seemed
more likely to prove a burden than a boon to his new
master. The poor fellow was quite downcast and said to
himself: "My brothers, by putting their goods together,
will be able to earn an honest livelihood; but as for myself, when I shall have eaten my cat, and sold his skin,
what is there left? Then I shall die of hunger."

The cat, who was sitting on the window-seat, overheard
these words, without seeming to do so, and, looking up,
said to him with a very serious, sober air—"Nay, dear
master, do not be downcast at your future prospects.
Only give me a bag, and get me a pair of boots made, such
as other folks wear, so that I may stride through the bram-
bles, and you will soon see that you have a better bargain
than you think for."

Although the cat's new master did not put much faith

in these promises, yet he had seen him perform so many clever tricks in catching rats and mice—such as hanging stiff by his hind legs, to make believe he were dead, and concealing himself in the meal-tub, as if he were nowhere about—that he did not quite despair of his helping him to better his fortunes. Besides, he knew not what else to do, and there was no harm in trying this.

As soon as the cat was provided with what he asked for, he drew on his boots, and, slinging the bag round his neck, took hold of the two strings with his fore-paws, and set off for a warren that he knew of, plentifully stocked with rabbits. He filled his bag with bran and sow-thistles, and then stretched himself out as stiff as though he had been dead, waiting patiently till some simple young rabbits, unused to worldly snares and wiles, should see the dainty feast and never think of the cat. He had scarcely lain a few moments in ambush before a thoughtless young rabbit caught at the bait, and went headlong into the bag, whereupon the cat drew the strings, and immediately strangled the foolish creature. The cat was vastly proud of his victory, and immediately went to the palace and asked to speak to the king. He was shown into the king's cabinet, when he bowed respectfully to his majesty, and said, "Sire, this is a rabbit from the warren of the Marquis of Carabas (such was the title the cat took it into his head to bestow on his master), which he desired me to present to your majesty."

"Tell your master that I am obliged by his courtesy, and that I accept his present with much pleasure," replied the king, looking graciously at him.

Another time the cat went and concealed himself in a cornfield, and held his bag open as before, and, very shortly after, two partridges were lured into the trap, when he drew the strings and made them both prisoners. He then went and presented them to the king, as he had done the rabbit. The king received the partridges very graciously, and ordered the messenger to be rewarded for his trouble.

For two or three months, Puss continued to carry game every now and then to the king, always presenting it in the name of his master, the Marquis of Carabas, who he said was a famous sportsman. At last he happened to hear that the king was going to take a drive on the banks of the river, in company with his daughter, who was the most beautiful princess in the world; and he said to his master, "If you will but follow my advice, your fortune is as good as made. You need only go and bathe in the river at the spot that I shall point out, and leave the rest to me."

The Marquis of Carabas did as his cat advised him, though it was too much for him to say what it was all coming to. Just as he was bathing, the king came driving past, when Puss began to bawl out as loud as he could "Help! help! the Marquis of Carabas is drowning! Save him!"

On hearing this, the king looked out of the carriage-window, and, recognizing the cat who had so frequently brought him game, ordered his body-guards to fly to the assistance of my Lord Marquis of Carabas.

While the poor marquis was being fished out of the river, Puss stepped up to the royal carriage, and informed his majesty, that, during the time his master was bathing, some robbers had stolen his clothes, although he had cried out "Stop thief!" with all his might. The rogue had really only hidden them under a large stone. The king immediately ordered the gentlemen of his wardrobe to go and fetch one of his most sumptuous dresses for the Marquis of Carabas.

When the marquis, who was a well-grown, handsome young fellow, came forth gayly dressed, he looked so elegant that the king took him for a very fine gentleman, and said the politest things in the world to him, while the princess was so struck with his appearance, that my Lord

Marquis of Carabas had scarcely made his obeisance to her, and looked at her once or twice with a very tender air, before she fell over head and ears in love with him.

The king insisted on his getting into the carriage and taking a drive with them. Puss, highly delighted at the turn things were taking, and determined that all should turn out in the very best way, now ran on before, and having reached a meadow where some peasants were mowing the grass, he thus accosted them: "I say, good folks, if you do not tell the king, when he comes this way, that the field you are mowing belongs to the Marquis of Carabas, you shall all be chopped as fine as mince-meat."

When the carriage came by, the king put his head out, and asked the mowers whose good grassland that was. "It belongs to the Marquis of Carabas, please your majesty," said they in a breath, for the cat's threats had frightened them mightily.

"Upon my word, marquis," observed the king, "that is a fine estate of yours."

"Yes, sire," replied the marquis, with an easy air, "it yields me a tolerable income every year."

Puss, who continued to run on before the carriage, presently came up to some reapers. "I say, you reapers," cried he, "mind you tell the king that all this corn belongs to the Marquis of Carabas or else you shall, every one of you, be chopped into mince-meat."

The king passed by a moment after, and inquired to whom those cornfields belonged.

"To the Marquis of Carabas, please your majesty," replied the reapers.

"Faith, it pleases our majesty right well to see our be-loved marquis is so wealthy!" quoth the king.

Puss kept still running on before the carriage, and re-peating the same instructions to all the laborers he met, and the king was astounded at the vast possessions of the Marquis of Carabas, and kept congratulating him, while the new-made nobleman received each fresh compliment more lightly than the last, so that one could see he was really a marquis, and a very grand one too.

At length Puss reached a magnificent castle belonging to an ogre, who was immensely rich, since all the lands the king had been riding through were a portion of his estate. Puss having inquired what sort of a person the ogre might be, and what he was able to do, sent in a mes-sage asking leave to speak with him, adding that he was unwilling to pass so near his castle without paying his re-spects to him.

The ogre received him as civilly as it is in the nature of an ogre to do, and bade him rest himself. "I have been told," said Puss, "that you have the power of transform-ing yourself into all sorts of animals, such, for instance, as a lion, or an elephant." "So I have," replied the ogre, sharply; "do you disbelieve it? then look, and you shall see me become a lion at once."

When Puss saw a lion before him, he was seized with such a fright that he scrambled up to the roof, although it was no easy job, owing to his boots, which were not intended for walking in a gutter and over tiles.

At last perceiving that the ogre had returned to his

natural shape, Puss came down again, and confessed he had been exceedingly frightened.

"But I have also been told," said Puss, "only I really cannot believe it, that you likewise possess the power of taking the shape of the smallest animals, and that, for instance, you could change yourself into a rat or a mouse; but that is really too much to believe; it is quite impossible."

"Impossible, indeed!" quoth the ogre, now put upon his mettle; "you shall see!"

So saying, he immediately took on the shape of a mouse, and began frisking about the floor, when Puss pounced upon him, gave him one shake, and that was the end of the ogre.

By this time the king had reached the gates of the ogre's magnificent castle, and expressed a wish to enter so splendid a building. Puss hearing the rumbling of the carriage across the drawbridge, now ran out to meet the king, saying, "Your majesty is welcome to the Marquis of Carabas's castle."

"What! my lord marquis," exclaimed the king, "does this castle likewise belong to you? Really, I never saw anything more splendid than the courtyard and the surrounding buildings; pray let us see if the inside be equal to the outside."

The marquis gracefully handed out the princess, and, following the king, they mounted a flight of steps, and were ushered by Puss, who danced before them, into a vast hall, where they found an elegant feast spread. Some of the ogre's friends were to have visited him that day, but the news went about that the king had come, and so they dared not go. The king was positively delighted, the castle was so magnificent and the Marquis of Carabas such an excellent young man; the princess, too, was evidently already in love with him so; after drinking five or six glasses of wine, his majesty hemmed and said—

"You have only to say the word, my lord marquis, to become the son-in-law of your sovereign."

The marquis bowed and looked at the princess, and that very same day they were married, and the old king gave them his blessing. Puss, who had brought it all about, looked on mightily pleased, and ever after lived there a great lord, and hunted mice for mere sport, just when he pleased.

EDWARD LEAR

# The Jumblies

ONE

They went to sea in a sieve, they did;
  In a sieve they went to sea:
In spite of all their friends could say,
On a winter's morn, on a stormy day,
  In a sieve they went to sea.
And when the sieve turned round and round,
And every one cried, "You'll all be drowned!"
They called aloud, "Our sieve ain't big;
But we don't care a button, we don't care a fig:
  In a sieve we'll go to sea!"
    Far and few, far and few,
      Are the lands where the Jumblies live:
    Their heads are green, and their hands are blue;
      And they went to sea in a sieve.


TWO

They sailed away in a sieve, they did,
  In a sieve they sailed so fast,

With only a beautiful pea-green veil
Tied with a ribbon, by way of a sail,
   To a small tobacco-pipe mast.
And every one said who saw them go,
"Oh! won't they be soon upset, you know?
For the sky is dark, and the voyage is long;
And, happen what may, it's extremely wrong
   In a sieve to sail so fast."
      Far and few, far and few,
         Are the lands where the Jumblies live:
       Their heads are green, and their hands are blue;
        And they went to sea in a sieve.

THREE

The water it soon came in, it did;
   The water it soon came in:
So, to keep them dry, they wrapped their feet
In a pinky paper all folded neat;
   And they fastened it down with a pin.
And they passed the night in a crockery-jar;
And each of them said, "How wise we are!
Though the sky be dark, and the voyage be long,
Yet we never can think we were rash or wrong,
   While round in our sieve we spin."
      Far and few, far and few,
         Are the lands where the Jumblies live:
       Their heads are green, and their hands are blue;
        And they went to sea in a sieve.

**FOUR**

And all night long they sailed away;
　And when the sun went down,
They whistled and warbled a moony song
To the echoing sound of a coppery gong,
　In the shade of the mountains brown.
"O Timballoo! How happy we are

*Illustration by Edward Lear*

When we live in a sieve and a crockery-jar!
And all night long, in the moonlight pale,
We sail away with a pea-green sail
　In the shade of the mountains brown."
　　　Far and few, far and few,
　　　　Are the lands where the Jumblies live:
　　　Their heads are green, and their hands are blue;
　　　　And they went to sea in a sieve.

**FIVE**

They sailed to the Western Sea, they did,—
　To a land all covered with trees:

And they bought an owl, and a useful cart,
And a pound of rice, and a cranberry-tart,
  And a hive of silvery bees;
And they bought a pig, and some green jackdaws,
And a lovely monkey with lollipop paws,
And forty bottles of ring-bo-ree,
  And no end of Stilton cheese.
    Far and few, far and few,
      Are the lands where the Jumblies live:
      Their heads are green, and their hands are blue;
      And they went to sea in a sieve.

SIX

And in twenty years they all came back,—
  In twenty years or more;
And every one said, "How tall they've grown!
For they've been to the Lakes, and the Torrible Zone,
  And the hills of the Chankly Bore."
And they drank their health, and gave them a feast
Of dumplings made of beautiful yeast;
And every one said, "If we only live,
We, too, will go to sea in a sieve,
  To the hills of the Chankly Bore."
    Far and few, far and few,
      Are the lands where the Jumblies live:
      Their heads are green, and their hands are blue;
      And they went to sea in a sieve.

# The Race Between Hare and Hedgehog

It was once upon a time on a Saturday morning in autumn, while the barley fields were still in bloom.

The sun was shining, the morning wind was blowing over the stubble, the larks were singing high in the air, the bees were buzzing in the barley blossoms, and the people were going blithely about their day's work. In short, all the world was happy, and the Hedgehog, too.

The Hedgehog stood in front of his door with folded arms, looked at the weather, and hummed a tune as only a hedgehog can hum on a Saturday morning.

Now, as he stood there humming, he thought to himself all at once that, while his wife was washing and dressing the children, he might as well go for a little walk in the fields and see how his turnips were getting on.

The turnips grew near his house, and as he and his family ate as many of them as ever they wanted, he looked upon them quite naturally as his own property.

Well, the Hedgehog slammed his door and started for the turnip field. He hadn't got very far, and was just sauntering round the brier bush that stood outside the field, when he met the Hare, who was out on the same errand—namely, to look at the cabbages, which he also considered as his own property.

When the Hedgehog caught sight of the Hare, he gave him a pleasant "Good morning."

But the Hare, who was a very aristocratic person in his own way, and very high and mighty in his manner, didn't answer the Hegehog's greeting, but said, with a nasty sneer:

"What are you running about the fields for so early in the morning?"

"I'm just walking," said the Hedgehog.

"Walking?" grinned the Hare. "I don't think your legs are very suited for walking!"

This remark annoyed the Hedgehog, for, though he was a good-natured fellow enough, he was touchy on the subject of his bandy legs.

"I suppose," he said tartly, "you think your legs are better than mine?"

"That I do," said the Hare.

"It remains to be seen," said the Hegehog. "I bet you that if we two were to run a race I should beat you."

"What a joke!" cried the Hare. "You with your bandy legs! But if you're so anxious to try, I've no objection. What will you bet?"

"A golden guinea," said the Hedgehog.

"Agreed!" said the Hare. "We'll start right away!"

"Oh, don't be in such a hurry," said the Hedgehog. "I haven't had my breakfast yet. I must go home first and get something to eat. I'll come back here in an hour."

So away he trotted, for the Hare made no objection.

Then he thought to himself:

"The Hare thinks a lot of his long legs, but I'll get the better of him all the same. For all his haughty ways, he's not so very clever, and I'll make him pay for his pride."

As soon as he got home, he said to his wife:

"Quick! go and get dressed. You must come out to the field with me."

"What's the matter?" said his wife.

"I've wagered the Hare a golden guinea that I will beat him in a race, and I want you to be there."

"Good gracious me!" cried the Hedgehog's wife. "Have you lost your senses? How can you think of racing the Hare?"

"Don't be so quick with your words, woman," said the Hedgehog. "That's my affair; you mustn't meddle with what you don't understand. Look sharp; put on your things, and come along."

What was the wife to do? She had to obey her husband, whether she liked it or not.

On the way to the field, the Hedgehog said:

"Now, listen to what I'm going to tell you. Do you see that plowed field over there? That's where we're to run our race. The Hare will run in one furrow, and I in the other. Now, all you've got to do is hide yourself at the

other end of my furrow, and directly the Hare comes up to you, you pop your head up and say:

" 'Here I am already!' "

With that they reached the field. The Hedgehog told his wife where to stand, and went on to the other end.

The Hare was there waiting for him.

"Shall we start?" asked the Hare.

"Right," said the Hedgehog.

"Now then!"

Each took up his place.

The Hare counted:

"One, two, three!"

And away he went like the wind.

But the Hedgehog took about three paces, then he went back, ducked down in his furrow, and stood there as comfortably as you please, and laughing as if he would split his sides.

Now, the moment the Hare came rushing up to the other end, the Hedgehog's wife called out to him:

"Here I am already!"

The Hare was quite taken aback, though he made sure it was the Hedgehog himself who was sitting there calling to him. But, as every one knows, a hedgehog's wife looks exactly like her husband.

"There's something not quite right here," said the Hare. "We must run again back to the starting point."

And away he flew like the wind, and his ears floated behind him. But the Hedgehog's wife never moved.

When the Hare got to the other end, the Hedgehog called out:

"Here I am already!"

Then the Hare, quite beside himself with jealousy, shouted:

"We must run again!"

"Right!" said the Hedgehog. "As often as you like."

And so the Hare went on, running backward and forward seventy-three times, and every time he was beaten. Every time the Hare arrived at one end or the other, the Hedgehog or his wife called out:

"Here I am already!"

But the seventy-fourth time the Hare dropped down dead tired before he got half-way. So the Hedgehog took his golden guinea, and he and his wife went home very well pleased with themselves. And so my tale is finished.

# Rumpelstiltskin

There was once a miller who was poor, but he had one beautiful daughter. It happened one day that he came to speak with the king, and to give himself consequence, he told him that he had a daughter who could spin gold out of straw. The king said to the miller,

"That is an art that pleases me well; if your daughter is as clever as you say, bring her to my castle tomorrow, that I may put her to the proof."

When the girl was brought to him, he led her into a room that was quite full of straw, and gave her a wheel and spindle, and said,

"Now set to work, and if by the early morning you have not spun this straw to gold you shall die." And he shut the door himself, and left her there alone.

And so the poor miller's daughter was left there sitting, and could not think what to do for her life; she had no notion how to set to work to spin gold from straw, and her distress grew so great that she began to weep. Then all at once the door opened, and in came a little man, who said,

"Good evening, miller's daughter, why are you crying?"

"Oh!" answered the girl, "I have got to spin gold out of straw, and I don't understand the business."

Then the little man said,

"What will you give me if I spin it for you?"

"My necklace," said the girl.

The little man took the necklace, seated himself before the wheel, and whirr, whirr, whirr! three times round and the bobbin was full; then he took up another, and whirr, whirr, whirr! three times round, and that was full; and so he went on till the morning, when all the straw had been spun and all the bobbins were full of gold.

At sunrise came the king, and when he saw the gold he was astonished and very much rejoiced, for he was very avaricious. He had the miller's daughter taken into another room filled with straw, much bigger than the last, and told her that as she valued her life she must spin it all in one night. The girl did not know what to do, so she began to cry, and then the door opened, and the little man appeared and said,

"What will you give me if I spin all this straw into gold?"

"The ring from my finger," answered the girl.

So the little man took the ring, and began again to send the wheel whirring round, and by the next morning all the straw was spun into glistening gold. The king was rejoiced beyond measure at the sight, but as he could never have enough of gold, he had the miller's daughter taken into a still larger room full of straw, and said,

"This, too, must be spun in one night, and if you accomplish it you shall be my wife." For he thought, "Although she is but a miller's daughter, I am not likely to find any one richer in the whole world."

As soon as the girl was left alone, the little man appeared for the third time and said,

"What will you give me if I spin the straw for you this time?"

"I have nothing left to give," answered the girl.

"Then you must promise me the first child you have after you are queen," said the little man.

"But who knows whether that will happen?" thought the girl; and as she did not know what else to do in her necessity, she promised the little man what he desired, upon which he began to spin, until all the straw was gold. And when in the morning the king came and found all done according to his wish, he caused the wedding to be held at once, and the miller's pretty daughter became a queen.

In a year's time she brought a fine child into the world, and thought no more of the little man; but one day he came suddenly into her room, and said,

"Now give me what you promised me."

The queen was terrified greatly, and offered the little man all the riches of the kingdom if he would only leave the child; but the little man said, "No, I would rather have something living than all the treasures of the world."

Then the queen began to lament and to weep, so that the little man had pity upon her.

' I will give you three days," said he, "and if at the end of that time you cannot tell my name, you must give up the child to me."

Then the queen spent the whole night in thinking over all the names that she had ever heard, and sent a messenger through the land to ask far and wide for all the names that could be found. And when the little man came next day (beginning with Casper, Melchior, Balthazar), she repeated all she knew, and went through the whole list, but after each the little man said,

"That is not my name."

The second day the queen sent to inquire of all the neighbours what the servants were called, and told the little man all the most unusual and singular names, saying,

"Perhaps you are called Roast-ribs, or Sheepshanks, or Spindleshanks?" But he answered nothing but

"That is not my name."

The third day the messenger came back again, and said,

"I have not been able to find one single new name; but as I passed through the woods I came to a high hill, and near it was a little house, and before the house burned a fire, and round the fire danced a comical little man, and he hopped on one leg and cried,

> *"To-day do I bake, to-morrow I brew,*
> *The day after that the queen's child comes in;*
> *And oh! I am glad that nobody knew*
> *That the name I am called is Rumpelstiltskin!"*

You cannot think how pleased the queen was to hear that name, and soon afterwards, when the little man walked in and said,

"Now, Mrs. Queen, what is my name?" she said at first,

"Are you called Jack?"

"No," he answered.

"Are you called Harry?" she asked again.

"No," answered he. And then she said,

"Then perhaps your name is Rumpelstiltskin!"

"The devil told you that! The devil told you that!" cried the little man, and in his anger he stamped with his right foot so hard that it went into the ground above his knee; then he seized his left foot with both his hands in such a fury that he split in two, and there was an end of him.

EMMA L. BROCK

# Sudden Mary

Once upon a time there was a little girl named
Mary. She was a very sudden little girl. She was sudden
when she tripped over the rugs. She was sudden when she
fell off the fence and tore her dress on a picket.

"I just could not stop," she would say to her mother.

She was sudden when she carried the plate of cookies
into the dining-room.

"Why, where are the cookies?" she would say when she
put the empty plate on the table.

She was sudden when she swept up the broken cookies
and swung the broom handle round in large circles, knocking over the milk bottle.

"Why, where did that bottle come from?" she would
say. That is how sudden Mary was.

She was sudden from early in the morning until she
went to bed at night. She was sudden from Monday morning to Tuesday morning to Wednesday morning and on
through the week until Monday morning came round
again.

Her mother was kept busy wondering what Mary would

do next. Her father bought new milk bottles and gave her pennies for being careful not to fall into the flower garden. Her grandmother said Mary was as lively as a very lively goat and no safer. That is how sudden Mary was.

Just one person liked the suddenness of Mary, and that person was her little sister. She was one quarter of the way from one year old to two years old. She could just totter around on her short fat legs.

Every time that Mary fell over a footstool or dropped a box of blocks or tipped over a mug of milk, Little Sister would clap her hands and shout. She did not mind how sudden Mary was.

One Saturday morning in the winter time after it had been snowing all the night before, Mary thought she would like to go for a visit to her grandmother, who lived on the other side of the town. The snow was thick and soft on the sidewalks. It had piled itself on the tops of the bushes until they looked like gnomes.

"And I could take Little Sister," said Mary.

So Mary put on her snowsuit and her toboggan cap. She zipped on her galoshes and pulled on her big red mittens. Little Sister had a snowsuit, too. When she was in it, she was just as wide as she was tall and she sat down every time she tried to walk. Mary and her mother put Little Sister on the low flat sled and showed her how to hold onto the sides.

"Take your time," said Mary's mother. "There is a whole morning to get there." She knew how sudden Mary was.

"And remember to turn to the right at the gas station and go straight down the hill and on past Mr. Tinkham's grocery store to the schoolhouse corner and then turn to the left to Grandmother's."

"I hope Grandmother is baking molasses cookies," said Mary.

Mary walked slowly and carefully along the walk, pulling Little Sister on the sled behind her. She scuffed through the snow. She kicked clouds of it high in the air. Little Sister laughed and laughed.

Mary skipped and slid through the snow. She made believe she was a horse. She snorted and stamped. Mary put her head down and stamped and tramped through the snow. She pranced right into the middle of old Mrs. Whittleby.

Mrs. Whittleby's pocketbook flew out of her hand and made a hole in the snow. The package of cat's meat flew out of the other hand and made another hole in the snow. And Mrs. Whittleby flew in still another direction and made a third hole in the snow. That is how sudden Mary was.

"Land sakes!" cried Mrs. Whittleby.

And while Mrs. Whittleby was doing all that, Mary bounced back into Little Sister's lap. Little Sister laughed and laughed. She did not care how sudden Mary was.

Mary picked herself up. She picked up the pocketbook and she picked up the cat's meat. Then she helped Mrs. Whittleby pick herself up.

"I don't know how all that happened," said Mary.

Mary walked slowly and carefully along the walk, pulling Little Sister on the sled behind her. She scuffed through the snow. She kicked clouds of it high in the air. She turned to the right by the red pumps of the filling station.

Mary skipped and slid over the snow down the hill. The snow was hard and slippery where the children had been sliding. Mary made believe she was skating. She made believe so hard that her feet flew up in the air. Her feet flew up in the air and the sled slid past her and carried Little Sister on down the hill.

It slid down the hill toward Mr. Tinkham's grocery store. It slid right into Mr. Tinkham's grocery store. It tipped over the snow shovels standing by the steps and spilled Little Sister out into the snow. That is how sudden Mary was.

Little Sister laughed and laughed. Mary ran and slid down the hill after her. She set the sled back on its runners and she picked up Little Sister. She leaned the snow shovels up against Mr. Tinkham's store.

"I don't know how all that happened," said Mary.

Little Sister laughed and laughed. She did not care how sudden Mary was.

Mary walked slowly and carefully along the walk, pulling Little Sister on the sled behind her. She scuffed through the snow. She kicked clouds of it high up in the air.

Mary skipped and slid through the snow. She made believe that Grandmother was mixing molasses cookies. The more she thought of the molasses cookies, the faster she went. She ran along the walk. She whirled round the schoolhouse corner. She whirled round the hedge and up the path that led to Grandmother's house.

"Grandmother," she called, "Grandmother!"

Grandmother came to the front door.

"Here I am, Grandmother," Mary shouted. "Here I am with Little Sister."

Mary ran up to the front steps and pulled the sled up beside her.

But the sled was empty. The sled was empty and there was no Little Sister, nor her snowsuit, nor her galoshes, nor her mittens anywhere. That is how sudden Mary was.

"Why, where is Little Sister?" cried Mary.

"Was she on the sled?" asked Grandmother.

"Well, she once was on the sled," said Mary.

Grandmother hurried into the house to put on her coat and rubbers.

Mary ran down the path pulling the empty sled behind her. She whirled out of the path and round the hedge. But there was no Little Sister nor her toboggan cap anywhere.

"Have you seen my little sister?" she asked Jimmy Green, who was pounding up a snow man in his front yard.

"No," said Jimmy Green. "There was nothing on your sled when you went past here."

"Have you seen my little sister?" she asked Johnny Brown, who was shoveling the snow from his front walk.

"No," said Johnny Brown. "There was nothing on your sled when you went past here."

Mary ran up the street toward the schoolhouse corner. There was no Little Sister nor her round blue snowsuit nor her red mittens anywhere.

"Have you seen my little sister?" Mary asked Mrs. Green, who was tucking her little baby into her carriage on the porch.

"Why, no, Mary. Have you lost her?"

"She once was on this sled," said Mary.

Mary ran to the schoolhouse door.

"Have you seen my little sister?" Mary asked the school janitor, who was brushing the snow from the steps.

"No, little girl," said the janitor. "Not a little sister nor a little brother. Have you lost one?"

"Well, she once was on this sled," said Mary.

She ran round the schoolhouse corner. And she saw people running. Mr. Tinkham was running from his grocery store and Mr. Peckham was running from his drug store. And Mr. Murphy, the big policeman, was running from across the street.

Mary looked at the spot they were running toward and there she saw something waving from a snowdrift. There, sticking out of the snowdrift, were two fat brown galoshes fastened to two fat blue snowsuit legs that were kicking in the air.

There was no sign of anything more. There was no sign of a face or of red mittens or of a toboggan cap. Just two legs kicking out of the snowbank.

Mary and Mr. Tinkham and Mr. Peckham and Mr. Murphy, the big policeman, all rushed up to the waving legs. Mr. Murphy took hold of them and pulled. And out of the snowdrift came the rest of Little Sister.

Little Sister was covered with snow. All the cracks were filled with snow. There was snow on her lashes. But Little Sister was laughing. She was laughing so hard that she could not stand up on her fat round legs.

"How ever did you get in a snowdrift?" asked Mary.

Mr. Peckham brushed and Mr. Tinkham brushed and Mr. Murphy wiped Little Sister's face with a big red bandanna handkerchief. Little Sister could not stop laughing. She did not care how sudden Mary was.

Then Grandmother came along and they put Little Sis-

ter on the low flat sled. And they thanked the kind gentlemen who had brushed her and wiped her.

Grandmother pulled the sled safely round the corner
to her house where the molasses cookies were waiting.

Grandmother said Mary was livelier than the very live-
liest goat and much less safe.

Her mother wondered what Mary would do next.

And her father said that if Little Sister should be at all
like Mary, he would have to build a fence around the
flower garden and around the china closet and perhaps
around the coal bin.

That is how sudden Mary was.

ROBERT LOUIS STEVENSON

# Looking Forward

When I am grown to man's estate
I shall be very proud and great.
And tell the other girls and boys
Not to meddle with my toys.

BEATRIX POTTER

# The Tale of Peter Rabbit

Once upon a time there were four little Rabbits, and their names were——

Flopsy,
Mopsy,
Cotton-tail,
and Peter.

They lived with their Mother in a sand-bank, underneath the root of a very big fir tree.

"Now, my dears," said old Mrs. Rabbit one morning, "you may go into the fields or down the lane, but don't go into Mr. McGregor's garden: your Father had an accident there; he was put in a pie by Mrs. McGregor. Now run along, and don't get into mischief; I am going out."

Then old Mrs. Rabbit took a basket and her umbrella, and went through the wood to the baker's. She bought a loaf of brown bread and five currant buns.

Flopsy, Mopsy, and Cotton-tail, who were good little

bunnies, went down the lane to gather blackberries; but Peter, who was very naughty, ran straight away to Mr. McGregor's garden, and squeezed under the gate!

First he ate some lettuces and some French beans; and

then he ate some radishes; and then, feeling rather sick, he went to look for some parsley.

But round the end of a cucumber frame, whom should he meet but Mr. McGregor!

Mr. McGregor was on his hands and knees planting out young cabbages, but he jumped up and ran after Peter, waving a rake and calling out, "Stop thief!"

Peter was most dreadfully frightened; he rushed all over the garden, for he had forgotten the way back to the gate.

He lost one of his shoes among the cabbages, and the other shoe amongst the potatoes.

After losing them, he ran on four legs and went faster, so that I think he might have got away altogether if he had not unfortunately run into a gooseberry net, and got caught by the large buttons on his jacket. It was a blue jacket with brass buttons, quite new.

Peter gave himself up for lost, and shed big tears; but his sobs were overheard by some friendly sparrows, who flew to him in great excitement, and implored him to exert himself.

Mr. McGregor came up with a sieve, which he intended to pop upon the top of Peter; but Peter wriggled out just in time, leaving his jacket behind him. And rushed into the tool shed, and jumped into a can. It would have been a beautiful thing to hide in, if it had not had so much water in it.

Mr. McGregor was quite sure that Peter was somewhere in the tool shed, perhaps hidden underneath a flower-pot. He began to turn them over carefully, looking under each.

Presently Peter sneezed—"Kertyschoo!" Mr. McGregor was after him in no time, and tried to put his foot upon Peter, who jumped out of the window, upsetting three plants. The window was too small for Mr. McGregor and he was tired of running after Peter. He went back to his work.

Peter sat down to rest; he was out of breath and trembling with fright, and he had not the least idea which way to go. Also he was very damp with sitting in that can.

After a time he began to wander about, going lippity ——lippity——not very fast, and looking all around.

He found a door in a wall; but it was locked, and there was no room for a fat little rabbit to squeeze underneath.

An old mouse was running in and out over the stone doorstep, carrying peas and beans to her family in the wood. Peter asked her the way to the gate, but she had such a large pea in her mouth that she could not answer. She only shook her head at him. Peter began to cry.

Then he tried to find his way straight across the garden, but he became more and more puzzled. Presently he came to a pond where Mr. McGregor filled his water cans. A white cat was staring at some goldfish; she sat very, very still, but now and then the tip of her tail twitched as if it were alive. Peter thought it best to go away without speaking to her; he had heard about cats from his cousin, little Benjamin Bunny.

He went back towards the tool shed, but suddenly, quite close to him, he heard the noise of a hoe—sc-r-ritch, scratch, scratch, scritch. Peter scuttered underneath the bushes. But presently, as nothing happened, he came out, and climbed upon a wheel-barrow, and peeped over. The first thing he saw was Mr. McGregor hoeing onions. His back was turned toward Peter, and beyond him was the gate!

Peter got down very quietly off the wheel-barrow, and started running as fast as he could go, along a straight walk behind some black-currant bushes.

Mr. McGregor caught sight of him at the corner, but Peter did not care. He slipped underneath the gate, and was safe at last in the wood outside the garden.

Mr. McGregor hung up the little jacket and the shoes for a scarecrow to frighten the blackbirds.

Peter never stopped running or looked behind him till he got home to the big fir tree.

He was so tired that he flopped down upon the nice soft sand on the floor of the rabbit hole, and shut his eyes. His mother was busy cooking; she wondered what he had done with his clothes. It was the second little jacket and pair of shoes that Peter had lost in a fortnight!

I am sorry to say that Peter was not very well during the evening.

His mother put him to bed, and made some camomile tea; and she gave a dose of it to Peter!

"One tablespoonful to be taken at bedtime."

But Flopsy, Mopsy, and Cotton-tail had bread and milk and blackberries for supper.

# Tattercoats

In a great Palace by the sea there once dwelt a very rich old lord, who had neither wife nor children living, only one little granddaughter, whose face he had never seen in all her life. He hated her bitterly, because at her birth his favourite daughter died; and when the old nurse brought him the baby, he swore that it might live or die as it liked, but he would never look on its face as long as it lived.

So he turned his back, and sat by his window looking out over the sea, and weeping great tears for his lost daughter, till his white hair and beard grew down over his shoulders and twined round his chair and crept into the chinks of the floor, and his tears, dropping on to the window-ledge, wore a channel through the stone, and ran away in a little river to the great sea. And, meanwhile, his granddaughter grew up with no one to care for her, or clothe her; only the old nurse, when no one was by, would sometimes give her a dish of scraps from the kitchen, or a torn petticoat from the rag-bag; while the other servants of the Palace would drive her from the house with blows and mocking words, calling her "Tattercoats," and pointing at her bare feet and shoulders, till she ran away crying, to hide among the bushes.

And so she grew up, with little to eat or wear, spending her days in the fields and lanes, with only the gooseherd for a companion, who would play to her so merrily on his little pipe, when she was hungry, or cold, or tired, that she forgot all her troubles, and fell to dancing, with his flock of noisy geese for partners.

But, one day, people told each other that the King was travelling through the land, and in the town near by was to give a great ball to all the lords and ladies of the country, when the Prince, his only son, was to choose a wife.

One of the royal invitations was brought to the Palace by the sea, and the servants carried it up to the old lord who still sat by his window, wrapped in his long white hair and weeping into the little river that was fed by his tears.

But when he heard the King's command, he dried his eyes and bade them bring shears to cut him loose, for his hair had bound him a fast prisoner and he could not move. And then he sent them for rich clothes, and jewels, which he put on; and he ordered them to saddle the white horse, with gold and silk, that he might ride to meet the King.

Meanwhile Tattercoats had heard of the great doings in the town, and she sat by the kitchen-door weeping because she could not go to see them. And when the old nurse heard her crying she went to the Lord of the Palace, and begged him to take his granddaughter with him to the King's ball.

But he only frowned and told her to be silent, while the servants laughed and said: "Tattercoats is happy in her rags, playing with the gooseherd, let her be—it is all she is fit for."

A second, and then a third time, the old nurse begged him to let the girl go with him, but she was answered only by black looks and fierce words, till she was driven from the room by the jeering servants, with blows and mocking words.

Weeping over her ill-success, the old nurse went to look for Tattercoats; but the girl had been turned from the door by the cook, and had run away to tell her friend the gooseherd how unhappy she was because she could not go to the King's ball.

But when the gooseherd had listened to her story, he bade her cheer up, and proposed that they should go together into the town to see the King, and all the fine things; and when she looked sorrowfully down at her rags and bare feet, he played a note or two upon his pipe, so gay and merry, that she forgot all about her tears and her troubles, and before she well knew, the herdboy had taken her by the hand, and she, and he, and the geese before them, were dancing down the road towards the town.

Before they had gone very far, a handsome young man, splendidly dressed, rode up and stopped to ask the way to the castle where the King was staying; and when he found that they too were going thither, he got off his horse and walked beside them along the road.

The herdboy pulled out his pipe and played a low

sweet tune, and the stranger looked again and again at Tattercoats' lovely face till he fell deeply in love with her, and begged her to marry him.

But she only laughed, and shook her golden head.

"You would be finely put to shame if you had a goose-girl for your wife!" said she; "go and ask one of the great ladies you will see to-night at the King's ball, and do not flout poor Tattercoats."

But the more she refused him the sweeter the pipe played, and the deeper the young man fell in love; till at last he begged her, as a proof of his sincerity, to come that night at twelve to the King's ball, just as she was, with the herdboy and his geese, and in her torn petticoat and bare feet, and he would dance with her before the King and the lords and ladies, and present her to them all, as his dear and honoured bride.

So when night came, and the hall in the castle was full of light and music, and the lords and ladies were dancing before the King, just as the clock struck twelve, Tattercoats and the herdboy, followed by his flock of noisy geese, entered at the great doors, and walked straight up the ballroom, while on either side the ladies whispered, the lords laughed, and the King seated at the far end stared in amazement.

But as they came in front of the throne, Tattercoats' lover rose from beside the King, and came to meet her. Taking her by the hand, he kissed her thrice before them all, and turned to the King.

"Father!" he said, for it was the Prince himself, "I

have made my choice, and here is my bride, the loveliest girl in all the land, and the sweetest as well!"

Before he had finished speaking, the herdboy put his pipe to his lips and played a few low notes that sounded like a bird singing far off in the woods; and as he played, Tattercoats' rags were changed to shining robes sewn with glittering jewels, a golden crown lay upon her golden hair, and the flock of geese behind her became a crowd of dainty pages, bearing her long train.

And as the King rose to greet her as his daughter, the trumpets sounded loudly in honour of the new Princess, and the people outside in the street said to each other:

"Ah! now the Prince has chosen for his wife the loveliest girl in all the land!"

But the gooseherd was never seen again, and no one knew what became of him; while the old lord went home once more to his Palace by the sea, for he could not stay at Court, when he had sworn never to look on his granddaughter's face.

So there he still sits by his window, if you could only see him, as you some day may, weeping more bitterly than ever, as he looks out over the sea.

From *More English Fairy Tales*, edited by Joseph Jacobs.

# Thumbelisa

There was once a woman who had the greatest longing for a little tiny child, but she had no idea where to get one; so she went to an old witch and said to her, "I do so long to have a little child, and will you tell me where I can get one?"

"Oh, we shall be able to manage that," said the witch. "Here is a barley corn for you; it is not at all the same kind as that which grows in the peasant's field, or with which chickens are fed; plant it in a flower pot and you will see what will appear."

"Thank you, oh, thank you!" said the woman, and she gave the witch twelve pennies, then went home and planted the barley corn, and a large, handsome flower sprang up at once; it looked exactly like a tulip, but the petals were tightly shut up, just as if they were still in bud. "That is a lovely flower," said the woman, and she kissed the pretty red and yellow petals; as she kissed it the flower burst open with a loud snap. It was a real tulip, you could see that; but right in the middle of the flower on the green stool sat a little tiny girl, most lovely and delicate;

she was not more than an inch in height, so she was called Thumbelisa.

Her cradle was a smartly varnished walnut shell, with the blue petals of violets for a mattress and a rose-leaf to cover her; she slept in it at night, but during the day she played about on the table where the woman had placed a plate, surrounded by a wreath of flowers on the outer edge with their stalks in water. A large tulip petal floated on the water, and on this little Thumbelisa sat and sailed about from one side of the plate to the other; she had two white horse hairs for oars. It was a pretty sight. She could sing, too, with such delicacy and charm as was never heard before.

One night as she lay in her pretty bed, a great ugly toad hopped in at the window, for there was a broken pane. Ugh! how hideous that great wet toad was; it hopped right down on to the table where Thumbelisa lay fast asleep, under the red rose-leaf.

"Here is a lovely wife for my son," said the toad, and then she took up the walnut shell where Thumbelisa slept and hopped away with it through the window, down into the garden. A great broad stream ran through it, but just at the edge it was swampy and muddy, and it was here that the toad lived with her son. Ugh! how ugly and hideous he was, too, exactly like his mother. "Koax, koax, brekke-ke-kex," that was all he had to say when he saw the lovely little girl in the walnut shell.

"Do not talk so loud or you will wake her," said the old toad; "she might escape us yet, for she is as light as thistledown! We will put her on one of the broad water lily leaves out in the stream; it will be just like an island to her, she is so small and light. She won't be able to run away from there while we get the stateroom ready down under the mud, which you are to inhabit."

A great many water lilies grew in the stream, their broad green leaves looked as if they were floating on the surface of the water. The leaf which was furthest from the shore was also the biggest, and to this one the old toad swam out with the walnut shell in which little Thumbelisa lay.

The poor, tiny little creature woke up quite early in the morning, and when she saw where she was she began to cry most bitterly, for there was water on every side of the big green leaf, and she could not reach the land at any point.

The old toad sat in the mud decking out her abode with grasses and the buds of the yellow water lilies, so as to have it very nice for the new daughter-in-law, and then she swam out with her ugly son to the leaf where Thumbelisa stood. They wanted to fetch her pretty bed to place it in the bridal chamber before they took her there. The old toad made a deep curtsey in the water before her, and said, "Here is my son, who is to be your husband, and you are to live together most comfortably down in the mud."

"Koax, koax, brekke-ke-kex," that was all the son could say.

Then they took the pretty little bed and swam away with it, but Thumbelisa sat quite alone on the green leaf and cried because she did not want to live with the ugly toad, or have her horrid son for a husband. The little fish which swam about in the water had no doubt seen the toad and heard what she said, so they stuck their heads up, wishing, I suppose, to see the little girl. As soon as they saw her, they were delighted with her, and were quite grieved to think that she was to go down to live with the ugly toad. No, that should never happen. They flocked together down in the water round about the green stem which held the leaf she stood upon, and gnawed at it with their teeth till it floated away down the stream carrying Thumbelisa away where the toad could not follow her.

Thumbelisa sailed past place after place, and the little birds in the bushes saw her and sang, "what a lovely little maid." The leaf with her on it floated further and further away and in this manner reached foreign lands.

A pretty little white butterfly fluttered round and round her for some time and at last settled on the leaf, for it had taken quite a fancy to Thumbelisa. She was so happy now, because the toad could not reach her and she was sailing through such lovely scenes; the sun shone on the water and it looked like liquid gold. Then she took her sash, and tied one end round the butterfly, and the other she made fast to the leaf which went gliding on quicker and quicker, and she with it, for she was standing on the leaf.

At this moment a big cockchafer came flying along, he caught sight of her and in an instant he fixed his claw round her slender waist and flew off with her, up into a tree, but the green leaf floated down the stream and the butterfly with it, for he was tied to it and could not get loose.

Heavens! how frightened poor little Thumbelisa was when the cockchafer carried her up into the tree, but she was most of all grieved about the pretty white butterfly which she had fastened to the leaf; if he could not succeed in getting loose he would be starved to death.

But the cockchafer cared nothing for that. He settled with her on the largest leaf on the tree, and fed her with honey from the flowers, and he said that she was lovely although she was not a bit like a chafer. Presently all the other chafers which lived in the tree came to visit them; they looked at Thumbelisa and the young lady chafers twitched their feelers and said, "she has also got two legs, what a good effect it has." "She has no feelers," said another. "She is so slender in the waist, fie, she looks like a human being." "How ugly she is," said all the mother chafers, and yet little Thumbelisa was so pretty. That was certainly also the opinion of the cockchafer who had captured her, but when all the others said she was ugly, he at last began to believe it too, and would not have anything more to do with her, she might go wherever she liked! They flew down from the tree with her and placed her on a daisy, where she cried because she was so ugly that the chafers would have nothing to do with her; and after all, she was more beautiful than anything you could imagine, as delicate and transparent as the finest rose-leaf.

Poor little Thumbelisa lived all the summer quite alone in the wood. She plaited a bed of grass for herself and hung it up under a big dock-leaf which sheltered her from the rain; she sucked the honey from the flowers for her food, and her drink was the dew which lay on the leaves in the morning. In this way the summer and autumn passed, but then came the winter. All the birds which used to sing so sweetly to her flew away, the great dock-leaf under which she had lived shriveled up leaving nothing but a dead yellow stalk, and she shivered with the cold, for her clothes were worn out. She was such a tiny creature, poor little Thumbelisa, she certainly must be frozen to death. It began to snow and every snowflake which fell upon her was like a whole shovelful upon one of us, for we are big and she was only one inch in height. Then she wrapped herself up in a withered leaf, but that did not warm her much, she trembled with the cold.

Close to the wood in which she had been living lay a large cornfield, but the corn had long ago been carried away and nothing remained but the bare, dry stubble which stood up out of the frozen ground. The stubble was quite a forest for her to walk about in: oh, how she shook with the cold. Then she came to the door of a field-mouse's home. It was a little hole down under the stubble. The field-mouse lived so cosily and warm there, her whole room was full of corn, and she had a beautiful kitchen and larder besides. Poor Thumbelisa stood just inside the door like any other poor beggar child and begged for a little piece of barley corn, for she had had nothing to eat for two whole days.

"You poor little thing," said the field-mouse, for she was at bottom a good old field-mouse. "Come into my warm room and dine with me." Then, as she took a fancy to Thumbelisa, she said, "you may with pleasure stay with me for the winter, but you must keep my room clean and tidy and tell me stories, for I am very fond of them," and Thumbelisa did what the good old field-mouse desired and was on the whole very comfortable.

"Now we shall soon have a visitor," said the field-mouse; "my neighbor generally comes to see me every week-day. He is even better housed than I am; his rooms are very large and he wears a most beautiful black velvet coat; if only you could get him for a husband you would indeed be well settled, but he can't see. You must tell him all the most beautiful stories you know."

But Thumbelisa did not like this, and she would have nothing to say to the neighbor for he was a mole. He came and paid a visit in his black velvet coat. He was very rich and wise, said the field-mouse, and his home was twenty times as large as hers; and he had much learning but he did not like the sun or the beautiful flowers, in fact he spoke slightingly of them for he had never seen them. Thumbelisa had to sing to him and she sang both "Fly away, cockchafer" and "A monk, he wandered through the meadow," then the mole fell in love with her because of her sweet voice, but he did not say anything for he was of a discreet turn of mind.

He had just made a long tunnel through the ground

from his house to theirs, and he gave the field-mouse and Thumbelisa leave to walk in it whenever they liked. He told them not to be afraid of the dead bird which was lying in the passage. It was a whole bird with feathers and beak which had probably died quite recently at the beginning of the winter and was now entombed just where he had made his tunnel.

The mole took a piece of tinder-wood in his mouth, for that shines like fire in the dark, and walked in front of them to light them in the long dark passage; when they came to the place where the dead bird lay, the mole thrust his broad nose up to the roof and pushed the earth up so as to make a big hole through which the daylight shone. In the middle of the floor lay a dead swallow, with its pretty wings closely pressed to its sides, and the legs and head drawn in under the feathers; no doubt the poor bird had died of cold. Thumbelisa was so sorry for it; she loved all the little birds, for they had twittered and sung so sweetly to her during the whole summer; but the mole kicked it with his short legs and said, "Now it will pipe no more! it must be a miserable fate to be born a little bird! Thank heaven! no child of mine can be a bird; a bird like that has nothing but its twitter and dies of hunger in the winter."

"Yes, as a sensible man, you may well say that," said the field-mouse. "What *has* a bird for all its twittering when the cold weather comes? it has to hunger and freeze, but then it must cut a dash."

Thumbelisa did not say anything, but when the others

turned their backs to the bird, she stooped down and stroked aside the feathers which lay over its head, and kissed its closed eyes. "Perhaps it was this very bird which sang so sweetly to me in the summer," she thought; "what pleasure it gave me, the dear pretty bird."

The mole now closed up the hole which let in the daylight and conducted the ladies to their home. Thumbelisa could not sleep at all in the night, so she got up out of her bed and plaited a large handsome mat of hay and then she carried it down and spread it all over the dead bird, and laid some soft cotton wool which she had found in the field-mouse's room close round its sides, so that it might have a warm bed on the cold ground.

"Good-bye, you sweet little bird," said she, "good-bye, and thank you for your sweet song through the summer when all the trees were green and the sun shone warmly upon us." Then she laid her head close up to the bird's breast, but was quite startled at a sound, as if something was thumping inside it. It was the bird's heart. It was not dead but lay in a swoon, and now that it had been warmed it began to revive.

In the autumn all the swallows fly away to warm countries, but if one happens to be belated, it feels the cold so much that it falls down like a dead thing, and remains lying where it falls till the snow covers it up. Thumbelisa quite shook with fright for the bird was very, very big beside her who was only one inch high, but she gathered up her courage, packed the wool closer round the poor bird, and fetched a leaf of mint which she had herself for a coverlet and laid it over the bird's head. The next night she stole down again to it and found it alive but so feeble that it could only just open its eyes for a moment to look at Thumbelisa who stood with a bit of tinder-wood in her hand, for she had no other lantern.

"Many, many thanks, you sweet child," said the sick swallow to her; "you have warmed me beautifully. I shall soon have strength to fly out into the warm sun again."

"Oh!" said she, "it is so cold outside, it snows and freezes, stay in your warm bed, I will tend you." Then she brought water to the swallow in a leaf, and when it had drunk some, it told her how it had torn its wing on a black thorn bush, and therefore could not fly as fast as the other swallows which were taking flight then for the distant warm lands. At last it fell down on the ground, but after that it remembered nothing, and did not in the least know how it had got into the tunnel.

It stayed there all the winter, and Thumbelisa was good to it and grew very fond of it. She did not tell either the mole or the field-mouse anything about it, for they did not like the poor unfortunate swallow.

As soon as the spring came and the warmth of the sun penetrated the ground, the swallow said good-bye to Thumbelisa, who opened the hole which the mole had made above. The sun streamed in deliciously upon them, and the swallow asked if she would not go with him, she could sit upon his back and they would fly far away into the green wood. But Thumbelisa knew that it would grieve the old field-mouse if she left her like that.

"No, I can't," said Thumbelisa.

"Good-bye, good-bye, then, you kind, pretty girl," said the swallow, and flew out into the sunshine. Thumbelisa looked after him and her eyes filled with tears, for she was very fond of the poor swallow.

"Tweet, tweet," sang the bird, and flew into the green wood.

Thumbelisa was very sad. She was not allowed to go out into the warm sunshine at all; the corn which was sown in the field near the field-mouse's house grew quite long, it was a thick forest for the poor little girl who was only an inch high.

"You must work at your trousseau this summer," said the mouse to her, for their neighbor the tiresome mole in his black velvet coat had asked her to marry him. "You shall have both woollen and linen, you shall have wherewith to clothe and cover yourself when you become the mole's wife." Thumbelisa had to turn the distaff and the field-mouse hired four spiders to spin and weave day and night. The mole paid a visit every evening and he was always saying that when the summer came to an end, the sun would not shine nearly so warmly, now it burnt the ground as hard as a stone. Yes, when the summer was over he would celebrate his marriage; but Thumbelisa was not at all pleased, for she did not care a bit for the tiresome mole. Every morning at sunrise and every evening at sunset she used to steal out to the door, and when the wind blew aside the tops of the cornstalks so that she could see the blue sky, she thought how bright and lovely it was out there, and wished so much to see the dear swallow again; but it never came back; no doubt it was a long way off, flying about in the beautiful green woods.

When the autumn came all Thumbelisa's outfit was ready.

"In four weeks you must be married," said the field-mouse to her. But Thumbelisa cried and said that she would not have the tiresome mole for a husband.

"Fiddle-dee-dee," said the field-mouse; "don't be obstinate or I shall bite you with my white tooth. You are going to have a splendid husband; the queen herself hasn't the equal of his black velvet coat; both his kitchen and his cellar are full. You should thank heaven for such a husband!"

So they were to be married; the mole had come to fetch Thumbelisa; she was to live deep down under the ground with him, and never to go out into the warm sunshine, for he could not bear it. The poor child was very sad at the thought of bidding good-bye to the beautiful sun; while she had been with the field-mouse she had at least been allowed to look at it from the door.

"Good-bye, you bright sun," she said as she stretched out her arms towards it and went a little way outside the field-mouse's house, for now the harvest was over and only the stubble remained. "Good-bye, good-bye!" she said, and threw her tiny arms round a little red flower growing there. "Give my love to the dear swallow if you happen to see him."

"Tweet, tweet," she heard at this moment above her

head. She looked up; it was the swallow just passing. As soon as it saw Thumbelisa it was delighted; she told it how unwilling she was to have the ugly mole for a husband, and that she was to live deep down underground where the sun never shone. She could not help crying about it.

"The cold winter is coming," said the swallow, "and I am going to fly away to warm countries. Will you go with me? You can sit upon my back! Tie yourself on with your

sash, then we will fly away from the ugly mole and his dark cavern, far away over the mountains to those warm countries where the sun shines with greater splendor than here, where it is always summer and there are heaps of flowers. Do fly with me, you sweet little Thumbelisa, who saved my life when I lay frozen in the dark earthy passage."

"Yes, I will go with you," said Thumbelisa, seating herself on the bird's back with her feet on its outspread wing. She tied her band tightly to one of the strongest feathers, and then the swallow flew away, high up in the air above forests and lakes, high up above the biggest mountains where the snow never melts; and Thumbelisa shivered in the cold air, but then she crept under the bird's warm feathers, and only stuck out her little head to look at the beautiful sights beneath her.

Then at last they reached the warm countries. The sun shone with a warmer glow than here; the sky was twice as high, and the most beautiful green and blue grapes grew in clusters on the banks and hedgerows. Oranges and lemons hung in the woods which were fragrant with myrtles and sweet herbs, and beautiful children ran about the roads playing with the large gorgeously-colored butterflies. But the swallow flew on and on, and the country grew more and more beautiful. Under magnificent green trees on the shores of the blue sea stood a dazzling white marble palace of ancient date; vines wreathed themselves round the stately pillars. At the head of these there were countless nests, and the swallow who carried Thumbelisa lived in one of them.

"Here is my house," said the swallow; "but if you will choose one of the gorgeous flowers growing down there, I will place you in it, and you will live as happily as you can wish."

"That would be delightful," she said, and clapped her little hands.

A great white marble column had fallen to the ground and lay there broken in three pieces, but between these the most lovely white flowers grew. The swallow flew down with Thumbelisa and put her upon one of the broad leaves; what was her astonishment to find a little man in the middle of the flower, as bright and transparent as if he had been made of glass. He had a lovely golden crown upon his head and the most beautiful bright wings upon his shoulders; he was no bigger than Thumbelisa. He was the angel of the flowers. There was a similar little man or woman in every flower, but he was the king of them all.

"Heavens, how beautiful he is," whispered Thumbelisa to the swallow. The little prince was quite frightened by the swallow, for it was a perfect giant of a bird to him, he who was so small and delicate, but when he saw Thumbelisa he was delighted; she was the very prettiest girl he had ever seen. He therefore took the golden crown off his own head and placed it on hers, and asked her name, and if she would be his wife, and then she would be queen of the flowers! Yes, he was certainly a very different kind of husband from the toad's son, or the mole with his black velvet coat. So she accepted the beautiful prince, and out of every flower stepped a little lady or a gentleman so lovely that it was a pleasure to look at them. Each one brought a gift to Thumbelisa, but the best of all was a pair of pretty wings from a large white fly; they were fastened on to her back, and then she too could fly from flower to flower. All was then delight and happiness, but the swallow sat alone in his nest and sang to them as well as he could, for his heart was heavy, he was so fond of Thumbelisa himself, and would have wished never to part from her.

"You shall not be called Thumbelisa," said the angel of the flower to her; "that is such an ugly name, and you are so pretty. We will call you May."

"Good-bye, good-bye," said the swallow, and flew away again from the warm countries, far away back to Denmark; there he had a little nest above the window where the man lived who wrote this story, and he sang his "tweet, tweet" to the man, and so we have the whole story.

ROBERT LOUIS STEVENSON

# Young Night Thought

All night long and every night,
When my mamma puts out the light,
I see the people marching by,
As plain as day, before my eye.

Armies and emperors and kings,
All carrying different kinds of things,
And marching in so grand a way,
You never saw the like by day.

So fine a show was never seen,
At the great circus on the green;
For every kind of beast and man
Is marching in that caravan.

At first they move a little slow,
But still the faster on they go,
And still beside them close I keep
Until we reach the town of Sleep.

# Tom Thumb

There was once a poor woodman sitting by the fire in his cottage, and his wife sat by his side spinning. "How lonely it is," said he, "for you and me to sit here by ourselves without any children to play about and amuse us, while other people seem so happy and merry with their children!" "What you say is very true," said the wife, sighing and turning round her wheel; "how happy should I be if I had but one child! and if it were ever so small, nay, if it were no bigger than my thumb, I should be very happy, and love it dearly." Now it came to pass that this good woman's wish was fulfilled just as she desired; for, some time afterwards, she had a little boy who was quite healthy and strong, but not much bigger than her thumb. So they said, "Well, we cannot say we have not got what we wished for, and, little as he is, we will love him dearly"; and they called him Tom Thumb.

They gave him plenty of food, yet he never grew bigger, but remained just the same size as when he was born; still his eyes were sharp and sparkling, and he soon showed himself to be a clever little fellow, who always knew well what he was about. One day, as the woodman was getting ready to go into the wood to cut fuel, he said, "I wish I had some one to bring the cart after me, for I want to make haste." "O father!" cried Tom, "I will take care of that; the cart shall be in the wood by the time you want it." Then the woodman laughed, and said, "How can that be? you cannot reach up to the horse's bridle." "Never mind that, father," said Tom: "if my

mother will only harness the horse, I will get into his ear, and tell him which way to go." "Well," said the father, "we will try for once."

When the time came, the mother harnessed the horse to the cart, and put Tom into his ear; and as he sat there, the little man told the beast how to go, crying out, "Go on," and "Stop," as he wanted; so the horse went on just as if the woodman had driven it himself into the wood. It

happened that, as the horse was going a little too fast, and
Tom was calling out "Gently! gently!" two strangers came
up. "What an odd thing that is!" said one, "there is a
cart going along, and I hear a carter talking to the horse,
but can see no one. "That is strange," said the other; "let
us follow the cart and see where it goes." So they went on
into the wood, till at last they came to the place where
the woodman was. Then Tom Thumb, seeing his father,
cried out, "See, father, here I am, with the cart, all right
and safe; now take me down." So his father took hold of
the horse with one hand, and with the other took his son
out of the ear; then he put him down upon a straw, where
he sat as merry as you please. The two strangers were all
this time looking on, and did not know what to say for
wonder. At last one took the other aside and said, "That
little urchin will make our fortune if we can get him, and
carry him about from town to town as a show: we must
buy him." So they went to the woodman and asked him
what he would take for the little man: "He will be better
off," said they, "with us than with you." "I won't sell him
at all," said the father, "my own flesh and blood is dearer
to me than all the silver and gold in the world." But Tom,
hearing of the bargain they wanted to make, crept up his
father's coat to his shoulder, and whispered in his ear,
"Take the money, father, and let them have me; I'll soon
come back to you."

So the woodman at last agreed to sell Tom to the
strangers for a large piece of gold. "Where do you like to
sit?" said one of them. "Oh, put me on the rim of your

hat, that will be a nice gallery for me; I can walk about there, and see the country as we go along." So they did as he wished; and when Tom had taken leave of his father, they took him away with them. They journeyed on till it began to be dusky, and then the little man said, "Let me get down, I'm tired." So the man took off his hat and set him down on a clod of earth in a plowed field by the side of the road. But Tom ran about amongst the furrows, and at last slipped into an old mouse-hole. "Good night, masters," said he, "I'm off! mind and look sharp after me the next time." They ran directly to the place, and poked the ends of their sticks into the mouse-hole, but all in vain; Tom only crawled farther and farther in, and at last it became quite dark, so that they were obliged to go their way without their prize, as sulky as you please.

When Tom found they were gone, he came out of his hiding-place. "What dangerous walking it is," said he, "in this ploughed field! If I were to fall from one of these great clods I should certainly break my neck." At last, by good luck, he found a large empty snail-shell. "This is lucky," said he, "I can sleep here very well," and in he crept. Just as he was falling asleep he heard two men passing, and one said to the other, "How shall we manage to steal that rich parson's silver and gold?" "I'll tell you," cried Tom. "What noise was that?" said the thief, frightened, "I am sure I heard some one speak." They stood still listening, and Tom said, "Take me with you, and I'll soon show you how to get the parson's money." "But where are you?" said they. "Look about on the ground,"

answered he, "and listen where the sound comes from."
At last the thieves found him out, and lifted him up in
their hands. "You little urchin!" said they, "what can you
do for us?" "Why I can get between the iron window-
bars of the parson's house, and throw you out whatever
you want." "That's a good thought," said the thieves;
"come along, we shall see what you can do."

When they came to the parson's house, Tom slipped
through the window-bars into the room, and then called
out as loud as he could bawl, "Will you have all that is
here?" At this the thieves were frightened, and said,
"Softly, softly! Speak low, that you may not awaken anybody." But Tom pretended not to understand them, and
bawled out again, "How much will you have? Shall I
throw it all out?" Now the cook lay in the next room, and
hearing a noise she raised herself in her bed and listened.
Meantime the thieves were frightened, and ran off to a
little distance; but at last they plucked up courage, and
said, "The little urchin is only trying to make fools of us."

So they came back and whispering softly said to him,
"Now let us have no more of your jokes, but throw out
some of the money." Then Tom called out as loud as he
could, "Very well: hold your hands, here it comes." The
cook heard this quite plain, so she sprang out of bed and
ran to open the door. The thieves ran off as if a wolf was
at their tails; and the maid, having groped about and
found nothing, went away for a light. By the time she
returned Tom had slipped off into the barn; and when the
cook had looked about and searched every hole and cor-

ner, and found nobody, she went to bed, thinking she must have been dreaming with her eyes open. The little man crawled about in the hay-loft, and at last found a glorious place to finish his night's rest in; so he laid himself down, meaning to sleep till daylight, and then find his way home to his father and mother. But, alas! how cruelly was he disappointed! what crosses and sorrows happen in this world! The cook got up early before daybreak to feed the cows: she went straight to the hay-loft, and carried away a large bundle of hay with the little man in the middle of it fast asleep. He still, however, slept on, and did not awake till he found himself in the mouth of the cow, who had taken him up with a mouthful of hay: "Good lack-a-day!" said he, "how did I manage to tumble into the mill?" But he soon found out where he really was, and was obliged to have all his wits about him in order that he might not get between the cow's teeth, and so be crushed to death. At last down he went into her stomach. "It is rather dark here," said he; "they forgot to build windows in this room to let the sun in; a candle would be no bad thing."

Though he made the best of his bad luck, he did not like his quarters at all; and the worst of it was, that more and more hay was always coming down, and the space in which he was became smaller and smaller. At last he cried out as loud as he could, "Don't bring me any more hay! Don't bring me any more hay!" The maid happened to be just then milking the cow, and hearing someone speak and seeing nobody, and yet being quite sure it was the same

voice that she had heard in the night, she was so frightened that she fell off her stool and overset the milk-pail.
She ran off as fast as she could to her master the parson,
and said, "Sir, sir, the cow is talking!" But the parson
said, "Woman, thou art surely mad!" However, he went
with her into the cow-house to see what was the matter.
Scarcely had they set their foot on the threshold when
Tom called out. "Don't bring me any more hay!"
Then the parson himself was frightened; and thinking the cow was surely bewitched, ordered that she
should be killed directly. So the cow was killed, and the
stomach, in which Tom lay, was thrown out upon a dung-
hill.

Tom soon set himself to work to get out, which was
not a very easy task; but at last, just as he had made room
to get his head out, a new misfortune befell him: a
hungry wolf sprang out, and swallowed the whole stomach, with Tom in it, at a single gulp, and ran away. Tom,
however, was not disheartened; and thinking the wolf
would not dislike having some chat with him as he was
going along, he called out, "My good friend, I can show
you a famous treat." "Where's that?" said the wolf. "In
such and such a house," said Tom, describing his father's
house, "you can crawl through the drain into the kitchen,
and there you will find cakes, ham, beef, and everything
your heart can desire." The wolf did not want to be asked
twice; so that very night he went to the house and
crawled through the drain into the kitchen, and ate and
drank there to his heart's content. As soon as he was satis-

fied he wanted to get away; but he had eaten so much that he could not get out the same way that he came in. This was just what Tom had reckoned upon; and he now began to set up a great shout, making all the noise he could. "Will you be quiet?" said the wolf: "you'll awaken everybody in the house." "What's that to me?" said the little man: "you have had your frolic, now I've a mind to be merry myself." And he began again singing and shouting as loud as he could.

The woodman and his wife, being awakened by the noise, peeped through a crack in the door; but when they saw that the wolf was there, you may well suppose that they were terribly frightened; and the woodman ran for his axe, and gave his wife a scythe. "Now do you stay behind," said the woodman; "and when I have knocked him on the head, do you rip up his belly for him with the scythe." Tom heard all this, and said, "Father, father! I am here, the wolf has swallowed me." And his father said, "Heaven be praised! we have found our dear child again"; and he told his wife not to use the scythe, for fear she should hurt him. Then he aimed a great blow, and struck the wolf on the head, and killed him on the spot; and when he was dead they cut open his body and set Tommy free. "Ah!" said the father, "what fears we have had for you!" "Yes, father," answered he, "I have traveled all over the world, since we parted, in one way or other; and now I am very glad to get fresh air again." "Why, where have you been?" said his father. "I have been in a mouse-hole, in a snail-shell, down a cow's throat, and in

the wolf's belly; and yet here I am again safe and sound."
"Well," said they, "we will not sell you again for all the
riches in the world." So they hugged and kissed their
dear little son, and gave him plenty to eat and drink, and
fetched new clothes for him, for his old ones were quite
spoiled on his journey.

# The Ugly Duckling

It was so glorious out in the country; it was summer; the cornfields were yellow, the oats were green, the hay had been put up in stacks in the green meadows, and the stork went about on his long red legs, and chattered Egyptian, for this was the language he had learned from his good mother. All around the fields and meadows were great forests, and in the midst of these forests lay deep lakes. Yes, it was right glorious out in the country. In the midst of the sunshine there lay an old farm, with deep canals about it, and from the wall down to the water grew great burdocks, so high that little children could stand upright under the loftiest of them. It was just as wild there as in the deepest wood, and here sat a Duck upon her nest; she had to hatch her ducklings; but she was almost tired out before the little ones came and then she so seldom had visitors. The other ducks liked better to swim about in the canals than to run up to sit down under a burdock, and cackle with her.

At last one egg-shell after another burst open. "Peep! Peep!" it cried, and in all the eggs there were little creatures that stuck out their heads.

"Quack! quack!" they said; and they all came quacking out as fast as they could, looking all round them under the green leaves; and the mother let them look as much as they chose, for green is good for the eyes.

"How wide the world is!" said all the young ones, for they certainly had much more room now than when they were in the eggs.

"D'ye think this is all the world?" said the mother. "That stretches far across the other side of the garden, quite into the parson's field; but I have never been there yet. I hope you are all here now," and she stood up. "No, I have not all. The largest egg still lies there. How long is that to last? I am really tired of it." And she sat down again.

"Well, how goes it?" asked an old Duck who had come to pay her a visit.

"It lasts a long time with that one egg," said the Duck who sat there. "It will not burst. Now, only look at the others; are they not the prettiest little ducks one could possibly see? They are all like their father: the rascal, he never comes to see me."

"Let me see the egg which will not burst," said the old visitor. "You may be sure it is a turkey's egg. I was once cheated in that way, and had much anxiety and trouble with the young ones, for they are afraid of the water. Must I say it to you, I could not get them to venture in. I quacked and I clacked, but it was no use. Let me see the egg. Yes, that's a turkey's egg. Let it lie there, and teach the other children to swim."

"I think I will sit on it a little longer," said the Duck. "I've sat so long now that I can sit a few days more."

"Just as you please," said the old Duck; and she went away.

At last the great egg burst. "Peep! peep!" said the little one, and crept forth. It was very large and very ugly. The Duck looked at it.

"It's a very large duckling," said she; "none of the others look like that: can it really be a turkey chick? Well, we shall soon find out. It must go into the water, even if I have to thrust it in myself."

The next day it was bright, beautiful weather; the sun shone on all the green trees. The Mother-Duck went down to the canal with all her family. Splash! she jumped into the water. "Quack! quack!" she said, and one duckling after another plunged in. The water closed over their heads, but they came up in an instant, and swam capitally; their legs went of themselves, and they were all in the water. The ugly gray Duckling swam with them.

"No, it's not a turkey," said she; "look how well it can use its legs, and how straight it holds itself. It is my own child! On the whole it's quite pretty, if one looks at it rightly. Quack! quack! come with me, and I'll lead you out into the great world, and present you in the duck-yard; but keep close to me, so that no one may tread on you, and take care of the cats!"

And so they came into the duck-yard. There was a terrible riot going on in there, for two families were quarreling about an eel's head, and the cat got it after all.

"See, that's how it goes in the world!" said the Mother-Duck; and she licked her beak, for she too wanted the eel's head. "Only use your legs," she said. "See that you can quack properly, and bow your heads before the old Duck yonder. She's the grandest of all here; she's of Spanish blood—that's why she's so fat; and d'ye see? she has a red rag round her leg; that's something particularly fine,

and the greatest distinction a duck can enjoy; it signifies that one does not want to lose her, and that she's to be recognized by animals and by men too. Shake yourselves —don't turn in your toes; a well brought-up duck turns its toes quite out, just like father and mother—so! Now bend your necks and say, 'Quack!' "

And they did so: but the other ducks round about looked at them, and said quite boldly—

"Look there! now we're to have these hanging on, as if there were not enough of us already! And—fie!—how that duckling yonder looks; we won't stand that!" And one duck flew up at it, and bit it in the neck.

"Let it alone," said the mother; "it does no harm to any one."

"Yes, but it's too large and peculiar," said the Duck who had bitten it; "and therefore it must be put down."

"Those are pretty children that the mother has there," said the old Duck with the rag round her leg. "They're all pretty but that one; that was rather unlucky. I wish she could make it over again."

"That cannot be done, my lady," replied the Mother-Duck. "It is not pretty, but it has a really good disposition, and swims as well as any other; yes, I may even say it swims better. I think it will grow up pretty, and become smaller in time; it has lain too long in the egg, and therefore is not properly shaped." And then she pinched it in the neck, and smoothed its feathers. "Moreover, it is a drake," she said, "and therefore it is not of so much consequence. I think he will be very strong: he makes his way already."

"The other ducklings are graceful enough," said the old Duck. "Make yourself at home; and if you find an eel's head, you may bring it to me."

And now they were at home. But the poor Duckling which had crept last out of the egg, and looked so ugly, was bitten and pushed and jeered, as much by the ducks as by the chickens.

"It is too big!" they all said. And the turkey-cock, who had been born with spurs, and therefore thought himself an emperor, blew himself up like a ship in full sail, and bore straight down upon it; then he gobbled and grew quite red in the face. The poor Duckling did not know where it should stand or walk; it was quite melancholy because it looked ugly, and was the butt of the whole duck-yard.

So it went on the first day; and afterwards it became worse and worse. The poor Duckling was hunted about by every one; even its brothers and sisters were quite angry with it, and said, "If the cat would only catch you, you ugly creature!" And the mother said, "If you were only far away!" And the ducks bit it, and the chickens beat it, and the girl who had to feed the poultry kicked at it with her foot.

Then it ran and flew over the fence, and the little birds in the bushes flew up in fear.

"That is because I am so ugly!" thought the Duckling; and it shut its eyes, but flew on farther, and so it came out into the great moor, where the wild ducks lived. Here it lay the whole night long; and it was weary and miserable.

Towards morning the wild ducks flew up, and looked at their new companion.

"What sort of a one are you?" they asked; and the Duckling turned in every direction, and bowed as well as it could. "You are remarkably ugly!" said the Wild Ducks.

"But that is nothing to us, so long as you do not marry into our family."

Poor thing! it certainly did not think of marrying, and only hoped to obtain leave to lie among the reeds and drink some of the swamp water.

Thus it lay two whole days; then came thither two wild geese, or, properly speaking, two wild ganders. It was not long since each had crept out of an egg, and that's why they were so saucy.

"Listen, comrade," said one of them. "You're so ugly that I like you. Will you go with us, and become a bird of passage? Near here, in another moor, there are a few sweet lovely wild geese, all unmarried, and all able to say *quack!* You've a chance of making your fortune, ugly as you are."

Bang! bang! resounded through the air; and the two ganders fell down dead in the swamp, and the water became blood red. Bang! bang! it sounded again, and the whole flock of wild geese rose up from the reeds. And then there was another report. A great hunt was going on. The sportsmen were lying in wait all round the moor, and some were even sitting up in the branches of the trees, which spread far over the reeds. The blue smoke rose up like clouds among the dark trees, and was wafted far away across the water; and the hunting dogs came—splash, splash!—into the swamp, and the rushes and the reeds bent down on every side. That was a fright for the poor Duckling! It turned its head, and put it under its wing; but at that moment a frightful great dog stood close by the Duckling. His tongue hung far out of his mouth, and his eyes gleamed horrible and ugly; he thrust out his nose close against the Duckling, showed his sharp teeth, and —splash, splash!—on he went, without seizing it.

"Oh, Heaven be thanked!" sighed the Duckling. "I am so ugly that even the dog does not like to bite me!"

And so it lay quite quiet, while the shots rattled through the reeds and gun after gun was fired. At last, late in the day, all was still; but the poor Duckling did not dare to rise up; it waited several hours before it looked round, and then hastened away out of the moor as fast as it could. It ran on over field and meadow; there was such a storm raging that it was difficult to get from one place to another.

Towards evening the Duck came to a little miserable peasant's hut. This hut was so dilapidated that it did not itself know on which side it should fall; and that's why it remained standing. The storm whistled round the Duckling in such a way that the poor creature was obliged to sit down, to stand against it; and the wind blew worse and worse. Then the Duckling noticed that one of the hinges of the door had given way, and the door hung so slanting that the Duckling could slip through the crack into the room; and that is what it did.

Here lived a woman, with her Cat and her Hen. And the Cat, whom she call Sonnie, could arch his back and purr, he could even give out sparks; but for that one had to stroke his fur the wrong way. The Hen had quite little, short legs, and therefore she was called Chickabiddy

Shortshanks; she laid good eggs, and the woman loved her as her own child.

In the morning the strange Duckling was at once noticed, and the Cat began to purr and the Hen to cluck.

"What's this?" said the woman, and looked all round; but she could not see well, and therefore she thought the Duckling was a fat duck that had strayed. "This is a rare prize!" she said. "Now I shall have duck's eggs. I hope it is not a drake. We must find out."

And so the Duckling was admitted on trial for three weeks; but no eggs came. And the Cat was master of the house, and the Hen was the lady, and always said "We and the world!" for she thought they were half the world, and by far the better half.

The Duckling thought one might have a different opinion, but the Hen would not allow it.

"Can you lay eggs?" she asked.

"No."

"Then will you hold your tongue!"

And the Cat said, "Can you curve your back, and purr, and give out sparks?"

"No."

"Then you will please give no opinion of your own when sensible folks are speaking."

And the Duckling sat in a corner and was melancholy; then the fresh air and the sunshine streamed in; and it was seized with such a strange longing to swim on the water, that it could not help telling the Hen of it.

"What are you thinking of?" cried the Hen. "You have

nothing to do, that's why you have these fancies. Lay eggs, or purr, and they will pass over."

"But it is so delicious to swim on the water!" said the Duckling, "so refreshing to let it close above one's head, and to dive down to the bottom."

"Yes, that must be a mighty pleasure, truly," quoth the Hen, "I fancy you must have gone crazy. Ask the Cat about it—he's the cleverest animal I know—ask him if he likes to swim on the water, or to dive down: I won't speak about myself. Ask our mistress, the old woman; no one in the world is cleverer than she. Do you think she has any desire to swim, and to let the water close above her head?"

"You don't understand me," said the Duckling.

"We don't understand you? Then pray who is to understand you? You surely don't pretend to be cleverer than the Cat and the woman—I won't say anything of myself. Don't be conceited, child, and thank your Maker for all the kindness you have received. Did you not get into a warm room, and have you not fallen into company from which you may learn something? But you are a silly fool, and it is not pleasant to associate with you. You may believe me, I speak for your good. I tell you disagreeable things, and by that one may always know one's true friends! Only take care that you learn to lay eggs, or to purr, and give out sparks!"

"I think I will go out into the wide world," said the Duckling.

"Yes, do go," replied the Hen.

And so the Duckling went away. It swam on the water, and dived, but it was slighted by every creature because of its ugliness.

Now came the autumn. The leaves in the forest turned yellow and brown; the wind caught them so that they danced about, and up in the air it was very cold. The clouds hung low, heavy with hail and snow-flakes, and on the fence stood the raven, crying, "Croak! croak!" for mere cold; yes, it was enough to make one feel cold to think of this. The poor little Duckling certainly had not a good time. One evening—the sun was just setting in his beauty—there came a whole flock of great, handsome birds out of the bushes; they were dazzlingly white, with long, flexible necks; they were swans. They uttered a very peculiar cry, spread forth their glorious great wings, and flew away from that cold region to warmer lands, to fair open lakes. They mounted so high, so high! and the ugly Duckling felt strangely uneasy as it watched them. It turned round and round in the water like a wheel, stretched out its neck towards them, and uttered such a strange, loud cry as to frighten itself. Oh! it could not forget those beautiful, happy birds; and as soon as it could see them no longer, it dived down to the very bottom, and when it came up again it was quite beside itself. It knew not the name of those birds, and knew not whither they were flying; but it felt more drawn to them than it had ever been by any other creatures before. It was not at all envious of them. How could it think of wishing to possess such loveliness as they had? It would have been glad if only the ducks would have endured its company—the poor, ugly creature!

And the winter grew cold, very cold! The Duckling was forced to swim about in the water, to prevent the surface from freezing entirely; but every night the hole in which it swam about became smaller and smaller. It froze so hard that the icy covering crackled again; and the Duckling was obliged to use its legs continually to prevent the hole from freezing up. At last it became exhausted, and lay quite still, and thus froze fast into the ice.

Early in the morning a peasant came by, and when he saw what had happened, he took his wooden shoe, broke the ice crust to pieces, and carried the Duckling home to his wife. Then it came to itself again. The children wanted to play with it; but the Duckling thought they wanted to hurt it, and in its terror fluttered up into the milk-pan, so that the milk spurted down into the room. The woman threw up her hands, at which the Duckling flew down into the butter-tub, and then into the meal-barrel and out again. How it looked then! The woman screamed, and struck at it with the fire-tongs; the children tumbled over one another in their efforts to catch the Duckling; and they laughed and they screamed!—lucky it was that the door stood open, and the poor creature was able to slip out between the shrubs into the newly-fallen snow—there it lay quite exhausted.

But it would be too melancholy if I were to tell all the misery and care which the Duckling had to endure in the hard winter. It lay out on the moor among the reeds,

when the sun began to shine again and the larks to sing:
it was a beautiful spring.

Then all at once the Duckling could flap its wings:
they beat the air more strongly than before, and bore it
off vigorously; and before it well knew how all this happened, it found itself in a great garden, where the lilac
trees smelt sweet, and bent their long green branches
down to the canal that wound through the region. Oh,
here it was so beautiful, such a gladness of spring! and
from the thicket came three glorious white swans; they
rustled their wings, and swam lightly on the water. The
Duckling knew the splendid creatures, and felt overcome
by a peculiar sadness.

"I will fly towards them, to the royal birds! and they
will beat me, because I, that am so ugly, dare to come
near them. But it is all the same. Better to be killed by
*them* than to be pursued by ducks, and beaten by fowls,
and pushed about by the girl who takes care of the poultry yard, and to suffer hunger in winter!" And it flew out
into the water, and swam towards the beautiful swans:
these looked at it, and came sailing down upon it with
outspread wings. "Kill me!" said the poor creature, and
bent its head down upon the water, expecting nothing but
death. But what was this that it saw in the clear water?
It beheld its own image; and, lo! it was no longer a
clumsy dark-gray bird, ugly and hateful to look at, but a
—swan!

It matters nothing if one is born in a duck-yard if one
has only come out of a swan's egg.

It felt quite glad at all the misery and misfortune it had suffered, now it appreciated its happiness and all the splendor that surrounded it. And the great swans swam round it, and stroked it with their beaks.

Into the garden came little children, who threw bread and corn into the water; and the youngest cried, "There is a new one!" and the other children shouted joyously, "Yes, a new one has arrived!" And they clapped their hands and danced about, and ran to their father and mother; and bread and cake were thrown into the water; and they all said, "The new one is the most beautiful of all! so young and handsome!" And the old swans bowed their heads before him. Then he felt quite ashamed, and hid his head under his wings, for he did not know what to do; he was so happy, and yet not at all proud. He thought how he had been persecuted and despised; and now he heard them saying that he was the most beautiful of all birds. Even the lilac tree bent its branches straight down into the water before him, and the sun shone warm and mild. Then his wings rustled, he lifted his slender neck, and cried rejoicingly from the depths of his heart—

"I never dreamed of so much happiness when I was the Ugly Duckling!"

CAROLYN HAYWOOD

# What Happened to the Only Pear

Close to the side porch of the Robinsons' house there grew a pear tree. It was a very special kind of pear tree and Mr. Robinson was very proud of it. He would always say to visitors, "This is a very fine pear tree. There isn't another like it for miles around. I am looking forward to having some good pears."

The visitors would always nod their heads and look very wise as though they knew all about pear trees.

In the spring the pear tree was covered with lovely white blossoms, but a late frost nipped them. Mr. Perkins said it was too bad, because it meant that the tree would not bear much fruit.

For a long time, it looked as though there were not going to be any pears, but one day Babs saw a tiny green pear hanging from one of the branches. She called Teddy to look at it.

"Sure 'nuff," said Teddy. "That's a pear, all right."

Off they ran to spread the news. Everyone was excited about the one pear.

Week after week, the children watched the pear grow. Teddy called it "Daddy's Pear," because Daddy said that he didn't want anything to happen to it.

The pear grew larger and larger. By September it was so big and heavy that it almost touched the porch roof. The pear was no longer green but a pale yellow.It showed very plainly against the green leaves. Babs could see it from her bedroom window. "If my arm was as long as a giraffe's neck, I could reach right out the window and pick the pear," thought Babs. But Babs knew that Daddy had said that no one should pick the pear.

Every time the children walked under the pear tree they would look up at the pear. Sometimes they would jump and make believe to pick it. Now that it was almost ripe, it didn't look as far away as it had when it was green.

One day the children were lying on the grass under the tree.

"You know what!" said Peter. "I'll bet if I stood on a ladder, I could reach that pear."

"Well, you better not," said Teddy. "Daddy says that no one is to pick that pear. It's Daddy's pear."

"Do you suppose it's soft yet?" said Jane.

"It looks soft," said Babs.

A few days later, Teddy and Babs and Peter came 'round the corner of the house. "Jane! Oh, Jane!" they called.

There was no answer.

"Where do you s'pose she is?" said Peter.

"Jane! Oh, Jane!" they cried. There was still no answer.

The children sat down under the pear tree. "That's funny," said Teddy. "Where do you suppose Jane went?"

"Maybe she went to the postoffice with your grandaddy," said Babs.

Teddy lay down on his back. "Why, there she is!" he cried; "up in the pear tree."

"Say, what are you doing up in the pear tree?" Peter called.

"I was just hiding, that was all," said Jane.

"I'll bet you were feeling that pear," said Babs.

"Well, it isn't soft yet," said Jane.

"You better leave Daddy's pear alone," said Teddy.

"I didn't hurt it," said Jane, as she climbed down.

"Did you smell it?" asked Babs.

"No, but I'll bet in another week it will be ripe," replied Jane.

"What do you suppose your daddy is going to do with it?" said Peter.

"I don't know," said Teddy. "I guess he's going to eat it."

The pear grew lovelier every day. One side turned a beautiful pink. Daddy warned the children again that they were not to pick the pear.

One day Mother went to the city. Teddy and Babs spent the morning playing trains on the stairs. Teddy's Uncle Bill had sent him a brand-new ticket puncher. Teddy went up and down the stairs punching the tickets of all the dolls and stuffed animals who were riding on the train. Sometimes he would let Babs be the conductor and she would punch the tickets. After a while Babs called out, "There goes Peter! I wonder where he is going with that little ladder?"

Teddy rushed to the door. "Peter," he called, "do you want to come and play?"

Peter didn't answer. Teddy ran after him. "Peter!" he cried. "Wait for me."

Peter turned 'round and waited for Teddy. "What were you doing with the ladder?" asked Teddy.

"Oh, I just needed it to get my ball," replied Peter.

"I've got a new ticket puncher," said Teddy.

"Can I punch with it?" asked Peter, as he stood the ladder in the tool shed.

The two little boys sat down behind the tool shed to

look at the ticket puncher.

Babs went upstairs to her room. She decided to change her best doll's dress. It was really very dirty. Babs took off all of her doll's clothes. Then she gave her a bath and dried her with a towel. After she was dressed in fresh, clean clothes, she looked very beautiful. Babs set her on the window-sill. Then she looked out of the window. The sun was shining on the sloping roof of the porch. It was a lovely warm September sun. Not hot like the summer sun. Babs suddenly thought it would be lovely to be on the porch roof. She had never thought of doing this before, but now she opened the screen and stepped out of the window. She lay down. It was nice to feel the warm sunshine on her arms and legs. She stayed quite a long time.

After a while Babs heard Jane calling her. Jane had spied her on the roof. "What are you doing up on the roof?" said Jane.

"Oh, nothing!" replied Babs. "I'm coming down now."

Babs climbed in the window and ran downstairs to Jane.

After lunch, Babs drove into town with Mr. Perkins. Teddy and Peter went off to the brook to run Peter's toy motor boat.

Jane didn't want to get her new blue and white striped dress dirty, so she decided to color pictures. She lay down under the pear tree and set to work.

Sometime later, Teddy came back from the brook alone. He had come back to get his little toy canoe. Jane was gone. There was no one around. As he went into the house, he could hear a fly buzzing on the screen-door. The house seemed very quiet.

Teddy went upstairs to his room. He found the little canoe on his mantelshelf. Then he wandered over to Babs' room. There didn't seem to be a soul in the house. The screen was still open at the window. Teddy walked over to the window and looked out.

Meanwhile, Peter sat beside the brook. He wondered what Teddy could be doing. He had been gone such a long time. Peter threw stones into the brook. Then he watched a frog catching flies. Finally, he decided to go home. When he reached the house, Jane was in the kitchen helping her grandmother to cut cookies. "Did you see Teddy?" asked Peter.

"No," replied Jane. "I haven't seen him all afternoon."

About five o'clock, Mother came back from the city. The children were nowhere in sight. She walked out on the porch. "I wonder where they are," she thought.

Just then she looked up into the pear tree. She looked for the pear. The beautiful pear was gone. There, hanging from the branch over the roof of the porch, was the core of the pear. The rest of it had been eaten away. She could still see the marks of little teeth. Just as she was turning away from the tree, she saw a piece of blue and white striped material hanging from a limb. "Oh!" said Mother. "I see! The one who ate the pear was wearing blue and white stripes." She took the little rag off the tree.

"Teddy!" she called. "Babs! Where are you?" All was quiet.

At last, Teddy came up from the pasture and Babs came back from town.

Mother sent Teddy for Peter and Jane. When the four children had gathered around Mrs. Robinson, she said, "Children, something terrible has happened."

She pointed up into the tree. The children looked up at the core of the pear. "Oh!" they gasped, and their faces were very grave.

"Jane," said Mrs. Robinson, "is this a piece of your dress?"

"Yes, Mrs. Robinson," said Jane.

"Did you climb up into the pear tree today?" Mrs. Robinson asked.

"Yes, I did," replied Jane, "but I didn't eat the pear."

Jane looked at Babs. "Babs, you were up on the roof this morning; I'll bet you ate it."

"Did you eat it, Babs?" asked Mother.

"No, Mother," said Babs, "but I saw Peter with a little ladder this morning."

"Peter," said Mrs. Robinson, "did you do it?"

"No, Mrs. Robinson," answered Peter. "I just had the ladder to get my ball. It went up on the window-sill."

Mrs. Robinson turned to Teddy. "Teddy," she said, "did you pick the pear?"

Teddy hung his head.

"Teddy," said Mother, "didn't Daddy tell you that you were not to pick that pear?"

"But, Mother," said Teddy, "I didn't pick it, I only ate it."

Mother marched Teddy upstairs. She put him right to bed. When dinner time came, she brought him a bowl of cereal. "Can't I have any dessert?" asked Teddy.

"No," replied Mother, "you had your dessert when you ate Daddy's pear."

"Is Daddy very angry with me?" asked Teddy.

"Very," said Mother.

"What do you think he will do to me?" Teddy asked.

"I don't know," answered Mother.

Teddy lay alone in the dark. He could hear Mother and Daddy talking downstairs. Sometimes he could hear Babs. He felt very lonely. Pretty soon, he heard Babs go to bed.

A long time afterwards he heard Mother and Daddy come upstairs. He wondered whether Daddy would come in and sit on his bed. He always did. Teddy waited and waited. All the lights were out now. The house was so quiet Teddy could hear the clock tick. "Daddy isn't coming," thought Teddy. "He isn't coming. Daddy is going to stay cross with me all night." Teddy began to cry. He wished, oh, how he wished, he had not eaten the pear!

After a while, Teddy got up and tip-toed to the door of Daddy's room. He opened the door. "Daddy!" he called, very softly. "Daddy!"

"Yes, Teddy," replied Daddy.

"I can't go to sleep, Daddy," said Teddy. "Can I come in your bed?"

"Come on," said Daddy.

Teddy climbed into bed with Daddy. He snuggled

up close beside him. "Daddy," he said, "I'll give you my new ticket puncher."

"Thanks, Teddy," replied Daddy.

"It's a very nice ticket puncher," said Teddy. "It punches little holes shaped like a star. I'll give you anything of mine you want, Daddy."

Daddy put his arm around his little boy.

"Daddy," said Teddy, "I didn't know that I was going to eat it. The window was open and I just thought that I would like to smell it. So I climbed out and it smelled so good, I thought I would take just a little tiny bite, where it wouldn't show. And then I took another bite and pretty soon it was all gone."

"Yes," said Daddy, "that is the way naughty things happen."

"Will you forgive me this time, Daddy?"

"Yes," said Daddy, "I'll forgive you. Now go to sleep."

"Daddy," said Teddy, "it was an awful good pear."

*from* A. A. MILNE'S

# Winnie-the-Pooh

*Winnie-the-Pooh is a teddy bear whose nonsense adventures with Piglet, the stuffed pig, Eeyore, the donkey (the kind you pin the tail to), Owl, Kanga, Roo, and his special friend Christopher Robin, have made boys and girls laugh for a long time. Here is the story of Eeyore's birthday party.*

## EEYORE HAS A BIRTHDAY AND GETS TWO PRESENTS

Eeyore, the old grey Donkey, stood by the side of the stream, and looked at himself in the water.

"Pathetic," he said. "That's what it is. Pathetic."

He turned and walked slowly down the stream for twenty yards, splashed across it, and walked slowly back on the other side. Then he looked at himself in the water again.

"As I thought," he said. "No better from *this* side. But nobody minds. Nobody cares. Pathetic, that's what it is."

There was a crackling noise in the bracken behind him, and out came Pooh.

"Good morning, Eeyore," said Pooh.

"Good morning, Pooh Bear," said Eeyore gloomily. "If it *is* a good morning," he said. "Which I doubt," said he.

"Why, what's the matter?"

"Nothing, Pooh Bear, nothing. We can't all, and some of us don't. That's all there is to it."

"Can't all *what?*" said Pooh, rubbing his nose.

"Gaiety. Song-and-dance. Here we go round the mulberry bush."

"Oh!" said Pooh. He thought for a long time, and then asked, "What mulberry bush is that?"

"Bon-hommy," went on Eeyore gloomily. "French word meaning bonhommy," he explained. "I'm not complaining, but There It Is."

Pooh sat down on a large stone, and tried to think this out. It sounded to him like a riddle, and he was never much good at riddles, being a Bear of Very Little Brain. So he sang *Cottleston Pie* instead:

> *Cottleston, Cottleston, Cottleston Pie.*
> *A fly can't bird, but a bird can fly.*
> *Ask me a riddle and I reply:*
> "Cottleston, Cottleston, Cottleston Pie."

That was the first verse. When he had finished it, Eeyore didn't actually say that he didn't like it, so Pooh very kindly sang the second verse to him:

> *Cottleston, Cottleston, Cottleston Pie,*
> *A fish can't whistle and neither can I.*
> *Ask me a riddle and I reply:*
> "Cottleston, Cottleston, Cottleston Pie."

Eeyore still said nothing at all, so Pooh hummed the third verse quietly to himself:

> *Cottleston, Cottleston, Cottleston Pie,*
> *Why does a chicken, I don't know why.*
> *Ask me a riddle and I reply:*
> *"Cottleston, Cottleston, Cottleston Pie."*

"That's right," said Eeyore. "Sing. Umty-tiddly, umty-too. Here we go gathering Nuts and May. Enjoy yourself."

"I am," said Pooh.

"Some can," said Eeyore.

"Why, what's the matter?"

"*Is* anything the matter?"

"You seem so sad, Eeyore."

"Sad? Why should I be sad? It's my birthday. The happiest day of the year."

"Your birthday?" said Pooh in great surprise.

"Of course it is. Can't you see? Look at all the presents I have had." He waved a foot from side to side. "Look at the birthday cake. Candles and pink sugar."

Pooh looked—first to the right and then to the left.

"Presents?" said Pooh. "Birthday cake?" said Pooh. "*Where?*"

"Can't you see them?"

"No," said Pooh.

"Neither can I," said Eeyore. "Joke," he explained. "Ha ha!"

Pooh scratched his head, being a little puzzled by all this.

"But is it really your birthday?" he asked.

"It is."

"Oh! Well, many happy returns of the day, Eeyore."

"And many happy returns to you, Pooh Bear."

"But it isn't *my* birthday."

"No, it's mine."

"But you said 'Many happy returns'——"

"Well, why not? You don't always want to be miserable on my birthday, do you?"

"Oh, I see," said Pooh.

"It's bad enough," said Eeyore, almost breaking down, "being miserable myself, what with no presents and no cake and no candles, and no proper notice taken of me at all, but if everybody else is going to be miserable too——"

This was too much for Pooh. "Stay there!" he called to Eeyore, as he turned and hurried back home as quick as he could; for he felt that he must get poor Eeyore a present of *some* sort at once, and he could always think of a proper one afterwards.

Outside his house he found Piglet, jumping up and down trying to reach the knocker.

"Hallo, Piglet," he said.

"Hallo, Pooh," said Piglet.

"What are *you* trying to do?"

"I was trying to reach the knocker," said Piglet. "I just came round——"

"Let me do it for you," said Pooh kindly. So he reached up and knocked at the door. "I have just seen Eeyore," he began, "and poor Eeyore is in a Very Sad

Condition, because it's his birthday, and nobody has taken any notice of it, and he's very Gloomy—you

*Illustration by E. H. Shepard*

know what Eeyore is—and there he was, and—— What a long time whoever lives here is answering this door." And he knocked again.

"But Pooh," said Piglet, "it's your own house!"

"Oh!" said Pooh. "So it is," he said. "Well, let's go in."

So in they went. The first thing Pooh did was to go to the cupboard to see if he had quite a small jar of honey left; and he had, so he took it down.

"I'm giving this to Eeyore," he explained, "as a present. What are *you* going to give?"

"Couldn't I give it too?" said Piglet. "From both of us?"

"No," said Pooh. "That would *not* be a good plan."

"All right, then, I'll give him a balloon. I've got one left from my party. I'll go and get it now, shall I?"

"That, Piglet, is a *very* good idea. It is just what

Eeyore wants to cheer him up. Nobody can be uncheered with a balloon."

So off Piglet trotted; and in the other direction went Pooh, with his jar of honey.

It was a warm day, and he had a long way to go. He hadn't gone more than half-way when a sort of funny feeling began to creep all over him. It began at the tip of his nose and trickled all through him and out at the soles of his feet. It was just as if somebody inside him were saying, "Now then, Pooh, time for a little something."

"Dear, dear," said Pooh, "I didn't know it was as late as that." So he sat down and took the top off his jar of honey. "Lucky I brought this with me," he thought. "Many a bear going out on a warm day like this would never have thought of bringing a little something with him." And he began to eat.

"Now let me see," he thought, as he took his last lick of the inside of the jar, "where was I going? Ah, yes, Eeyore." He got up slowly.

And then, suddenly, he remembered. He had eaten Eeyore's birthday present!

"*Bother!*" said Pooh. "What *shall* I do? I *must* give him *something*."

For a little while he couldn't think of anything. Then he thought: "Well, it's a very nice pot, even if there's no honey in it, and if I washed it clean, and got somebody to write 'A *Happy Birthday*' on it, Eeyore could keep things in it, which might be Useful." So, as he was just passing the Hundred Acre Wood, he went inside to call on Owl, who lived there.

"Good morning, Owl," he said.

"Good morning, Pooh," said Owl.

"Many happy returns of Eeyore's birthday," said Pooh.

"Oh, is that what it is?"

"What are you giving him, Owl?"

"What are *you* giving him, Pooh?"

"I'm giving him a Useful Pot to Keep Things In, and I wanted to ask you——"

"Is this it?" said Owl, taking it out of Pooh's paw.

"Yes, and I wanted to ask you——"

"Somebody has been keeping honey in it," said Owl.

"You can keep *anything* in it," said Pooh earnestly. "It's Very Useful like that. And I wanted to ask you——"

"You ought to write 'A *Happy Birthday*' on it."

"*That* was what I wanted to ask you," said Pooh. "Because my spelling is Wobbly. It's good spelling but it Wobbles, and the letters get in the wrong places. Would *you* write 'A Happy Birthday' on it for me?"

"It's a nice pot," said Owl, looking at it all round. "Couldn't I give it too? From both of us?"

"No," said Pooh. "That would *not* be a good plan. Now I'll just wash it first, and then you can write on it."

Well, he washed the pot out, and dried it, while Owl licked the end of his pencil, and wondered how to spell "birthday."

"Can you read, Pooh?" he asked, a little anxiously. "There's a notice about knocking and ringing outside my door, which Christopher Robin wrote. Could you read it?"

"Christopher Robin told me what it said, and *then* I could."

"Well, I'll tell you what *this* says, and then you'll be able to."

So Owl wrote . . . and this is what he wrote:

HIPY PAPY BTHUTHDTH
THUTHDA BTHUTHDY.

Pooh looked on admiringly.

"I'm just saying 'A Happy Birthday,'" said Owl carelessly.

"It's a nice long one," said Pooh, very much impressed by it.

"Well, *actually*, of course, I'm saying 'A Very Happy Birthday with love from Pooh.' Naturally it takes a good deal of pencil to say a long thing like that."

"Oh, I see," said Pooh.

While all this was happening, Piglet had gone back to his own house to get Eeyore's balloon. He held it very tightly against himself, so that it shouldn't blow away, and he ran as fast as he could so as to get to Eeyore before Pooh did; for he thought that he would like to be the first one to give a present, just as if he had thought of it without being told by anybody. And running along, and thinking how pleased Eeyore would be, he didn't look where he was going . . . and suddenly he put his foot in a rabbit hole, and fell down flat on his face.

BANG!!!???***!!!

Piglet lay there, wondering what had happened. At

first he thought that the whole world had blown up; and then he thought that perhaps only the Forest part of it had; and then he thought that perhaps only *he* had, and he was now alone in the moon or somewhere, and would never see Christopher Robin or Pooh or Eeyore again. And then he thought, "Well, even if I'm in the moon, I needn't be face downwards all the time," so he got cautiously up and looked about him.

He was still in the Forest!

*Illustration by E. H. Shepard*

"Well, that's funny," he thought. "I wonder what that bang was. I couldn't have made such a noise just falling down. And where's my balloon? And what's that small piece of damp rag doing?"

It was the balloon!

"Oh, dear!" said Piglet. "Oh, dear, oh, dearie, dearie, dear! Well, it's too late now. I can't go back, and I haven't another balloon, and perhaps Eeyore doesn't *like* balloons so *very* much."

So he trotted on, rather sadly now, and down he came to the side of the stream where Eeyore was, and called out to him.

"Good morning, Eeyore," shouted Piglet.

"Good morning, Little Piglet," said Eeyore. "If it *is* a

good morning," he said. "Which I doubt," said he. "Not that it matters," he said.

"Many happy returns of the day," said Piglet, having now got closer.

Eeyore stopped looking at himself in the stream, and turned to stare at Piglet.

"Just say that again," he said.

"Many hap——"

"Wait a moment."

Balancing on three legs, he began to bring his fourth leg very cautiously up to his ear. "I did this yesterday," he explained, as he fell down for the third time. "It's quite easy. It's so as I can hear better. . . . There, that's done it! Now then, what were you saying?" He pushed his ear forward with his hoof.

"Many happy returns of the day," said Piglet again.

"Meaning me?"

"Of course, Eeyore."

"My birthday?"

"Yes."

"Me having a real birthday?"

"Yes, Eeyore, and I've brought you a present."

Eeyore took down his right hoof from his right ear, turned round, and with great difficulty put up his left hoof.

"I must have that in the other ear," he said. "Now then."

"A present," said Piglet very loudly.

"Meaning me again?"

"Yes."

"My birthday still?"

"Of course, Eeyore."

"Me going on having a real birthday?"

"Yes, Eeyore, and I brought you a balloon."

"*Balloon?*" said Eeyore. "You did say balloon? One of those big coloured things you blow up? Gaiety, song-and-dance, here we are and there we are?"

"Yes, but I'm afraid—I'm very sorry, Eeyore—but when I was running along to bring it you, I fell down."

"Dear, dear, how unlucky! You ran too fast, I expect. You didn't hurt yourself, Little Piglet?"

"No, but I—I —oh, Eeyore, I burst the balloon!"

There was a very long silence.

"My balloon?" said Eeyore at last.

Piglet nodded.

"My birthday balloon?"

"Yes, Eeyore," said Piglet sniffing a little. "Here it is. With—with many happy returns of the day." And he gave Eeyore the small piece of damp rag.

"Is this it?" said Eeyore, a little surprised.

Piglet nodded.

"My present?"

Piglet nodded again.

"The balloon?"

"Yes."

"Thank you, Piglet," said Eeyore. "You don't mind my asking," he went on, "but what colour was this balloon when it—when it *was* a balloon?"

"Red."

"I just wondered. . . . Red," he murmured to himself. "My favourite colour. . . . How big was it?"

"About as big as me."

"I just wondered. . . . About as big as Piglet," he said to himself sadly. "My favourite size. Well, well."

Piglet felt very miserable, and didn't know what to say. He was still opening his mouth to begin something, and then deciding that it wasn't any good saying *that*, when he heard a shout from the other side of the river, and there was Pooh.

"Many happy returns of the day," called out Pooh, forgetting that he had said it already.

"Thank you, Pooh, I'm having them," said Eeyore gloomily.

"I've brought you a little present," said Pooh excitedly.

"I've had it," said Eeyore.

Pooh had now splashed across the stream to Eeyore, and Piglet was sitting a little way off, his head in his paws, snuffling to himself.

"It's a Useful Pot," said Pooh. "Here it is. And it's got 'A Very Happy Birthday with love from Pooh' written on it. That's what all that writing is. And it's for putting things in. There!"

When Eeyore saw the pot, he became quite excited.

"Why!" he said. "I believe my Balloon will just go into that Pot!"

"Oh, no, Eeyore," said Pooh. "Balloons are much too

big to go into Pots. What you do with a balloon is, you hold the balloon——"

"Not mine," said Eeyore proudly. "Look, Piglet!" And as Piglet looked sorrowfully round, Eeyore picked the balloon up with his teeth, and placed it carefully in the pot; picked it out and put it on the ground; and then picked it up again and put it carefully back.

"So it does!" said Pooh. "It goes in!"

"So it does!" said Piglet. "And it comes out!"

"Doesn't it?" said Eeyore. "It goes in and out like anything."

"I'm very glad," said Pooh happily, "that I thought of giving you a Useful Pot to put things in."

"I'm very glad," said Piglet happily, "that I thought of giving you Something to put in a Useful Pot."

But Eeyore wasn't listening. He was taking the balloon out, and putting it back again, as happy as could be. . . .

"And didn't *I* give him anything?" asked Christopher Robin sadly.

"Of course you did," I said. "You gave him—don't you remember—a little—a little——"

"I gave him a box of paint to paint things with."

"That was it."

"Why didn't I give it to him in the morning?"

"You were so busy getting his party ready for him. He had a cake with icing on the top, and three candles, and his name in pink sugar, and——"

"Yes, *I* remember," said Christopher Robin.

RICHARD HUGHES

# The Wishing-Shell

There was once a little boy making sand castles
while the tide came in. He was very good at building
sand castles and used to make the most grand kind of ones,
with a square keep in the middle and a wall all round,
and a moat, and a bridge at the way in. The exciting time
of course was when the tide reached them, and filled the
moat first. Then presently there would be sea all round
the whole castle, rising up till it broke down a chunk of
the wall and poured into the inside of the castle itself.

While he was building one of these castles, the little
boy noticed a very pretty little shell in some sand he was
handling. He picked it out, and it seemed to have some
tiny writing on it, much too small for a person's eye to
read. The little boy peered and peered, but he didn't have
a magnifying glass.

"Oh, I wish I were small enough to read that writing!" he sadly said.

No sooner had he said that than he found himself
shrinking, until before long he was no bigger than the
top of your finger. When he was that size the shell

seemed to him about the size of a table, and he could read what was written on it easily:

"I am the Magic Wishing-Shell," it said, which explained of course why his wish to become small had come true.

But the tide, you remember, was coming in, and suddenly the little boy found it was almost up to where he was standing. Now anybody the size he was can't run very fast, because his legs are too short, and he soon realized the tide was coming in much too fast for him to be able to get away from it. Then he got in a fright and forgot all about the magic wishing-shell (which might have helped him). Instead he ran to his castle that he had built. It looked so big and solid (for now it was as big to him as an ordinary castle is to you and me), and the grains of sand looked almost as big as bricks or stones.

"I'll go in that fine castle I have made," he said. "The sea cannot *possibly* get in there!"

So he scuttled through the tunnel at the entrance, and scrambled up the steep sides of the ramparts, and finally got right on top of the keep itself, and there he thought he was safe.

But not a bit of it, as you can guess! The sea was coming in quickly, and the sea was hungry. In no time it was swallowing great chunks of his castle, and it was impossible now to run away, for the sea stretched many yards inland from where the castle stood!

Just as he thought he was bound to be drowned in a minute, the little boy noticed a match-box floating in the water. By good luck it had floated right against the castle itself. It was his only chance, so he jumped into it, and hoped it would make a good boat. There was nothing to row it with, but there was one match inside, so he set it up as a mast, and fastened his coat to it as a sail, and hoped the wind would blow him ashore.

Now, all the time the little boy had been building his sand castle, his sister had been riding her donkey. She had galloped it far up the beach, and now she had galloped it back again, and was looking for her brother. But he was nowhere to be seen.

"I expect he has gone home," she said to herself, and then she had the fine idea of riding her donkey into the water. The donkey did not want to go, at first, and did not seem to like the little waves tickling his legs, but she made him, and presently he was walking through the sea, up to his knees.

That was when the little girl noticed the match-box, floating in the water with its little sail up. There was a tiny pink thing inside it: but it never entered her head of course that the tiny pink thing was her brother!

"Oh, look!" she thought. "Some child has been making a boat, and put a shrimp in for a sailor."

Leaning down out of the saddle (which she was rather proud of being able to do) she picked the boat and the sailor too out of the water. When the little boy knew it was his sister who had picked him up like this, he was ashamed of letting her see him so small, so he scuttled out of the boat into the donkey's mane, and tried to hold on to the hair and hide there. But he was afraid she would find him, even there, so he scrambled as fast as he could up the donkey's neck, and hid in one of the donkey's ears.

Now it so happens that the inside of a donkey's ears is one of the most ticklish parts of him, and when the little boy settled down among the soft fur there, the donkey did not like it a bit. He wriggled his ear until the little boy was giddy, and then he shook his head until the little boy's teeth chattered. But the donkey could not shake the little boy out. At that the donkey lost his temper altogether and began to kick. He kicked so hard that with the third kick he sent the little boy's sister clean over his head, splash into the sea. Then he bolted up the beach with the stirrups flapping, and the little boy still clinging on for dear life to the inside of his ear. As for the sister, the water of course was not very deep, but it was deep enough to give her a thorough sousing. But, wet as she was, she wasn't going to let the donkey go, and instead of going home to change, she chased him all over the sandy shore.

The donkey was not going to be caught—not so long as he had that horrible tickly thing in his ear. It drove him half crazy. He saw a tent on the sands and tried to rub his head on it, but all he succeeded in doing was pushing the tent over. The people inside the tent struggled under the canvas to get out. They looked so queer that it frightened him, and off he went again.

Next he came to a bungalow, where a party of people were having tea on a little table outside. He charged straight up to them, and tried to rub his head on the table. They shouted and squawked and tried to stop him. That made him angry with them, so he turned round and gave another of his famous kicks. This time it landed fair and square under the tea-table. The tea-table, tea, cups and saucers—everything went up in the air with a loud bang, like a curious kind of fountain, and fell with splashes and crashes on the people who were having tea.

But that last kick did finally shake the little boy out of the donkey's ear, and once that was done the donkey became good again, and trotted off home—where he arrived long before his mistress.

But meanwhile, the little boy had fallen flump on a man's lap, slipped on to his knee, tumbled the whole way down his shin, and landed in the turned-up bottom of his trousers.

"Here I stop for a bit," said the little boy. "For if I get onto the ground, with so much trampling going on I am bound to be trodden on."

Presently the man got up and walked, and that was a very funny feeling for the little boy. It was like being in a ship when there is a long swell. In fact it nearly made him seasick, the long slow swing of the man's legs.

Now it so happened that the turn-up belonged to trousers which belonged to a leg which belonged to a man who was not a good man at all, but in fact a robber, and now that his tea had been spoilt he felt in the mood to go off and rob. If it had been night-time, he would have set about some big robbery. He would have taken a gun and his best robbing tools, and broken into a bank (for instance) to steal the money that was locked up there. But it was still daylight, and moreover there were no banks near. In fact there was no one in sight but a fat toddling baby flying a balloon.

"Well," he thought, "I feel I must rob something, and even a baby's balloon is better than nothing!"

So he marched along in a frightening sort of way up to the baby, and snatched away its balloon. Of course the baby set up a frightful howling, but that only pleased the wicked robber, because he always enjoyed his robbing more if the people really minded being robbed. Then he noticed the baby had a shell in its other hand, so he snatched that too.

"Ha!" he said as he walked away carrying the balloon and the shell, "but I do wish there was a bank or something here really worth robbing!"

Now no sooner had he said that than a bank suddenly grew up out of the sand. It was all complete, with a shiny brass plate on the door saying that it was "The Sand Bank," and "Open Every Day except Saturdays from 10 till 3." The robber of course was delighted, and started pulling burglaring tools out of every pocket, and set to work to bust in the door. He never stopped to wonder why the bank had come. He did not know of course that the shell he had taken from the baby was the wishing-shell, and he carelessly dropped it. And by good luck it fell into the turn-up of his trousers where the little boy was.

**And** there is another thing. The robber did not notice
(so busy was he working on the door) that the tide was
still coming in, and that presently it was round him and
the bank too. But the little boy noticed, of course, as
soon as the water was splashing over the robber's ankles.
He knew he must escape at once, or again he ran the risk
of being drowned. The robber did not care tuppence for
the balloon either, now, and was just going to let go of the
string when the little boy managed to get hold of the end
with one hand, while with the other he hung onto the
wishing-shell with all his might. Then the balloon floated
away into the air, with the little boy hanging on to it,
up and up into the sky.

"Oh, dear!" said the little boy to himself when he was
about a hundred feet above the sea, "I wish I was big
again."

Now no ordinary-sized boy is going to be held up in
the air by a little rubber balloon, so the moment he was
big again he began to fall. Quick as thought he wished
once more:

"I wish this was a real balloon," he said, and then in a
second it was one—one of those big flying-balloons,
round, with a basket underneath for a man to sit in, such
as people used for flying before they had aeroplanes. And
there was the little boy sitting in the basket, and once
more rising up into the sky.

Now it was very interesting to see all the places he knew
from so high up in the air, spread out under him like a
map. But he soon noticed that the wind was blowing out

to sea, and of course blowing the balloon along with it. The little boy had not the faintest idea how wide the sea was, or what lay on the other side, but it was evening now, and he did not a bit want to spend the night alone in a balloon lost out over the sea.

"I wish," he said, "I wish I were safe home again."

As soon as he said that the balloon seemed to rock and sway in the most giddy-making way, and then to blow up with a loud bang. The little boy felt himself falling, falling, falling . . . and suddenly landed with a thump in his own bed. He sat up and rubbed his eyes. He looked at himself: and sure enough he had got his pyjamas on.

"Oh, dear," he thought, "can it have been only a dream, or did I really have these adventures?"

Then he looked across the room to where his sister's bed was. It was empty. So he slipped out and crept quietly down the stairs to see where she was, and into the kitchen. There she sat, wrapped in a dressing-gown drinking hot milk by the fire, while her mother was drying her wet clothes and scolding her:

"You really ought to have more sense than to ride your donkey into the sea like that, and then get kicked off!"

So she really had ridden her donkey into the sea! When he heard that the little boy crept back to bed, and knew indeed that all his adventures had been true and not a dream at all.

# The Wolf and the Seven Little Kids

There was once an old goat who had seven little ones, and was as fond of them as ever mother was of her children. One day she had to go into the wood to fetch food for them, so she called them all round her.

"Dear children," said she, "I am going out into the wood; and while I am gone, be on your guard against the wolf, for if he were once to get inside he would eat you up, skin, bones, and all. The wretch often disguises himself, but he may always be known by his hoarse voice and black paws."

"Dear mother," answered the kids, "you need not be afraid, we will take good care of ourselves." And the mother bleated good-bye, and went on her way with an easy mind.

It was not long before some one came knocking at the house-door, and crying out,

"Open the door, my dear children, your mother is come back, and has brought each of you something."

But the little kids knew it was the wolf by the hoarse voice.

"We will not open the door," cried they; "you are not our mother, she has a delicate and sweet voice, and your voice is hoarse; you must be the wolf."

Then off went the wolf to a shop and bought a big lump of chalk, and ate it up to make his voice soft. And then he came back, knocked at the house-door, and cried,

"Open the door, my dear children, your mother is here, and has brought each of you something."

But the wolf had put up his black paws against the window, and the kids seeing this, cried out,

"We will not open the door; our mother has no black paws like you; you must be the wolf."

The wolf then ran to a baker.

"Baker," said he, "I am hurt in the foot; pray spread some dough over the place."

And when the baker had plastered his feet, he ran to the miller.

"Miller," said he, "strew me some white meal over my paws." But the miller refused, thinking the wolf must be meaning harm to some one.

"If you don't do it," cried the wolf, "I'll eat you up!"

And the miller was afraid and did as he was told. And that just shows what men are.

And now came the rogue the third time to the door and knocked. "Open, children!" cried he. "Your dear mother has come home, and brought you each something from the wood."

"First show us your paws," said the kids, "so that we may know if you are really our mother or not."

And he put up his paws against the window, and when they saw that they were white, all seemed right, and they opened the door; and when he was inside they saw it was the wolf, and they were terrified and tried to hide themselves. One ran under the table, the second got into the bed, the third into the oven, the fourth in the kitchen, the fifth in the cupboard, the sixth under the sink, the seventh in the clock-case. But the wolf found them all, and gave them short shrift; one after the other he swallowed down, all but the youngest, who was hid in the clock-case. And so the wolf, having got what he wanted, strolled forth into the green meadows, and laying himself down under a tree, he fell asleep.

Not long after, the mother goat came back from the wood; and, oh! what a sight met her eyes! the door was standing wide open, table, chairs, and stools all thrown about, dishes broken, quilt and pillows torn off the bed. She sought her children, they were nowhere to be found. She called to each of them by name, but nobody answered, until she came to the name of the youngest.

"Here I am, mother," a little voice cried, "here, in the clock-case."

And so she helped him out, and heard how the wolf had come, and eaten all the rest. And you may think how she cried for the loss of her dear children. At last in her grief she wandered out of doors, and the youngest kid with her; and when they came into the meadow, there

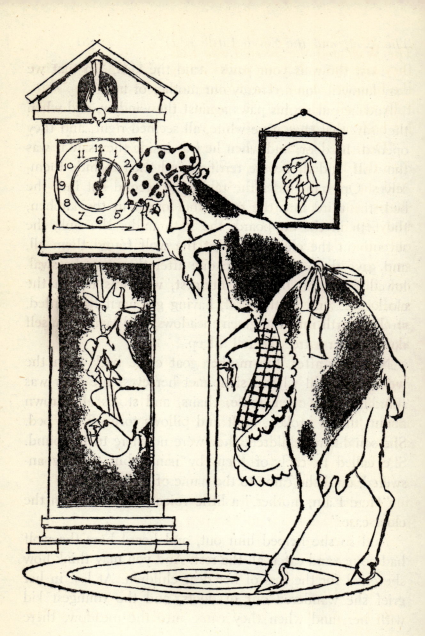

they saw the wolf lying under a tree, and snoring so that the branches shook. The mother goat looked at him carefully on all sides and she noticed how something inside his body was moving and struggling.

"Dear me!" thought she, "can it be that my poor children that he devoured for his evening meal are still alive?" And she sent the little kid back to the house for a pair of shears, and needle, and thread. Then she cut the wolf's body open, and no sooner had she made one snip than out came the head of one of the kids, and then another snip, and then one after the other the six kids all jumped out alive and well, for in his greediness the rogue had swallowed them down whole. How delightful this was! so they comforted their dear mother and hopped about like tailors at a wedding.

"Now fetch some good hard stones," said the mother, "and we will fill his body with them, as he lies asleep."

And so they fetched some in all haste, and put them inside him, and the mother sewed him up so quickly again that he was none the wiser.

When the wolf at last awoke, and got up, the stones inside him made him feel very thirsty, and as he was going to the brook to drink, they struck and rattled one against another. And so he cried out:

> "What is this I feel inside me
> Knocking hard against my bones?
> How should such a thing betide me!
> They were kids, and now they're stones."

So he came to the brook, and stooped to drink, but the

heavy stones weighed him down, so he fell over into the water and was drowned. And when the seven little kids saw it they came up running.

"The wolf is dead, the wolf is dead!" they cried, and taking hands, they danced with their mother all about the place.